# Purple Death

# Purple Death

*Brian L Porter*

## Dedication

*This work is dedicated to the memory of my mother, Enid Ann Porter (1914 – 2004). Her love and support never failed me, and to my wife Juliet, who supplies those commodities in our everyday lives together.*

# Acknowledgements

Purple Death owes much of its existence to a small group of people scattered across the globe whose help and support, both in reading and critiquing the manuscript has proved invaluable. Covering a wide spectrum of ages and occupations these volunteers have helped to shape the final story that is about to be laid before you, and for that reason I wish to express my heartfelt thanks to Malcolm Davies, Sheila Noakes and Ken Copley (UK), Jean Pike (USA), Graeme S Houston, (Malaysia), and last but not least to my wife Juliet, whose help and support through the long hours of writing the novel has been inspirational.

# Introduction

The London Borough of Richmond-on-Thames sits sedately at the south-eastern fringes of the boundaries of Greater London. Hampton Court Palace, Kew Gardens and Twickenham, the home of English Rugby are all to be found within its borders, as is the National Physical Laboratory. There are over one hundred parks within its borders, and the River Thames flows sedately through twenty one miles of the borough which has royal connections that date back some nine hundred years.

It is into this tranquil and unlikely setting that a killer with terrifying motives begins a spree of murders that soon lead the police to a connection with a decades old case. Unfortunately for Detective Inspector Sean Connor and his assistant Sergeant Lucy Clay, all roads seem to lead to nowhere in this baffling investigation as they begin to realise that the man behind the murders is a master of the art of misdirection who appears to assume a new identity with almost every passing day. Witnesses are thin on the ground, clues non-existent, and every potential suspect soon turns out to be yet another victim of the invidious killer. Connor is faced with question after question as to the killer's motives and yet the answers are never going to be easy to find.

Who is the unknown but deadly female accomplice of the murderer whom the police soon dub The Chocolate Woman? Who is directing her in the prosecution of these apparently pointless and motiveless crimes? Why does the driver die at the controls as an express train arrives at Birmingham station, and how does his murder on the opposite side of the country connect with the horrendous series of killings taking place in quiet, leafy Richmond-on-Thames? What, if anything connects the victims to a thirty two year old unsolved murder investigation?

Each and every time that Connor and his team feel they are about to discover a new lead, they find they have been led into yet another 'blind alley' by the merciless yet fiendishly clever mastermind behind the murders. Time is running out for those still on the killers 'murder list' and the detectives must work fast to prevent the serial killer from completing his gruesome task as they begin their investigation into the catalogue of murders that would soon come to be known collectively as 'The Purple Death'.

Author's note: Although the towns and cities named in this fiction and the borough of Richmond-on-Thames are genuine, any and all references to local place names, streets and individuals are purely the inventions of the author's mind and bear no connection to any place or person in real life. Any similarity to real places or persons is thus a pure coincidence and is entirely unintentional.

# Prologue

The man pulled the grey cardboard box file from its place in the bottom of the well-worn metal filing cabinet that stood in the darkest corner of his office. The heavy box file bulged from the bulk of its contents. It bore no file name or label in the space that had been provided for the purpose. Placing it on his desk the man removed the pink ribbon that held it closed and slowly began to remove the contents. Old newspaper cuttings, yellow with age, were soon joined on his desk by photographs of a diverse collection of men and women, of streets that betrayed their history by the collection of motor cars of a previous generation, notebooks with discoloured, crumpled pages and a single, leather bound album that contained yet more photographs, this time of a more personal nature.

He spent a good ten minutes perusing the contents of the file before slowly replacing each item in the reverse of the order in which he'd removed it. Finally he spent a few minutes looking at the photos in the personal album, tenderly fingering the face of the central character in each and every one of the pictures that the well preserved photograph album contained. A smile played across his lips and he appeared lost in thoughts of a happier time, but eventually he added the album to the other items back in the box file which he soon replaced in its place in the filing cabinet. He pushed the protruding pop-out auto-lock on the cabinet. His secrets were safe until the next time he decided to delve into his own personal museum of what his life had been, and what, under other circumstances, it might have been.

Unlocking a drawer in his desk, he next took out a polished wooden box. Hand-made from the finest quality oak, it bore a distinctly aged and old-fashioned appearance. He knew it had once belonged to a retired sea-captain who'd sailed the world long ago on one of the old clipper ships, carrying tea and other treasures from one corner of the empire to another. He'd acquired it at an antiques auction, and had put it to good use.

Opening it with a key he kept on a chain around his neck he surveyed the contents with a look of satisfaction. Five small glass tubes, rather like test tubes from a chemical laboratory lay in a bed of green velvet within the box. Each was securely topped off with a closely fitting cork top, and sealed around the edges with strong corrosive resistant black tape. Only the sharpest of syringes would serve to pry the contents of those vials from within their glass homes. He touched each of the vials in turn, his gaze lingering upon the clear, innocent looking liquid that each one contained and then, with a smile of satisfaction on his face, he slowly closed the box, turned the key in the lock and returned the box to its allotted place in the drawer.

Picking up the telephone, the man prepared to make a call, checking the number on a pad on his desk. He smiled again as he began to dial. The game was about to begin!

# Chapter 1
# The First Taste

Looking out at the world through his office window Sam Gabriel had every reason to feel pleased with himself. As he took in the sights of the people enjoying the warmth of the sun in the park that lay directly below his office building he wondered if any of them could possibly feel as happy as he did at that particular moment in his life. Just forty years old and already he'd been propelled upwards towards the higher reaches of the promotion ladder. It had been less than an hour since old Lawrence Betts called Sam into his office and handed him the prize he'd been seeking for so long, a partnership! To be offered the role of partner in the firm of Betts, Cowan and Ford was something Sam had dreamed about ever since he'd joined the city law firm just four years ago, but he'd never envisaged would happen this soon. He'd earlier made a name for himself with a smaller firm specialising in criminal matters and had been head-hunted by the larger, more prosperous firm for whom he now worked. He wanted so much to call Lynne, his wife of the last six years but he knew that she was en-route to Edinburgh to visit her mother and Lynne would never, ever dream of answering her phone while she was driving. She'd always been too safety conscious to take such a risk.

As Sam was thinking of Lynne he first noticed the slight burning sensation, accompanied by an unexplained tingling in his mouth. Putting it down to excitement Sam ignored the discomfort at first but, as he watched two children chasing a small Yorkshire terrier through the park below his window he became aware of another disturbing sensation, when his mouth began to feel numb, as though he'd received a large dose of novocaine, and the tingling sensation increased, as did the burning which now spread from his mouth and took a firm hold of his abdomen.

Sam staggered back against his desk while the burning increased and his motor functions suddenly failed him. He wanted to move his arms and legs but they didn't want to obey his brain's commands. *What the hell was happening?* Sam reached for the telephone which sat invitingly on his desk intending to call for Maggie, his secretary. He knew he must have eaten something that had disagreed with his stomach. This could only be a virulent attack of food poisoning, surely. For some reason, at the same time as he reached across the desk the telephone seemed to keep moving away from his outstretched hand; no matter how hard he tried he just couldn't make his hand connect with the inanimate but elusive plastic object that had become the absolute focus of his life in the last few seconds.

He couldn't do it. The telephone wouldn't allow him to pick it up, so he tried for the next best option. He'd walk across the floor to the door, open it and call Maggie into the office. He'd done it a thousand times before, why not now? The answer came in less than two seconds when Sam Gabriel tried to move his legs and instead fell in a crumpled heap on his office floor. He felt more than just 'ill' now and fear gripped Sam while the sweat on his brow began to run down into his eyes. He felt a constriction in his chest which felt as though someone had suddenly placed an iron barrel ring around him and was tightening it by the second. The life was rapidly being crushed out of his body, but with nothing and no-one there with him in the office to offer help. Sam Gabriel had never felt so frightened and alone.

Why didn't anyone come to his aid? He couldn't think of a reason why no-one came until he remembered that he'd told Maggie he wasn't to be disturbed under any circumstances. Sam had wanted to enjoy his big moment, to savour it and then make a few phone calls to friends and family to share his news. Then he'd have gone for lunch, meeting as usual with his colleagues from inside and outside the firm at The Harrow Arms, the local watering hole for the legal and upmarket business set.

His pulse was slowing and his skin appeared to him to be on fire and the sensations of heat were rapidly spreading over his whole body. He could almost feel the throbbing of his own heartbeat in his temples and he knew that along with his pulse, his heart rate was getting slower by the minute.

"What the hell's happening to me?" he managed to voice out loud, but they were the last words he managed before he felt his stomach lurch and heave, and Sam Gabriel began to vomit uncontrollably. He lurched violently while a spasm shook his body, he felt the cold hardness of his desk behind his back, and then Sam began to sob as he realised that no-one was about to come to his aid, and that whatever was happening to him could have potentially lethal consequences for him. This was no simple case of food poisoning, he concluded. Some bastard had deliberately poisoned him. But who, and with what? He tried desperately to think of something he might have ingested that could have caused this type of reaction but his poor tortured brain could think of nothing.

The pain in his gut increased exponentially and Sam managed to assume a foetal position, his arms gripping his belly tightly in an effort to dull the agony and control the retching that now wracked his weary body every few minutes. It became harder to breathe. Little did he know at that stage, but Sam was slowly being starved of air, his lungs were beginning to fail due to asphyxiation. Lucid to the end, Sam Gabriel lived out the last minutes of his life on the floor of his office, recognising the approach of imminent death, but being unable to summon help, unable even to call out to his secretary in the next office. Sam thought of Lynne and the child she was carrying, the son or daughter he'd never know, and then, as the pain in his abdomen reached a crescendo and his lungs felt as though they were being crushed in a vice, Sam closed his eyes for the last time, and the children in the park chased the little terrier, and the lunchtime crowd gathered on the park benches to enjoy their sandwiches and pre-packaged drinks.

Knowing that he'd want to be on time to celebrate the good news of his promotion with the lunchtime crowd Maggie Lucas dared to knock and enter Sam Gabriel's office less than ten minutes after he'd drawn his last agonizing breath. The screams that accompanied her discovery of the painfully contorted body of her boss brought the staff and the senior partners of the firm of Betts, Cowan and Ford running to the office of their newly promoted and recently deceased junior partner. Sam Gabriel had lived less than two hours to enjoy his promotion.

# Chapter 2
# Second Helpings

An hour after Sam Gabriel expired on the floor of his office, David Arnold, thirty- eight year old father of two and a driver for Great Eastern Railways pulled his train to rest at platform two of New Street Station in Birmingham. The journey from the south coast resort of Penzance had been uneventful and David had coasted to a halt at the platform at Birmingham dead on time. The burning in his stomach had started about ten miles from the city, but he'd put it down to having eaten his breakfast in a hurry that morning. Now he was paying the price.

It wasn't until he felt the burning and tingling sensations in his mouth and began to feel the cramping feeling in his gut that David realised there might be something more seriously wrong with him. He knew he couldn't continue to drive for the rest of his shift which would take the train as far as his home town of Liverpool, where he'd hand over to a new driver for the rest of the train's journey to Glasgow. In his current condition he'd be a liability to himself and his passengers and so he responsibly decided to exit from his cab and get help before handing over the train to a relief driver if one could be found.

It was at that moment, at the same time as he tried to rise from his seat and move to the door of the cab that he realised just how bad things were. Though his brain continued to function perfectly well, David Arnold found himself rooted to his seat. He wanted to move, but couldn't. All his motor functions seemed to have deserted him. Hell, he couldn't even reach out his arm to lean through the window and call for help. He felt sick and a heavy tightness began to form in his chest, breathing becoming difficult. David knew he was in trouble.

Carriage doors slammed, the guard's whistle blew, and the hundred and forty passengers aboard the train waited for the mighty diesel-electric locomotive to begin its slow glide as it pulled the snake of carriages away from the station before gradually picking up speed as it moved out of the city.

When the train failed to move, the guard tried the whistle once more, thinking that perhaps the driver had failed to hear the shrill piercing sound intended to send him on his way. When the second whistle produced the same abortive effect the guard walked briskly down the platform to the front of the train. He was joined as he neared the locomotive by a platform supervisor, whose job it was to ensure that the train's carriages were in a safe condition with all doors closed before it moved off. The two men arrived at the door to the driver's cab simultaneously and the guard, a veteran of twenty years working on the rail system reached out to open the door. Normally, the door to the cab would be automatically locked while the train was in motion, but now it allowed the guard to depress the latch and open it to reveal the interior of the cab.

The floor of the cab lay awash, stained with the vomit that David Arnold had spewed in his final moments. He'd remained conscious and clear-minded to the end, and had been horrified to feel the massive constrictions in his chest and lungs, to feel himself being gradually strangled as if by an invisible assailant, his need for air being met with nothing but more pain, more burning and numbness while his body closed down cell by cell, and the tears ran down his face. David Arnold thought of Vicky and Tracy, his two young daughters, and Angela his wife waiting at home for him to finish his shift and return to them as he always did. He could see their faces in his mind when that final awful constriction hit him and the struggle to breathe became superseded by the need to give in, to let the inevitable consequences of this sudden painful attack take their course. David Arnold died just ten seconds before Ray Fellows the guard opened his cab.

The horrified faces of Ray Fellows and Mike Smith the platform supervisor mirrored each other as they gawped at the horrific sight that met their eyes when they looked into the drivers cab. Smith looked away and vomited himself, right there on the platform. Fellows, despite the shock of finding the driver in such a state, managed to gasp a call for help into his radio and requested both the police and paramedics be summoned.

The police were there first of course, since the local force maintained a strong presence on all the major stations on the rail network as part of the modern-day deterrent against the scourge of terrorism. A sergeant and a police constable arrived at the entrance to the cab within two minutes of Fellows' call and the sergeant needed no second look in order for him to determine that the driver was unlikely to be alive. The grim rictus of pain on his face, frozen at the moment of death, served to advertise his deceased state and the sergeant ordered the constable to seal off the area around the cab until the paramedics and a more senior police officer arrived to take charge.

"What about the train?" asked Fellows.

"Eh?" the sergeant responded.

"The train, Sergeant! There are probably over a hundred people in these carriages waiting to continue their journey. What are we supposed to do with the bloody train?"

Sergeant Peter Seddon thought quickly, and came to a decision.

"I'm sorry, but until we know for sure that this was an accidental death, they'll have to stay here until a senior officer decides to release them."

"You're joking surely," the guard responded. "How do we keep them all on the train? We don't exactly have a massive security force here you know. They could just open the doors and leave the station and we'd never know a thing would we?"

"Davies," the sergeant spoke to his constable. "Get on the radio and get as many men as we've got on duty at the station to get over here.

I want the names and addresses of every passenger and I want them quick!"

"I'm on it, Sergeant," the constable replied.

People were already opening carriage doors all along the length of the eight carriage train. It was going to take a superhuman and miraculous effort by the police to keep them all in place until the detectives arrived. Thanks to the sterling efforts of Sergeant Seddon, Constable Paul Davies, and four men from the transport police office at New Street Station, they achieved the near-impossible. As far as they knew, no-one left the train before the arrival some thirty minutes later, of Detective Inspector Charles Carrick and his assistant, Detective Sergeant Lewis Cole.

The detectives soon set to work, though there was little that could be gleaned from either the passengers or the rail staff on duty on Platform Two. The likelihood that anyone on board the train could have had anything to do with the driver's death was miniscule in the extreme in the detective's minds, and after ensuring that the constables had noted the names and addresses of the passengers they were released to continue on their journeys as best as they could.

The paramedics were certain that the driver was dead, (the policemen could have told them that) and Carrick demanded that the body remain untouched until it could be examined by the police doctor and officially pronounced as such. The whole procedure took about an hour from start to finish and eventually paramedics removed the body of David Arnold from the cab with as much care as possible, placed it in a black body bag, and removed the deceased to the local mortuary where he would soon be subjected to a rigorous examination and autopsy in an effort to determine the cause of the unfortunate driver's demise. The locomotive would be treated as a potential crime scene for the time being, forcing the station master into the inconvenience of having to shut down all operations on that platform, thus causing severe disruption to the whole rail network, until the police allowed the loco to be moved to a siding.

Carrick's words as he watched the ambulance carry away the unfortunate driver towards his date with the medical examiner's scalpel would eventually prove to be quite prophetic when he said to Cole,

"I wouldn't like to see one like that every day Sergeant, no sir, I wouldn't. Gives a man the creeps to see a body like that. The poor sod must have been in agony at the end, from the look on his face. No-one should die like that, no-one. I hope I never see a face like that again as long as I live."

"Right, Sir," Cole replied.

He could think of nothing else to say at the time. He was too busy trying to hold back the bile and vomit that he'd been fighting against since he too had seen the corpse of the once strong and vibrant engine driver.

At the time, neither man could think ahead any further than the inevitable autopsy, which they hoped would prove that the man had died from some awful but natural death, food poisoning perhaps.

That hope proved to be short-lived, as was Carrick's hope that this was the first and last time he'd see such a tortured sight as the body of David Arnold!

# Chapter 3
# Questions Without Answers

The death of Sam Gabriel had caused more than a stir within the hallowed portals of the old-established law firm. Senior partner Lawrence Betts, having so recently shaken the hand of his newly promoted junior partner had taken it upon himself to notify the authorities as soon as Sam's secretary had informed him of the tragedy that had taken place in Sam's office. Sixty-nine year old Betts, looking visibly shaken and every one of his years, now sat at his desk, his hands filled with a restless energy all of their own as Detective Inspector Sean Connor sat in the comfortable leather client chair that Betts provided for those who consulted him in his professional capacity. At that moment however, Connor saw only a sad old man with a head of white hair and wrinkled temples, hands pocked here and there with liver spots, a man with a look of defeat in his eyes.

"So, Mr Betts," he began, "what can you tell me that might throw some light on what took place here today? I understand that Mr Gabriel had been with you in your office shortly before his death and that you'd just handed him a big promotion?"

Betts paused for a second before answering. Obviously Maggie or one of the other secretaries or para-legals had already given the inspector the news of Sam's promotion.

"Mm, yes, quite so Inspector," he eventually responded. "Sam Gabriel was one of the brighter lights shining against an increasingly dull horizon. In modern legal terms he performed quite brilliantly and had a dazzling career ahead of him. I would have promoted him a year ago, but I wanted him to gain a little more trial experience before confirming what I already knew deep down inside. This is nothing short of a catastrophic tragedy Inspector, a catastrophic tragedy!"

"Yes sir, I'm sure you're quite right. Do you have any idea what might have happened to cause this, this...whatever it was to happen to him?"

"I can assure you Inspector that I have no idea whatsoever what could have happened to poor Samuel. Let me tell you right now though, that Sam had no time for drugs, so the thought that he might have overdosed on some illegal substance is positively out of the question."

"Why on earth do you think that I might be thinking along those lines Mr Betts?" asked the inspector.

"I don't know Inspector. It's just that I know from years of experience that when someone dies in suspicious circumstances with no visible outward signs of bodily trauma, the police tend to think along those lines, don't they?"

"You do have a poor opinion of us don't you Mr Betts? For all I know Mr Gabriel could have had a heart attack, a stroke, a brain haemorrhage, any number of things that could be attributed to natural causes, and yet you automatically think of controlled substances. I know you're a lawyer, but I think that perhaps it's you who are jumping to conclusions. Is it that you think he really *might* have taken something that contributed to his death?"

"No Inspector, I don't think that at all, and you must forgive me for having brought the subject into our conversation. I'm shocked, that's all, shocked at losing a colleague with such a brilliant young mind and shocked at the effect his death is going to have on his wife and family."

"Of course Mr Betts, of course. So, you have no idea what happened in Mr Gabriel's office after he left you following your conversation together?"

"That's right. Samuel left my office at around eleven a.m. and as far as I know from talking to my staff he returned to his office and after a few words with his secretary asking that she allow no-one to disturb him he was never seen alive again."

"Wasn't that a little strange sir, you know, him just having received a big promotion and then not sharing it with everyone straight away?"

"Not at all Inspector. Samuel Gabriel was a modest and a respectful man. He would have wanted his wife to be the first to share in his good fortune. He told me that she was travelling north today, to Edinburgh I think to visit her family and he wouldn't have dreamed of disturbing her by telephoning her whilst she were driving. He'd have waited until she'd arrived north of the border, and then phoned her before telling anyone else."

"But the office staff, the other members of your firm, they all knew I suppose?"

"Of course, but they would have kept that to themselves until such times as they left the building. Besides, apart from his family and friends it wasn't really of much importance to anyone outside of the office was it Inspector? It was just a work promotion after all and could have had no possible bearing on his death."

"Perhaps Mr Betts, and perhaps not. We'll have to wait and see what the autopsy throws up won't we? Until that's carried out, anything else would be sheer speculation on our part, and hardly worthy of either of our professional statuses wouldn't you agree?"

Betts nodded in agreement as a knock sounded at the door. The diminutive figure of Detective Sergeant Lucy Clay followed her polite knock by pushing the door open and peering around it until she caught sight of Connor.

"Yes, Sergeant, what is it?"

"It's the crime scene people Sir, and the doctor. They want to know if they can move the body."

"As soon as the doctor pronounces the man deceased and makes his initial examination of the body they can take him away," Connor replied.

Betts could be of little further help to the police officers, his knowledge of Sam Gabriel extending little beyond the doors of the law firm's offices, so Connor and Clay spent the next two hours questioning the other partners and the staff of Betts, Cowan and Ford with the result that they ended up knowing almost nothing about the deceased apart from his record as a lawyer and the most basic details about his wife and home life. That he was happily married seemed to be a universally accepted fact, and everyone in the office professed the firm belief that Sam Gabriel had been the victim of some tragic accident, or that he'd been struck down by some hideous but as yet unknown disease, and a couple of the staff had even gone so far as to ask the police if they would be screening everyone for the disease that had killed their colleague.

It was with a sense of relief that Connor and Clay eventually left the building and headed back to police headquarters. It remained too early for any post-mortem results, and they decided to use the time at their disposal to check and cross reference the statements they'd received from the employees of the law firm and to contact the police in Edinburgh, where Sam Gabriel's unfortunate widow was expected to arrive at any time. It would fall on the shoulders of some poor unfortunate Scottish officer to break the sad news to the widow, but it would be Sean Connor who would have to deal with her grief and her questions upon her return.

# Chapter 4
# Arsenic and Old Lace

Catherine Nickels tied her hair back, pulled on her scrubs and gloves and strode purposefully into the autopsy room. As chief forensic medical examiner for the town, thirty-eight year old Catherine had been called in to perform the examination of the body of the newly deceased Sam Gabriel. Her assistant, Doctor Gunther Schmidt was waiting for her. Gunther was Austrian by birth, of German parents, and had come to England ten years earlier to further his studies in forensic medicine. Tall and good looking in a Teutonic sort of way, Gunther had fallen in love with the country and its people and had been only too pleased to accept the job as Assistant Medical Examiner for Richmond when the post was offered to him. He'd been with Catherine for four years and the two of them worked together with a seamless ease that at times belied the meticulous professionalism that they applied to every case.

"Morning, Gunther", Catherine greeted her assistant with a warmth that came from their close and at times intense professional relationship.

"Same to you," he replied as he continued to wash down the body on the table in front of him ready for the process of autopsy to begin. "Looks like we have a small mystery on our hands today, according to the police."

"What have I told you Gunther? There are no mysteries in forensics, simply answers that have yet to be found."

"Of course Doctor, as you say, but this is a little out of the ordinary wouldn't you say?"

"Perhaps Gunther, perhaps," was all Catherine would say as the two of them moved into their well-practised routine of opening up the deceased's remains. There was little or no verbal communication between the two specialists as the internal organs were swiftly removed from the chest and abdominal cavities, and the whirring of the high powered circular saw heralded the removal of the brain from its position within the skull. Within the next few hours various tests and procedures would be carried out on the various tissue samples taken by Catherine and Gunther, and if all went well they would soon be able to provide the police with the cause of death of the unfortunate Sam Gabriel.

As they left the autopsy room, the door at the end of the well lit corridor opened towards them to admit a tall dark-haired figure in a smart but slightly crumpled grey suit. Sean Connor passed through the entrance and moved briskly towards the two pathologists.

"Any word for me, Doc?" he asked Catherine.

"Sorry Inspector, not yet I'm afraid. If there was evidence of gunshot wounds or blunt force trauma I could give you a rough guess at the cause of death, but in this case he appeared to be a healthy and well-nourished man with nothing out of the ordinary to categorise in a visual scan of the organs. I've sent tissue samples and stomach contents to the lab for analysis, and we should have some preliminary answers for you by tomorrow afternoon."

"As long as that eh, Doc?" Connor spoke with a smile on his face. He knew that Catherine Nickels was good at her job. If she could give him an answer sooner he knew that she would. Sean Connor trusted her to be meticulous. After all, a future prosecution could depend on the reliability and accuracy of her findings. He'd never try to rush the good doctor, though he might sound as if he would.

"As long as that, Inspector." she retorted.

"I know it's not in your usual remit to do so Doc, but, if I were to tell you that your life depended upon taking a complete shot in the dark and giving me an inkling of what secret thoughts are going through your head about this one, what would you say to me? Come on, Doc, you must have a private opinion of some sort."

"Inspector Connor," Catherine grinned, "I do believe you're pushing me to speculate."

"Maybe Doc, but go on, just tell me what you think it *might* be, please."

"Listen Inspector Connor, as you seem to want to push me into a corner on this one, I'll tell you what went through my mind when I looked into the chest cavity of that poor young man a few minutes ago."

"Yes Doc?"

"Well, there was no direct evidence of course, and I won't be sure until we get the test results back from the lab, but..."

"Oh, come on Doc, don't muck about."

"OK. There was evidence of some kind of trauma in the trachea and oesophagus, as though he'd been struggling for breath, and I mean in a big way. The slight discolouration on his lips added to my feelings that we are dealing with a victim of asphyxia, and yet..."

"Are you saying he was strangled?"

"There's nothing to suggest that, I'm afraid."

"Please Doc, you're holding back on me, I know you are."

Catherine Nickels took a deep breath. Speculation wasn't her forte but Connor had pressed her and she *had* entertained a private speculative thought about the circumstances of this death as she'd looked at the victim's internal organs.

"If you were to press me, and I stress that this is just a wild shot in the dark, I'd say we're dealing with a case of poisoning of some sort."

"Poison?" Connor was stunned.

"Like I said, we won't know until we get the results back from the lab, but I'd say we're dealing with some fast acting and highly lethal toxin, though I can't tell you how or when it was administered, not yet. Maybe the stomach contents will tell us something. There were no puncture marks on the body though, I can tell you that. Now, if you don't mind, Doctor Schmidt and I have notes to write up and other work to do.

"Yes, right, well, thanks Doc," said Connor, turning and heading back for the door. "You'll let me know, right?"

"As soon as I know, you'll know Inspector," she replied as she and Gunther disappeared through the door to her office.

As he climbed back into his car which he'd left parked in the tree-lined lane that ran along the back of the mortuary building, he picked up his phone, and dialled Lucy Clay's mobile number. She replied within seconds of the phone ringing.

"Any word from the widow yet Lucy?" Connor asked.

"Not yet Sir, we're still waiting. Anything on the cause of death yet?"

"Nothing definite yet Sergeant, but according to the doc, we could be looking at a good old Christie style mystery here, if she's proved right by the lab reports of course."

"Sorry Sir, but you're talking in riddles?"

"Oh, yes, sorry Sergeant. Let's just say that in the case of Mr Sam Gabriel we could be looking at a case of good old-fashioned arsenic and old lace."

"You've lost me now Sir," Lucy spoke in exasperation into her phone.

"Forgive me Sergeant, I'm daydreaming of the books of my own youth. Poison, Lucy, that's what we could be looking at. Good old-fashioned poisoning, and you know what?"

"What, Sir?" was all the bemused detective sergeant could ask down the phone.

"In all my years on the force, I've never had a poisoning before. This could be something to really get our teeth into."

With that unfortunate remark Connor brought the conversation to a close. Before Clay could respond, he shouted into the phone;

"See you back at the office," and then broke the connection.

Sitting at her desk in the Criminal Investigation Department (C.I.D.) operations room at police headquarters, Lucy Clay looked in bewilderment at Detective Constable Harry Drew who just happened to be walking past, pointed an agitated finger at the phone to indicate whomever she'd been speaking to and shouted at Drew;

"He's gone crazy, absolutely bloody crazy."

Constable Drew kept walking. He had nowhere to hurry to but he'd think of somewhere to get away from the demented Sergeant who sat staring at the phone in her hand, looking a little on the crazy side and muttering to herself,

"Old lace and arsenic, arsenic and old lace? What the hell does he mean by that?"

Unfortunately, Lucy Clay's education into classic Victorian style English literature was soon to escalate at an unheard of and decidedly unwanted rate.

# Chapter 5
# Trolley Dash

As Catherine Nickels slid the corpse of the unfortunate Sam Gabriel into its resting place in the cold room of the Richmond mortuary her counterpart in Birmingham, Doctor Gary Hudson was just beginning his examination of the mortal remains of David Arnold, the sadly demised locomotive driver. It would be some time before Inspectors Carrick and Connor would realise that they were investigating cases that may have been related and for now Gary Hudson worked steadily on the post-mortem examination of David Arnold knowing only that the police were extremely anxious to discover the poor man's cause of death and whether it could be attributed to natural causes, or whether they were looking at a case of foul play, i.e. murder.

Hudson, who'd been doing this job for over twenty years knew a strange case when he saw one and the possibility of poisoning by sources as yet unknown were strong in his mind as he began to cut open the chest cavity of the engine driver, revealing the interior organs to his expert gaze..

Had he known that Catherine Nickels was working on a similar case a number of miles to the south of his location then maybe, just maybe, the police would have been better informed than they were when the next unfortunate victim was brought to the attention of the guardians of the law. As it was Hudson was working 'blind' in the same way as Catherine Nickels, each specialist believing theirs to be the only such case under investigation at the time. Something about the body of David Arnold bothered him. The grim rictus of pain etched into the dead man's face affected him in the way most of his 'clients' failed to do. Something terrible had happened to this man, and Hudson knew from past experience that the one thing guaranteed to produce such a look of horror on a dying person's face was the effect of a particularly toxic and fast acting poison, one that would leave the victim in little or no doubt that he was about to breathe his last. Who had administered such a poison to the victim and why they'd done so was of no relevance to Gary Hudson. His task was simply to determine what poison if any had been used to bring about the death of the man whose body now lay exposed to his scalpels, retractors and cutting saws.

As Hudson worked, back in Richmond Sean Connor and Lucy Clay had just completed their initial interview with the grieving widow of Sam Gabriel. Five months pregnant, Lynne Hudson had been met by local police officers from the Lothian and Borders Police Force the moment she arrived at her parents' house in Leith just outside Edinburgh. Having been informed of the tragic death of her husband her father had immediately offered to drive her home and the two of them had gone straight to the police station upon their arrival in Richmond, where Connor and Clay sympathetically carried out their duty in the presence of Lynne's father, Harold Butcher.

During the course of the interview it transpired that no, Lynne knew of no-one who held a grudge against her husband, no, he hadn't been taking any drugs either illegal or prescription and no, she could think of nothing he might have eaten or drunk that could have caused him to collapse in such a state. He had no serious or non-serious health worries, and hadn't seen a doctor for over a year so she could think of nothing that might have brought about the death of her husband. They appeared to have had a happy marriage and were looking forward to the birth of their first child.

When Lynne eventually collapsed in a flood of tears, obviously unable to go on with the interview Connor sensitively brought the proceedings to a close and diplomatically asked Harold Butcher to carry out the official identification of the body. At first the widow protested, saying that she wanted to see her husband, but good sense prevailed and after being assured that she wouldn't want to see Sam in the condition he was in at the moment she deferred to the police and her father, having been promised that she could see him later. The body would be made presentable after all the autopsy procedures had been concluded, and no trace of Catherine's incisions would be visible to the untrained eye.

Lucy Clay remained with Lynne while her father accompanied Connor to the viewing room where the formal identification was carried out. That done, the grieving widow and her father left for Lynne and Sam's home with a promise from Connor that he would be in touch the moment he had some news about the cause of Sam's death. Lynne also made him promise that she could see Sam as soon as possible. Quite naturally she wanted to say her own private farewell to the man she loved, to the father of her unborn child.

As Lynne and her father made their way across town in the car and Connor and Clay sat down to enjoy a welcome cup of coffee in Connor's office, a few miles away housewife Virginia Remick was pushing her shopping trolley around her local supermarket. She was intent on picking up everything that she'd written down on the shopping list she carried in her hand. As she reached out to take a packet of her husband Pete's favourite biscuits from the top shelf of the aisle she was suddenly gripped by a fierce tingling and burning sensation in her mouth and throat. These symptoms were soon followed by the numbness, the shortness of breath and the lack of motor functions though her brain remained totally focussed and lucid. Virginia's four-wheeled shopping trolley seemed to develop a life of its own and she could only watch in shocked horror as the trolley appeared to wrench itself from her increasingly feeble grasp and it careered into a pyramid display of cans of baked beans, bringing the whole edifice crashing to the ground. As she lost her grip on the real world Virginia's head began to swirl and swim on her shoulders, the overhead lights of the supermarket became dizzy whirlpools of white fluorescence and the pain in her chest grew to monumental proportions to the extent that she barely felt herself hitting the ground as her legs collapsed from beneath her, nor did she hear the concerned voices of the two staff members and fellow shopper who rushed to her aid as they saw her obvious predicament.

She heard a disembodied voice calling out "Someone send for a doctor", and then her throat felt as though someone were tightening a garrotte around it and breathing become an impossibility. Virginia lay on the hard, cool supermarket floor, looking up in horror and fear as a battery of concerned faces peered down at her as though from a great height.

Another voice penetrated her fear and pain, "Is she drunk?"

Virginia wanted to protest at this inference but her voice box wouldn't obey her brain's commands and instead she felt her mouth opening and closing in silence, like that of a peacefully swimming fish; though there was nothing peaceful about what was happening to her at that moment.

As her airway began to close for what would be the last time Virginia Remick could do no more than look at the bright white light that beamed down at her from the supermarket ceiling, the bright white light that now beckoned her into another world, one where breathing would no longer be so difficult, one where breathing wouldn't matter anymore. With a final gasp of pain and panic Virginia took one last look at the bright white light that called her into that other world, then, unable to fight against the pain, the numbness and the burning sensations any longer Catherine Nickels's next case closed her eyes for the last time, the packet of biscuits still clutched in her right hand crushed in a final death grip.

The stunned supermarket manager ordered his staff to call the police and the ambulance service then instructed his assistant to clear the store, close the doors and await the arrival of the emergency services. Less than ten minutes passed before the noise of approaching sirens announced the approach of both police and an ambulance, and a further ten minutes was all it took for the paramedics to pronounce the patient dead and remove the body from the aisle of the supermarket. Only thirty five minutes after she'd breathed her last breath Virginia Remick's body was delivered into the hands of the Medical Examiner. It wouldn't be long before Catherine Nickels would be able to give Inspector Connor the unwelcome news that they had a second mystery death on their hands.

# Chapter 6
# Purple Death

"You're sure, Doc?" Connor asked Catherine as they sat in her neat and functional office two days after the deaths of Sam Gabriel and Virginia Remick. He noticed, not for the first time, how attractive the pathologist was, even with her hair tied back functionally for the purposes of her work. He tried to imagine how her fair hair would look if it were allowed to cascade down into its natural position. Catherine's answer quickly snapped him back to reality.

"There's absolutely no doubt," she replied. "They were both poisoned, and by a particularly nasty little villain that goes by the name of Aconite."

"The name isn't familiar to me Doc, tell me more."

"Well, apart from what's happened here, if you know anything about history, it was the preferred method of despatching her victims as used by Lucrezia Borgia."

"Ah, now there's a name I recognise," said Connor. "Exactly what is this stuff?"

"Purple Death, Sean. It's derived from a plant. Its Latin name is *Ranunculaceae* which belongs to the buttercup family would you believe? Its full name is aconitum, but it's also known as aconite, monkshood and wolfsbane. The last name came from the middle ages when archers would dip their arrows in the poison made from the roots of the flowers which they believed made their arrows particularly deadly when used against wolves. Monkshood is simple. The flowers are shaped just like the hoods worn by monks. Anyway, the roots of one genus of the plant are well documented as being used in Nepal and India to supply the poison known as *bikh*, or *bish*, which is a deadly toxin. Other variants have been used all around the world as poisons for hunting and warfare through the ages. Funnily enough a lot of people have these things growing in their gardens even here in England without truly knowing what they are or what they're capable of. They all bear particularly beautiful flowers, with purple monkshood being one of the most common. Oh yes, and aconite is supposedly highly efficacious in dealing with werewolves."

"Werewolves eh? Very interesting. So it's the root that carries the toxin, is that right Doc?"

"Yes, and believe it or not, it's still used in certain herbal and home-opathic cures, in very small amounts of course. Personally, I'd avoid anything that contains the stuff."

"How does it kill then, Doc? Just what did those poor people go through?"

Catherine thought carefully for a moment or two, wanting to make the explanation as easy to follow as possible. It wasn't necessary for Connor to know the technicalities at this stage. She knew him well enough to know that he wanted a basic and succinct delivery of the facts, so, after the brief pause, she continued.

"Basically, they would have felt a numbing or tingling sensation in the mouth and lips to begin with. The pulse would slow, they'd feel a burning in their lungs, and there'd be a massive drop in blood pressure. They'd begin to struggle for breath. They'd feel as though they were being strangled as the airways closed and their throat constricted. There'd be tingling and pain in the nerve endings, and yet through all of this the brain and the mind would function normally. They'd be aware of what was happening to them but would be unable to do anything about it as their motor functions gradually ceased to operate. Respiration gradually slows due to a paralytic action on the respiratory centre and the activity of the spinal cord is depressed. So the collapse of the respiratory system is what actually kills the victim rather than the stopping of the heart which comes after respiration ceases. Is that fairly clear?"

Connor swallowed hard. The thought of those symptoms was enough to make his own heart miss a beat.

"Jesus Christ, Catherine!" he exclaimed at last. "You'd have to hate someone pretty badly to want to put them through a death like that, surely."

"It certainly wasn't quick, and it definitely wasn't painless," Catherine replied to his observation. "As to the motive of whoever did this I'm afraid that's your department Inspector, not mine. I'm just a simple scientist. I can tell you the how, but not the why."

"I need to speak to the constables who answered the call to the supermarket, and to the family of that poor woman," Connor said quietly. "There must be some connection between her and Sam Gabriel but for the life of me I can't imagine what. They seem to be miles apart in their lifestyles and I can't see that they would have moved in the same social circles."

"Well, someone didn't like them very much that's for sure Sean,"

Catherine had relaxed enough to use his first name. They'd known each other for three years and had even dated once or twice since Connor's divorce, so a certain familiarity had crept into their relationship though they kept it on ice while discussing the real nuts and bolts of a case.

"I have to go," said Connor. "One was bad enough, two is more than coincidence."

"Find him Sean," said Catherine with a note of urgency in her voice. "Whoever he or maybe she is, find whoever it is before they do this again."

"I will Catherine, don't worry. I'll get the poisoning bastard if it's the last thing I do. No-one is going to get away with doing this to people in *my* town."

A sudden thought came to him as he rose to leave. He couldn't believe that he'd failed to ask the question before now.

"One last thing Catherine. Could you tell from your examinations just how the poison was administered to the victims?"

"All I can tell you is that the stomach contents of both victims showed significant levels of aconite to be present. How it was actually administered is another one for you to solve I'm afraid. I can tell you that there were no needle marks on the bodies to indicate an intravenous administration. Funny thing is there was little undigested food residue in either case so I can't be sure if it was introduced in something they ate on the day of death. You have a very clever killer out there Sean. Just be careful."

"Don't worry; I'll be more than careful. It's time I wasn't here. See you soon Catherine. If you find anything else you'll let me know of course?"

"Of course," she replied as Sean Connor made his way out of the office.

An hour later Police Constables Rogers and Thompson, both of whom had responded to the call to the supermarket found themselves seated in Detective Inspector Connor's office. Connor praised both men for their prompt and efficient handling of the situation before asking both of them if they'd spoken to the dead woman's next of kin or any other family members.

"Yes Sir," said Rogers, a thick-set and cheerful looking officer, an old-fashioned 'copper' with fifteen years service under his belt. "I volunteered to inform the husband. Poor chap, he was totally devastated. They'd only been married for a year. It was a second marriage for both of them. No kids or anything, but her first husband had been a bit of a sod to her, if you know what I mean Sir."

"I get your drift Constable. Do you think the ex-husband might have had enough of a grudge against her to have wanted to do her some harm?"

Connor wondered if there might be a connection between the two victims. Could Sam Gabriel have been her divorce solicitor for example?

"I doubt it Sir," said Rogers. "The ex moved away after the divorce, about three years ago and according to Mr Remick he now lives and works abroad. He thinks he might be in Germany or Holland."

"Hang on Sir," Constable Thompson interjected. "Are you saying that this wasn't death by natural causes?"

"That's precisely what I'm saying Constable. She was poisoned, and by a particularly nasty and painful poison at that. Added to which, a couple of hours before that a junior partner in a law firm in town was killed by exactly the same method."

"Bloody hell Sir," said Thompson, who at twenty three was very much the junior amongst the three men present in the room.

"Do you think there's a connection, sir?" asked Rogers, keeping a calm head despite the inspector's revelation,

"I'd be very surprised if there wasn't," said Connor. "I doubt we'd have two totally separate killers wandering around the town using aconite to poison people, wouldn't you agree?"

"When you put it like that Sir, well, yes, it would be hard to imagine," Rogers concurred with the D.I.

"Right," said Connor. "I've cleared it with your own inspector. I want you both to go and report to my sergeant out there", he pointed to the outer office. "She'll tell you what to do but basically I want you to make inquiries with all of Mrs Remick's friends and relatives. I need to know everything that you can find out about the lady and her past. I especially want to know who the solicitor was who handled her divorce from her first husband, and I most definitely want you to find out and confirm that man's whereabouts. Germany and Holland aren't so far away that he couldn't have hopped back across the channel to carry out a couple of murders and then hopped back again."

"Yes Sir, right you are Sir," said Rogers, his words echoed by Thompson's "Yes sir."

Though it wasn't much to go on, Connor felt that he had to start somewhere and this was his only tenuous line of inquiry at that point. He was of course still ignorant of the death of David Arnold and as the two uniformed constables left his office and reported to Lucy Clay, little did the detective know just how complex his inquiry was about to become.

# Chapter 7
# Painful Memories

Angela Stride heard the click of the latch as the front gate opened and closed. She turned to the young man sitting on the sofa. He appeared to be staring into nowhere through the heavy, thick dark glasses that obscured his eyes.

"Mary's home Mikey", she exclaimed. "I told you she wouldn't be long."

"Where did you say she'd gone to?" the handsome but totally blind man asked his sister.

"I told you. She went to the shops to get some of your favourite biscuits, those chocolate cream ones, remember?"

"I hope she got me some cigarettes." Mikey grumbled quietly.

The front door opened and closed and a few seconds later Mary Stride walked into the room and smiled a greeting at her brother and sister

"Hey, you two," she beamed at them. "Have you missed me?"

"Mikey forgot where you'd gone," said Angela.

"Did you get my cigarettes?" asked Mikey.

"Of course little brother, and your biscuits."

Mary pressed the packet of cigarettes into Mikey's hand, and let him feel the round wrapper of the biscuits she'd picked up on her way home. Mikey smiled and gripped her hand in thanks.

"Did you get everything done that you wanted while you were out?" asked Angela.

"Yes, Sis, everything," she replied.

"Do you think I might have some coffee to go with those biscuits you brought home?" Mikey asked from his position on the sofa.

"Hey, no problem little brother," Angela said cheerfully. "I'll go put the kettle on. Come and give me a hand Mary, won't you?"

Mary nodded at her sister and followed her out of the room, turning as she went through the door to say;

"Won't be long Mikey. Just take it easy 'til we get back."

As his two sisters disappeared into the kitchen, Michael Stride allowed his head to loll back against the back of the sofa. His unseeing eyes were pointing up towards the ceiling, though he'd never know what that ceiling looked like. He was forty two, though he looked much younger, and Mikey, as his sisters had always referred to him had been blind ever since the trauma that had struck the family thirty years earlier. The doctors had said it was shock that had caused him to wake one morning, having been perfectly sighted the night before, only to find himself in total darkness. The darkness had persisted and Michael had never seen a thing since that day. To lose one parent in such an agonising way had been bad enough, but then, when their mother had followed their father to the grave within a short space of time and by the same hideous means, it had been too much for Mikey. If it hadn't been for his sisters he didn't know what he would have done. They'd cared for him from that day forward as though he was the most important thing in their lives. They were both older than he was of course, and he knew that they'd sacrificed much in order to be able to look after him the way they did. Angela especially had given up a promising career in nursing and now worked part-time in a restaurant near their home. She was an excellent cook and her employer was always trying to get her to work full-time, to take courses at college and become a certified chef, but always, Angela insisted, she needed to be able to look after her brother. She was happy as a part-time cook, the money was good and she had plenty of time to spend with her darling brother who, after all, needed her more than Mr Grafton at the restaurant.

Mary, on the other hand, had managed to combine the needs of Mikey with her chosen career, and had qualified as a doctor some few years after the death of their mother. After spending ten years working in various departments of their local hospital she had managed to secure a post as a part-time member of the local general practitioners panel and, with the excellent money that she earned, Mary was able to work hours that suited her. The highly respected Doctor Stride had made quite a name for herself in the local community and at the same time she could liaise with Angela so that they could provide what they saw as the necessary care for their brother. Being blind was one thing, but the fact that Mikey had been born with only one leg; well, that and a whole raft of other medical problems made him a full-time job.

Now, according to the news, it was all happening again. Someone was killing people and the radio announcer said that aconite had been used in the murders. Mikey had been discussing it with Angela before Mary had arrived home. He couldn't believe that someone could be doing these terrible things and he just knew that he'd have nightmares about it. Angela had tried to placate and soothe him, but for Mikey it had all seemed too much. Now, Mikey closed his unseeing eyes behind his shades, and as the screeching sound of the boiling kettle in the kitchen reached his ears, and Mary called out, "Won't be long Mikey", the memories came flooding back, and Michael Stride began to cry into his blindness.

# Chapter 8
# A Meeting of Minds

Doctor Gary Hudson had just completed his post mortem report on the death of David Arnold. Aconite poisoning wasn't something he'd ever had to record on a report before but he knew that there was always a first time for everything, particularly in his chosen profession. As he signed his name to the dotted line that ran along the bottom of the document on his desk, Claire Forrester knocked and entered through his half open office door.

"Hello Claire my dear," said Hudson. He and Claire had worked together for over a year and he'd got to know the youngest pathologist on the staff quite well in that time.

"Got a minute, Boss?" she enquired.

"Only one measly minute? For you Claire, I've got ten," he joked in reply.

"I take it that's the report on the train driver?" she asked, nodding towards the papers on his desk.

"Indeed it is Claire. Why do you ask?"

"Is it what you thought it was? You know, at the morning conference you said you were sure it was a poisoning of some kind and you were waiting on the toxicology results before confirming it?"

"Well, yes Claire, it seems I was right. It was most definitely a case of poisoning."

"It wasn't by any chance aconite that did the deed was it Gary?" she asked, suddenly very serious.

Gary Hudson's head seemed to jerk upwards and his eyes bulged in his face. The look of shock he displayed would have been quite humorous if it hadn't been such a serious matter.

"As a matter of fact Claire, it was aconite poisoning, but how in the name of God did you guess at that one out of all the poisons in the world to choose from?"

"Well, in a way it was a guess, but what you might call an informed guess. You see, it's just been on the radio that the police in Richmond-on-Thames in Surrey are investigating two sudden deaths in the town, both from aconite poisoning. Please don't tell me that this could just be a coincidence."

"Bloody hell Claire. You're right. It's too way out for this to be a coincidence. There must be a connection somewhere or my name's not Gary Hudson. Do me a favour. Please go and find the number of the chief medical examiner for Richmond. I need to speak to someone down there in a hurry."

Claire Forrester nodded and dashed away, returning five minutes later with a piece of paper with the name Dr C Nickels, and a telephone number neatly written underneath it. This time when she left the office she closed the door as Hudson had requested, and in less time than Claire had taken to discover Catherine's office telephone number, Gary Hudson and Catherine Nickels were engaged in conversation.

Within minutes of her putting the phone back on its receiver after her conversation with Gary Hudson in Birmingham Catherine was connected by the police switchboard operator to Sean Connor.

"Hello Catherine, what's the latest?" asked the detective inspector cheerfully.

"Sean, we've got another aconite poisoning," said Catherine into the phone.

"Hell! How come I haven't heard about it? I asked to be informed of any suspicious looking deaths the minute they were picked up," Connor went on.

"That's just it," continued the pathologist. "It's not here in Richmond. This one was in Birmingham on the same day as Remick and Gabriel, and that's not all. This third victim adds another dimension to the whole scenario. He was a locomotive driver with a home in Liverpool, but who was driving a train that set off that morning from Penzance, and he was apparently struck down by the poison just as the train arrived at Birmingham, New Street Station."

"Shit!" Connor was perplexed. Catherine was right in her statement that this added another dimension to the case. How did this engine driver fit in with the others, and how was the poison administered to him? He was driving a speeding train from the south coast to the Midlands. His home was in the northwest in Liverpool, meaning that it was highly unlikely he could have any connection with the two victims in Richmond.

"Do you know who's in charge of the case in the West Midlands?" he asked.

"I asked the medical examiner who phoned me. His name is Gary Hudson by the way. The man you need to speak to is a Detective Inspector Charles Carrick. According to Doctor Hudson he's a good man Sean, a really top notch detective. By the sounds of it you won't have any trouble getting co-operation from him. He'll be as anxious as you are to solve the case, I'm sure."

"Let's hope so Catherine. I think he and I may have to work quite closely together to solve this one."

"Call him Sean, call him soon. You need to get a grip on this before we end up with more victims. I've got a feeling that the clock is ticking on this one, and I'd hate the alarm to go off!"

"Well put Catherine, well put," said Connor as he said his goodbyes and prepared to call his counterpart on the investigation in the West Midlands

The United Kingdom, like many nations of the world is unfortunately not blessed with either a single national police force, or with a single medical records office. In other words, it is quite possible for a crime to be committed by a perpetrator in, say, Yorkshire, and followed up by a similar crime in Norfolk, and because two separate police forces and two different labs are involved in each case, the first investigating force wouldn't necessarily have any knowledge of the second crime. Only when the information relating to the two murders (assuming the crimes to *be* murders) was placed onto a central computer programme that collated and circulated details of particularly violent crimes (e.g., murder, rape, kidnapping etc.), was there the possibility that the second force would discover the connection between the two crimes, unless of course the first case had been high profile enough to make the national TV and radio news. That was much easier of course. Had the local radio station in Richmond been a nationally broadcast station perhaps the Birmingham force would have known about the Richmond cases sooner. It wasn't of course, and it had only been today, three days after the event that the national news media had thought it newsworthy enough to fit into one of their bulletins. After all there was little or no consumer titillation to be had from the deaths of a solicitor and a housewife in leafy suburban Richmond. The editor of the BBC's national news broadcast however saw enough in the strange case of poisoning by this strange substance to have purloined the local station's tapes and inserted a report on the Richmond case into the national hourly news broadcasts. This had been the report heard by both Claire Forrester and Michael Stride, and which had caused them both such consternation in differing ways, but of equal gravity.

Now, the full force of the law in two separate regions of England would be brought to bear on the investigation. Two highly regarded and very professional investigators in the forms of Carrick and Connor would lend their best efforts to finding the solution to the case. Unfortunately for them, just as Carrick and Connor were beginning their first telephone conversation and swapping verbal case notes, the next twist in the case was about to jump up and bite them both in the metaphorical backsides.

# Chapter 9
# Aconite and Old Judges

Connor and Carrick felt a rapport for each other almost from the opening of their conversation. It was evident to each man that the other was, like himself a consummate professional and a man who would let nothing get in the way of the search for the truth. There was a warmth about each of them that transmitted itself across the miles through the telephone connection and the two detective inspectors were soon engaged in an honest and very open discussion about their respective cases. They soon agreed that so far neither of them had anything approaching a single lead to go on, much less any idea of the motive for the poisonings. Normally in a murder case the first twenty four hours after the murder were crucial to any investigation. In these cases however, it had been more than twenty four hours after the deaths before the police were even aware that foul play had been responsible for the deaths, and the two detectives agreed that whoever the killer may be, they had a head start on the police in terms of covering their tracks and making a getaway, if indeed the murderer felt that they even needed to get away. That conclusion in itself did however lead them to their first major point of agreement.

"So you agree that they must be connected then?" asked Connor.

"There surely can't be any doubt," Carrick replied. "Let's face it; the chances of two independent and unconnected murderers going around the country killing people by the use of an obscure poison like aconite would be remote in the extreme."

"Nigh on non-existent if you ask me," Connor added.

"So, how do you suggest we proceed?" Carrick asked his counterpart, perhaps already knowing what Connor's answer would be.

"We need to meet," Connor went on, "and soon, if we're to catch this sod before he or she kills again."

"You think it could be a woman then?"

"Why not? According to all we know about the history of crime, poisoning has invariably been the instrument of choice of the fairer sex, or am I wrong?"

"You're quite correct of course," Carrick responded, "though I don't suppose the brass would want us to be jumping to stereotypical conclusions."

Both men were only too aware of the modern politically-correct culture that had forced its way into modern policing methods and though they would never knowingly show discrimination of any kind towards anyone involved in a case, suspect or victim, they were both realists and it was true that, sexist or not, women *were* historically the chief exponents of the use of poison.

"We need to keep an open mind I suppose," said Connor.

"Of course, I agree entirely" Carrick replied.

"About this meeting?" asked Connor.

"Seeing as how you've got two victims at your end, I suggest my sergeant and I drive down to Richmond and see you there," Carrick suggested.

"That's fine by me," Connor replied. "How soon can you get here?"

"How about we pull all the files together and Sergeant Cole and I will drive down to your place first thing tomorrow? We should be able to get to your office by ten or ten-thirty if the traffic's not too bad."

"Sounds good to me. I'll make sure my sergeant, her name's Lucy Clay incidentally, sends you directions by e-mail. You should find us quite easily."

"Until tomorrow then Inspector," said Carrick.

"Until tomorrow it is then, and the name's Sean by the way."

"Charles!" Carrick responded.

"OK, see you tomorrow then Charles."

"And you Sean."

As he replaced the phone on its cradle Sean Connor swivelled his office chair and glanced out of the window, trying to allow his thought processes to decode any scrap of inspiration from his conversation with Charles Carrick. The sun was shining, and Connor watched the comings and goings in the police station car park for a couple of minutes, vehicle doors opening and closing, men and women entering and leaving the hot metal boxes that formed twenty-first century man's chief method of personal transportation. He was glad that he didn't have to go and climb into his car right at that moment. With the sun having been beating down on the roof for the last couple of hours it would be like a hot box in there, a true torture chamber on wheels that even the aircon would struggle to cope with in anything less than ten minutes. As his thoughts focussed again on the conversation with Carrick he concluded that the only thing they knew for certain was that three people were dead, they had all died from aconite poisoning, and it was a fairly safe assumption that they had all been the victims of the same killer who may or may not be female, and that there appeared to be no connection whatsoever between the three deceased persons who even now lay on ice in the respective mortuaries of Richmond-on-Thames and Birmingham. In short, Sean Connor concluded that they really knew damn all and he failed to see what the meeting with Charles Carrick and Sergeant Cole the next day could achieve. He knew of course that such a meeting was absolutely necessary, as the two forces would have to work together on this case and he and Carrick needed to set up a fast and efficient means of communication between them. If nothing else tomorrow would see that procedure hammered out and put in place.

A blue Ford Mondeo pulled up in the car park and Sean Connor watched as his assistant extricated herself from the vehicle and began walking towards the main entrance to the station. Sergeant Lucy Clay waved a cheery greeting to another officer who passed her on her way in; it was another sergeant, Peter Newell, who Connor had worked with on a previous case. "Good man", he thought to himself. In less than two minutes a knock on his door was followed by the person of Lucy Clay, who smiled a cheerful greeting at her boss as she walked into the room and sat in the visitor's chair directly opposite Connor. Her skirt was almost the same colour as a picture Catherine had shown him of the purple monkshood plant, topped off by a pale blue shirt-style blouse. She looked very hot and flustered. Connor resisted the temptation to comment on her choice of colour scheme for her outfit.

"It's bloody hot out there Sir," she gasped as she fanned herself with the grey manila file that she held in her right hand.

"Come in and sit down Sergeant Clay, why don't you?" said Connor in amusement at Lucy's very 'forward' entrance, and use of the chair.

"What? Oh yes, sorry Sir, but listen, it's so hot, and I've been rushing about all morning trying to get this information, and anyway here it is, and I thought you'd want it as soon as possible."

"Right, yes, well, what information are we talking about exactly, Sergeant?"

"Aconite Sir! We know of course that it's a poison. We know that it was used to kill people. We also know that they died pretty horribly, but the one thing we don't know is just how the aconite got into their systems. They were all different people from different backgrounds, and in different places so we can assume that they didn't all ingest it from some common source, right?"

"My, you have been busy haven't you Sergeant? Come on Lucy, where is all this heading? What have you got in that folder in your sweaty little hand?"

"Well, I thought that in order to find out how the aconite got into their systems we might need the help of an expert on the subject. I talked to Doctor Nickels, and she's good but even she couldn't answer the big question. She did however give me the name of someone who might be able to help, and hey presto! I made a couple of calls to the National Police Forensic and Toxicology Lab in Oxford and the senior toxicologist there gave me the name of the world's foremost expert in the toxicology of certain plant based alkalis who just happens to live in this country. I pulled all the information I could get on the guy from the police national computer system and even more info from a search on the internet, (that's mostly what's in this file), and then I called the professor at his home. He works from his own lab in the basement of his house, would you believe? But anyway, he's agreed to see me this afternoon, and with a bit of luck we might just find out how the aconite could possibly have been given to three separate people in three separate places, presumably all at around the same time, and in three different locations."

"You're a bloody genius Lucy. Well thought out. Just who is this genius by the way?"

"Professor Simon Medwin, Sir. He's Australian apparently, but seems to have spent most of his life either in this country or the USA. Seems his research is more appreciated here than anywhere else."

"When you said you were seeing him this afternoon, I have to presume that he lives not too far away from here?

"That's the spooky thing Sir. He lives right here! His house is just outside town, less than ten miles from where we're sitting right now."

"That's too much of a coincidence Lucy, surely. We get three murders in one day, all from aconite poisoning, two of them here in town and the world's leading expert on the bloody stuff has a private laboratory right where it's all happening? Something tells me that Professor Medwin has just jumped to the top of our list of suspects. Well, to be fair he's our only suspect."

"That's what I thought, but according to the Senor Toxicologist at the National Police Lab, Medwin is unimpeachable. He's helped the police out on a number of occasions in the past all over the country and there's no way he could be involved in the murders."

"No one's *that* unimpeachable Lucy. What time are you seeing him?"

"Three o'clock. I thought you might want to come and lead the interview?"

"Hey, no Sergeant. This was your idea. You tracked him down, so you follow it up for now. You talk to him. See what you can find out. If you think there's anything worth following up I can jump on the bandwagon later. Let him think he's our only hope of solving the case. Lead him on a bit. See if you think he might be hiding something. Use those instincts of yours Lucy. Heaven knows we need a break. Professor Medwin might just be it!"

Clay left Connor's office feeling rather pleased with herself. She'd used a large slice of initiative and it appeared to have paid off. Whether Professor Simon Medwin proved to be a viable suspect or simply as she'd thought at first a great source of professional assistance she knew that Connor was pleased with her work that morning and that meant a lot to Lucy Clay. When she'd been selected by Connor for the post of his assistant there'd been a few raised eyebrows amongst a small minority of the older and more experienced officers at the station but Connor had insisted she was the sergeant he wanted. She'd worked under Connor on a couple of previous murder investigations and he'd been impressed by her work, hence the role she now filled within the local Criminal Investigation Division.

As she prepared a few notes for her meeting with Simon Medwin and as Sean Connor left the building for a working lunch with his own boss, Detective Chief Inspector Harry Lewis, the one thing that no-one wanted to happen, happened. That twist, the aforementioned proverbial kick in the backside that had been waiting to jump up and surprise them all took place less than five miles from Richmond Central Police Station, and less than five miles from the home of Professor Simon Medwin.

At the beautiful Georgian-style house known as 'Badgers Holt' situated on a leafy lane that no-one could possibly connect with heinous murder eighty-five year old retired High Court Judge Nathan Tolliver had just finished his lunch, served to him by Henry, his faithful manservant of many years, when he suddenly complained of a tingling sensation in his mouth and lips. As Henry tried his best to help his employer the burning sensations and the numbness arrived to ravage the old man's age-weakened body and as Henry, in fear and panic dialled 999 on the telephone, Judge Tolliver jerked in one last violent spasm and expired on the dining room floor, his coffee still warm and untouched where Henry had placed it less than ten minutes before.

The poisoner had claimed his or her first high-profile victim and, rightly or wrongly Connor and Carrick would soon begin to feel a mounting pressure from quarters hitherto silent in the affair.

As he drove to his lunch with Harry Lewis at The Swan and Anchor hotel, Connor heard the screeching sound of an ambulance siren heading for an unknown destination in the opposite direction.

"Not for me this time," he thought to himself.

Of course, he was wrong.

# Chapter 10
# Going Nowhere, Running Backwards

Connor's pager sounded less than ten minutes after he'd sat down to a lunch of tuna salad and cold beer with Chief Inspector Lewis, who'd been out of the office all morning but who wanted Connor to brief him on the case over lunch. He'd immediately called the station to be informed by Lucy Clay that a report had been received which indicated that Judge Nathan Tolliver, retired, had just been reported as having died suddenly at his home. The responding officers, being well aware of the poisoning cases currently under investigation had immediately informed their senior officer on being appraised of the circumstances of the judge's last minutes on Earth by Henry DeVere, the judge's manservant. Their boss, Inspector Maurice Black had immediately called Connor's office: Lucy had responded to the call and now Connor's lunch was about to be curtailed before he'd barely managed to raise his glass to his lips.

Detective Chief Inspector Lewis was aghast at the latest development in the case and insisted that Connor go immediately to the scene, which of course he would have done anyway.

The sight that met his eyes when he walked into the judge's dining room was one of apparent mayhem. Food and plates were strewn across the floor and the table and it was obvious that old Judge Tolliver had flailed around in panic as the effects of the poison had taken hold. The body itself was still exactly where the victim had fallen and come to rest at the moment of death. The two officers who'd responded to the emergency call, Sergeant Beresford and Constable Lee had acted with all due caution and strictly in accordance with procedures. Nothing had been moved and no-one had been allowed to touch the body so far with the exception of the paramedics who'd first answered the 999 emergency call, and the police doctor who'd arrived at the scene only minutes before Connor.

Sean was impressed by the efficiency of the two uniformed officers and made a note of their names for future reference. One never knew when one might need a good man on one's team, and these appeared to be two very good officers by Connor's reckoning.

Tolliver's body lay at a grotesquely unnatural angle, his head and neck seemingly at odds with the position of the torso and legs. His fists were clenched as though in a spasm of great pain, and his shoulders appeared hunched into his body. Sean Connor had no doubt that the judge's death had not been a pleasant one, if indeed any death could ever be described as pleasant. This was different though. The old man, who could surely have done no harm to anyone in his advanced state of years had been subjected to a painful and horrific last few minutes on the planet and no-one, Connor believed, deserved to meet with such a fate. Lucy Clay was in the sitting room talking to Henry DeVere and after ascertaining all he could from his initial examination of the death scene, Connor decided to join her in the less oppressive surroundings in which she was now conducting her interview with the judge's manservant.

He nodded to Lucy as he entered the room. She rose from her seat and introduced Connor to Henry DeVere, who struck the detective as being an archetypal manservant. Strong of build, with a military bearing, possibly an ex-guardsman, and fiercely loyal to his employer, Henry DeVere looked crestfallen and in deep shock as he shook the hand of the detective inspector. Connor bade him to sit once again and also asked Lucy to continue the interview. He would simply sit in and listen.

As he listened, Connor felt as though he were listening to his own previous interview with Lawrence Betts, the employer of the first victim Sam Gabriel. DeVere could think of no-one with a reason to do the judge any harm and no, he hadn't received any threatening phone calls or letters recently, *that DeVere knew of*, and no, the judge hadn't expressed any fears or worries to his faithful manservant who, it transpired was indeed an ex-Coldstream guardsman, and who had served the judge for over ten years, becoming more of a friend than a servant to his employer. He'd left the house for about an hour that morning to go shopping, but apart from that he'd spent all day up to the time of his death with the judge. Henry DeVere was most insulted when asked if he might know whether he was a beneficiary in Tolliver's will. He had no idea if the judge had left him anything and was appalled that the detective could even think that any such bequest if it existed, could have provided him with a motive for murdering his employer. Henry DeVere was clever enough to know what Connor had been hinting at. Connor apologised to the man whilst at the same time reminding him that a murder had most likely been committed and that it was his job to apprehend whoever had done this terrible thing and that meant that everyone close to the judge had to be scrutinised and eliminated from his enquiries in order to narrow the list of suspects down.

Henry DeVere calmed down. He wanted to see the killer caught and promised to do all he could to help the police. Truth be told however, neither Clay nor Connor felt that there was much that DeVere could tell them that would be of help in finding the murderer of Judge Tolliver. As with all the other victims, this one had no known enemies, *though a retired judge certainly might have enemies they didn't know about yet*, and though they couldn't be sure as yet, Connor suspected that the judge neither knew nor had any connection to the three earlier victims.

After dismissing DeVere, who left to try and busy himself in the kitchen, Connor turned to his sergeant and asked: "Well, Lucy, what do you think of it so far?"

"Shit, Sir. That's what I think. We're getting nowhere fast, almost running backwards in fact. We've got nothing to connect the victims, and not a single idea of motive or even a hint of a suspect."

"Ah, that's unless you count your professor of poisons or whatever he is, who you're seeing this afternoon. By the way, I hope you realise you're going to be late for that appointment now that this has happened?"

"Don't worry. I called him as soon as I got the call to come here. I told him I'd likely be delayed, and he said he'd be at home all day so there was no need to worry about what time I arrived. You don't seriously suspect Professor Medwin do you Sir?"

"I don't know what to think Lucy, and that's the truth. Maybe we'll know more once you've spoken to him."

"You know, we really don't know for sure that the judge died from aconite poisoning yet. This could be unconnected with the other deaths for all we know."

"Do you really think that Sergeant? I think that would be stretching coincidence a little too far. I know we have to wait for the post-mortem to confirm it but I'm almost a hundred percent certain that Judge Tolliver is the fourth victim of our phantom poisoner."

"I know Sir, so am I, but I just thought I'd mention the possibility of natural or some other cause of death."

"Quite right too Lucy, but no, I've no doubt that this is another victim. I'm going to have a closer look around and then let you get off to your meeting with Medwin. Then I'd better ring Charles Carrick and let him know what's happened. Hell, the poor guy hasn't even got here yet and we've got another body on the mortuary slab. This is getting to be like murder city Sergeant and I tell you, I don't like it, not one little bit. Go on, find out what you can from the Professor, we need something more tangible to go on. We have to know how the poison is being administered for one thing, and then we might at least know where to start looking for our murderer."

Sean Connor made a brief but thorough search of the murder scene, neither expecting nor actually finding anything to help his investigation. Lucy Clay set off for the home of Professor Medwin and the paramedics placed the body of the unfortunate judge in a body bag and reverently and respectfully carried the body out of the house and into the waiting ambulance. From there they drove the short distance to the mortuary where Catherine Nickels would once again find herself getting up close and personal with the aftermath of the aconite poisoner's handiwork.

Connor eventually returned to his office from where he called Charles Carrick. The West Midlands detective was surprised to be told of yet another victim in Richmond. He concurred with Connor that things were rapidly getting out of hand, then told him that his own investigation had thrown up precisely nothing in the way of leads or suspects, much the same as Connor's inquiries. Carrick promised to be in Richmond as early as he could the next day and wished Connor a good evening before the two men hung up on each other and then, in their respective offices miles apart from each other both men independently first buried their heads in their hands, scratched their heads in a vain search for inspiration, and then rose from their desks and headed for their respective police canteens where they both felt in need of strong coffee and something to fill the increasingly large voids that had developed in their stomachs.

An hour later, having gorged himself on coffee and three large cream cakes Sean Connor returned to his office to await the return of his sergeant with her report on her meeting with Professor Medwin. Chief Inspector Lewis came to his office as he sat rifling through his notes on the case so far but there was little that Connor could tell his boss. He promised Lewis that he'd give him regular updates on the case but that there could be very little to report until Lucy Clay filed her report on the meeting with Medwin and until Connor had held his conference with the detective from Birmingham the following morning.

Meanwhile the local newshounds had had their ears so close to the ground that the death of Judge Tolliver had made the four o'clock radio news bulleting. Without waiting for confirmation from either the police or the coroner, the news hacks were already ascribing the judge's death to the same killer who had poisoned the earlier victims.

From his position of rest on the chintz sofa in the sitting room of his home Michael Stride heard the news report on the death of the judge and his sightless eyes could suddenly see the events from all those years ago or at least, that's how it felt. Of course, it was all in his mind. Michael knew that. The sound of the boiling kettle in the kitchen broke into his dark and private world and his sister's cheerful voice called out: 'Won't be long Mikey. Tea's ready!"

As the door creaked a little on opening and Angela walked into the room with two steaming cups of tea and a plate of biscuits on a tray, Michael Stride put all thoughts of the past to the back of his mind. After all, such things were safest there.

# Chapter 11
# Haunting Memories

Far from leaving the station and going home to enjoy a quiet evening at home, *it was always quiet since the divorce,* Connor decided to pay a visit to the widow of Sam Gabriel. Someone, somewhere had to know something that would lead him to a connection between the victims, and there was a connection, of that he was sure. Perhaps the families of the victims didn't know or realise what linked them, but if he probed deep enough Connor was sure that someone would volunteer that vital spark, the piece of information or evidence that may be so small in itself, but which would provide him with the kick-start his investigation needed.

Lynne Gabriel was still in a state of shock at the death of her husband. The pregnant widow sat in a high-backed armchair as Connor sank into the comfortable dralon covered sofa in her well-furnished sitting room. It was obvious as Connor looked around the room, that Sam Gabriel had provided a very high standard of living for his wife and himself and would have done equally so for the child that Lynne was expecting, the child he would never see and who would never know him.

The red rings around her eyes betrayed the fact that Lynne Gabriel had been crying just before his arrival and though she'd done her best with a tissue there were still tear stains on her face. Connor knew that he'd have to be very diplomatic in his questioning of the woman, something he was well-accustomed to in interviewing the grieving spouses of murder victims.

"I'm sorry if this an inconvenient time to call, Mrs Gabriel," he began.

"That's alright Inspector," she replied. "I'm afraid I'm not at my best at the moment, as I'm sure you understand."

Connor nodded, saying nothing and allowing her to say whatever she wanted to for a minute. He felt sure that being left here alone in her home meant that she needed to let out some of the pent-up stresses and strains that she must undoubtedly be feeling.

"I still can't believe it you know. He was so, so alive if you know what I mean," said Lynne, with tears beginning to well up in her eyes once more. "My father has been wonderful, but he left me this morning to drive up to Edinburgh and bring my mother back with him. They'll be here later tonight but these last few hours here on my own have been pretty awful I'm afraid. I'm sorry; I shouldn't be burdening you with all this should I? You came to ask me some questions?"

"There's no need to apologize Mrs Gabriel, really. You wouldn't be human if you weren't feeling just the way you do at the moment. This whole thing has to have been absolutely dreadful for you. I'm just sorry that I have to intrude upon your grief, but I'm sure you understand that I have to ask these questions, that I have to try and find out who did this to your husband?"

"Of course. I want to help in whatever way I can. Just promise me Inspector Connor, promise that you'll find out who did this to poor Sam, and that they'll be locked away for ever."

"I promise you that I'll do everything in my power to bring the murderer to justice, Mrs Gabriel. As for how long they'll be locked away for, that's a matter for the judge I'm afraid if and when we get the bastard to trial."

Sean Connor had sat with enough grieving spouses in his time to know that he needn't apologize for the small profanity in his last sentence. The recently bereaved often appeared to see it as a sign of strength when he adopted a show of naked belligerence towards the as yet unidentified perpetrators of the murder of their nearest and dearest.

"What do you want to know, Inspector?"

"We already know your husband's movements on the day of his death Mrs Gabriel. We know what he ate for breakfast before leaving home, and even what he ate the day before his death. As yet we aren't sure how the poison got into his system, but we're working on it. The real reason for my calling on you this evening is to try and see if we can find something that connects Sam to the other victims in this case. There has to be something that the killer sees as linking Sam, Virginia Remick, David Arnold the train driver, and Judge Tolliver together. You may not know what it is, but it's there somewhere, so I'm hoping that you'll give me a guided tour of your husband's past, as best as you know it, right back to his childhood if you can."

"I'll do my best Inspector. It's a shame that Sam's parents are both dead. They'd have been far better at relating his childhood days to you I'm sure."

"That's OK Mrs Gabriel. Please, just tell me as much as you know."

For the next half hour, Lynne Gabriel gave Connor his requested guided tour of her husband's childhood, adolescence, teenage years and early adulthood, right up to the time the two of them met. She backed up her story with photographs, both from his childhood, and of their life together. As she related the tale to him, Sean Connor could see nothing at that point that would join any of the dots in his case; that would link Sam Gabriel to the others.

He knew it had been a long shot that he would strike lucky on his first call. It may be that something in Lynne Gabriel's statement would eventually tie in with something from the other victims' relative's statements. For now, he made painstaking notes of everything she related to him, knowing that any detail, no matter how insignificant it might appear at present might eventually prove decisive in bringing the case to a successful conclusion.

As Lynne cleared away the scrapbooks and photograph albums, one particular snapshot caught his eye. It was a picture of Sam's parents, standing next to a black limousine, obviously taken in their younger days as the couple appeared to be no more than in their early twenties when the photo had been taken.

"Do you know when or where this was taken?" he asked.

"I'm sorry Inspector; I can't help you with that one. Sam would have been able to tell you where they were I'm sure, and he might have mentioned it to me in the past, but I can't be sure. I probably wasn't taking much notice. His parents died before we met so I never knew them and though they were obviously important to Sam, I might have been a little lackadaisical in listening to some of stories about them, you know how it is?"

Connor nodded. He understood just what the lady was saying. Sam Gabriel had probably spent hours telling his wife all about his parents, and much of it had probably gone in one ear and straight out the other one. She wasn't being cruel, but never having met them they would have appeared unreal and to some extent unimportant to her as she began her life with her new husband. She'd probably nodded her head and said "Yes, that's nice" or something similar whilst missing much of what Sam had told her.

Oh yes, Sean Connor knew just what she meant and he couldn't bring himself to push her any further on the subject that evening, so he made a polite but hasty retreat from the home of the grieving widow and made his way back to his own home, picking up a Chinese Take-Away meal on the way which he devoured as soon as he arrived at the now lonely house he'd once shared with his own wife in the days when he too had been part of a couple, before the bad times set in and he ended up on his own with just memories to haunt his evenings and nights much as Lynne Gabriel would now find herself being haunted by the memories, albeit mostly happy ones probably, of her newly deceased and much loved husband Sam.

After finishing his meal, Connor cleared away and disposed of the cardboard and foil containers that had held his sweet and sour chicken and rice, and then proceeded to down two bottles of strong beer in quick succession. Whether it was the effect of the alcohol or the memory of his meeting with Lynne Gabriel, or a mixture of both, some kind of morbid desire crept into his mind and Sean Connor went to the bottom draw of his bedside table and returned downstairs to spend the next hour going through the photograph albums his ex-wife hadn't wanted to take with her when their marriage had ended. He knew that he'd end up being haunted himself through the night, as memories of the good times he'd shared with Marilyn reared up into sharp focus in his mind, intertwined with the pain that he'd felt at discovering her betrayal of their love and the eventual sadness and heartbreak of the final separation.

Finally, the detective laid aside the albums and rose from the sofa, trudged into the kitchen and rescued another bottle of beer from its place of confinement in the fridge. He followed that with another, and another until his mind relaxed sufficiently to allow his body to sink into the welcome black oblivion of sleep.

When he woke the next morning, still with his feet up and his head at an odd angle on the arm of the sofa, with a stiff neck and sore bones, the first thing Sean Connor did was to consign those photograph albums to the dustbin. Despite the amount of alcohol he'd consumed the night before he'd had a troubled, disturbed night with dreams he'd rather not have dreamed. He'd had enough personal haunting to last him a lifetime.

He glanced at the clock. He just had time for a quick shower and a change of clothes. He had a meeting with his counterpart from Birmingham to attend that morning. He skipped breakfast. The police canteen would satisfy his needs when he arrived at the station, and within thirty minutes of opening his eyes he was in his car and on his way to work. As he reflected on the death of his own marriage he concluded that yesterday was gone, tomorrow had yet to dawn, and for now he would concentrate on today.

# Chapter 12
# Medwin's Theory

As he drove the eight miles from his home to the station, Connor wound down the driver's window, hoping that the cool draught would help to clear the fuzziness from his head. As coherent thought began to replace the effects of his minor hangover he reflected on why he hadn't heard from Lucy Clay since she left the station the day before in order to interview Professor Medwin. She'd left his presence quite late of course, having been delayed by their attendance at the death scene at Judge Tolliver's house. She hadn't returned to the station by the time Connor had left so he assumed her session with the professor had turned out to be a long one, though he thought it strange that she hadn't rung him later that evening as she normally would, to fill him in on the results of her inquiries. A sudden thought hit him as his mind became clearer, and as he sat at a red light waiting for the green to appear he took the opportunity to pull his mobile phone from his pocket and took a quick look at the screen.

Damn! Two missed calls. He felt sure that they would be from Clay, and as the lights changed and he engaged first gear, he promised himself that he would check the phone as soon as he arrived at the station. The next question he posed himself in his mind was why his sergeant hadn't called him at home. Then again he hadn't checked his answering machine when he'd got home but he knew he'd have heard the phone ring anytime later in the evening, wouldn't he?

Shortly after eight a.m. Connor rolled into the police station car park, wound up the window and stepped from his car feeling more like his usual self. Perhaps disposing of the photographs the night before had had a cathartic effect on him, but he certainly felt better in himself than he had for a long time. He checked his phone and confirmed that the missed calls had been from Lucy Clay. He'd soon put matters right when he got upstairs to the office.

As he stepped out of the elevator on the third floor and walked along the corridor towards his office he was met by his assistant, who approached him from the opposite direction with a worried look on her face.

"Are you alright Sir?" she asked, with a note of concern in her voice.

"Of course I'm alright Lucy. Why shouldn't I be?"

"I tried to call you last night, and there was no reply. I was a bit worried in case something was wrong."

"Yes, I'm sorry. I found your calls on my mobile this morning. I went to see Mrs Gabriel after I left here yesterday and then went for something to eat and a couple of drinks and got back late and…"

"But I tried to phone you at home as well, about ten o'clock it was, and there was no answer."

*"My God"* thought Connor, *"that beer must have been strong."* He'd been at home when Lucy had rung but hadn't heard the phone ring at all. He'd been in too deep a sleep.

"I left you two messages," she went on.

Such was Connor's state of mind and body when he'd awoken that he hadn't even checked his answering machine that morning. An apology was in order and he wasn't too big or too proud to provide it.

"Look, I'm sorry Lucy. I had a bit too much to drink to tell the truth, and I fell asleep on the sofa. I didn't surface until this morning and I must have slept through your calls. I had a hangover when I woke up and didn't check my answering machine, so I've no excuse. Like I said, I'm sorry."

Lucy Clay smiled. She'd suspected as much and was flattered that her boss had gone to the extent of apologising to her when it hadn't really been necessary. He was, after all, a grown man and fully entitled to drink himself into a stupor after working hours if he so wished.

"No apologies necessary Sir," she replied. "I just thought you'd want to know how the interview with Professor Medwin had gone, that's all. It was nothing that couldn't have waited until today anyway."

"You bet I want to know," said Connor, engaging his professional head to the full. "Let's retire to my office and you can tell me all about it. We've got plenty of time before Carrick and his sergeant arrive from Birmingham."

Connor and Clay armed themselves with two coffees in styrene cups from the machine that stood in the corridor and walked into his office, closing the door behind them.

As the noise of everyday police station hubbub retreated into oblivion behind the closed door they sat down on either side of Connor's desk and he nodded at his sergeant, who took that as a sign to begin her report.

"Well, I think that the first thing I should say is that I'm pretty sure we can dispense with any notion that Professor Medwin is our killer. For one thing, the reason he works at home is that he's in a wheelchair. He suffers from Multiple Sclerosis and has barely left his house for the last year. He's a genius in his field alright, but I doubt he'd have been able to administer poison to people in different locations with the speed our killer must have done all in the space of a day."

"He could have had an accomplice," said Connor, clutching at a final dwindling straw. He knew deep down of course that Medwin had never really been a serious suspect; there was nothing at all to link him to the victims.

"Sir, believe me, it wasn't him. He's as upright and honest as the day is long, I'd swear to it, and he was very, very helpful yesterday."

"Go on then Sergeant, impress me," said Connor with a smile on his face and in his voice.

"Well, for one thing, aconite isn't that hard to get hold of. It was quite a surprise when Professor Medwin told me that thousands of people probably have the stuff growing in their gardens all over the world, not just here in Britain, and don't even know what they really possess. Anyway, it comes in many different varieties but the one thing they all have in common is that they can be used to produce a deadly poison. The poison itself is usually obtained from the root of the plant, though the flowers themselves can have a harmful effect if swallowed.

As to the physical nature of the stuff, the aconite can be ground to a pulp and made into a liquid which could be drunk or even injected intravenously, or it can be dried and powdered, thus making it possible that it can be made into tablets or, and this was Professor Medwin's best guess bearing in mind the nature of our victims deaths, the powder could be placed into capsules, even tiny time release capsules, allowing the killer to be well away from the scene of the crime by the time the poison took hold."

"Ha!" said Connor. "Good for the professor. Why didn't I think of that? Of course, it makes sense. The killer, whoever he or she was, could have forced the victims to ingest a capsule containing the poison and then simply moved on to the next one on his list. But, and this is the big but, Lucy, if that were the case, why didn't the victims protest or refuse to swallow the capsules? Even if they had swallowed them, don't you think they'd have told someone?"

"Yes, of course, that's what I said, but the professor had another idea on that as well."

"Oh, did he now?" Connor went on. "Do tell me what our learned professor thinks Lucy. I'm intrigued as to what his theory might be."

"Well Sir, it needn't have been a capsule in the real sense of the word, as you or I would think of anyway. The professor suggested that the poison could have been wrapped in a slowly digestible covering, even something a simple as sugar or rice paper, and then inserted into another foodstuff in such a way that the victim might never know they'd ingested the stuff at all. Equally, it could have been injected into a food product. The killer could have hidden the poison in a bar of chocolate for example, or a cream cake, or…"

"OK, OK, I get the picture," said Connor. I must say I rather like your Professor Medwin. He seems to have given us a working hypothesis if nothing else, though it still doesn't get us any nearer to identifying the killer."

"I'm sorry to differ from your opinion Sir, but it does," Clay exclaimed.

"It does?" asked Connor.

"Yes indeed. According to the professor, although raw aconite itself is easy to obtain, making it into the poison in the form required to murder all those people would require at least a modicum of professional and technical knowledge. Professor Medwin thinks that when and if we find the killer he'll turn out to have some medical or pharmaceutical knowledge."

"You mean we're looking for a mad doctor or chemist, is that it Sergeant?"

"It's a possibility that's all Sir, but a good one based on what the professor told me."

"I agree with you Sergeant. I think your afternoon was far more productive than mine, that's for sure. While we're waiting for Carrick to arrive, why don't you get on that computer of yours and see if you can find any history of similar or related cases in the past involving members of the medical or pharmaceutical professions? Also, see if we have any records anywhere of any doctors who may have been struck off for misuse of poisons and who might therefore have a grudge against society. It might not be much but it's a place to start."

"I'm on it Sir," said Clay, as she rose from her chair, grabbed the manila folder containing the notes of her interview with Medwin and made for the door.

"Just find out what you can before Carrick arrives," he called to her disappearing back.

After Clay had left his office Sean Connor leaned back in his chair and tried to assess what little knowledge they'd gleaned so far. Whoever had killed the four victims had moved swiftly and professionally, that much was certain. Connor knew that poison was usually a very personal way of killing, and was usually associated with women. All four victims died in agony, and had given no clues as to what or who had introduced the poison into their systems. The more he thought about it, the more Connor kept returning to the word 'personal' There had to be something intensely personal about the either the killer's relationship to the victims, or in the victims' relationships to each other and somehow that must indirectly link them to the motive of the killer. It was there, he knew it was. Something just out of reach, something he was missing in the whole case scenario. If he could just put his finger on it Connor felt he could crack the case wide open, but, for now, that niggling clue, the link he sought remained elusive, at arms length, waiting, like time itself, real yet not real, without form or substance, for something to happen.

Before he knew it the hands of the clock had moved around to almost ten a.m. and he was disturbed from his thoughts by a knock on his door. As Clay showed Detective Inspector Charles Carrick and Detective Sergeant Lewis Cole into his office, he hoped that the presence of the West Midlands detectives might just herald the arrival of the cavalry!

# Chapter 13
# Tea and Biscuits

"We should do something, tell someone what we know," said Michael Stride from his usual position on the sofa.

"But what *do* we know?" asked his sister Angela as she sat in the arm-chair opposite her brother. "What took place was years ago and can't possibly have any bearing on what's happening now Mikey. You're just overreacting."

"I don't care", her brother continued. "There might be a connection. You never know. If we at least tell the police they might find something to connect the two cases."

"Oh please Mikey, don't be so stupid. How can something that happened thirty years ago possibly be connected to these random killings? I'm sure Mary would agree with me. We've had enough tragedy in our family haven't we? Why go dredging up the past when it should stay dead and buried?"

Michael Stride leaned back against his supporting cushions and sighed heavily. His disabilities made him dependent on his sisters and he knew that Angela was probably right. If both she and Mary saw no need to go to the police then he had little choice but to accept their decision. He knew they'd never desert him of course, but arguing with them would only antagonise them and Michael had always held a dread deep down inside of what life would be like for him if his sisters weren't there to take care of him. He knew only too well that without their constant care he would probably end up in a soulless and impersonal home for the disabled, or worse still be permanently hospitalized, neither of which scenarios were in any way attractive to him.

"I just thought we might be able to offer some help, that's all," he said quietly, knowing already that the argument was lost.

"Listen Mikey, I'll talk to Mary when she comes home OK? We'll see what she thinks and then decide what to do, alright?"

Michael nodded his acquiescence.

"After all, "Angela went on, "thirty years is almost a lifetime ago Mikey. There can't be any reason why the police would be interested in what happened to us. It was another time, another world, and this is today Mikey. Time's moved on and so have we. I'm sure none of us want to have to live through those old memories again, now do we?"

If Angela Stride could have put herself inside her brother's head she would have realised that those 'old' memories were still very fresh in her brother's mind. Not a single day went by without the horrors of the past replaying themselves, often in terrible slow motion, deep within Michael's sightless and often pain-wracked world. Neither one of his sisters could even begin to imagine what it was like to live the way he did, with the knowledge that his sight was robbed from him not by birth, accident or illness, but by those very events which Angela now seemed to want to make sure were buried for ever. For Michael Stride the cause of his blindness, the shock that took away his view of the world could never be buried, not even for a day. He knew though that now wasn't the time to try to argue the point or to try to explain his inner feelings for the umpteenth time to his sister. After all, both Angela and Mary had their health and strength; they hadn't been affected by it the way he had. He knew also that though they loved him and cared for his needs each and every day, the time might come when they would see him as an encumbrance, a weight around their necks, and that he had to do everything he could to keep them from being angry with him, or thinking him 'difficult'.

So, Michael said nothing to his sister and would say nothing to anyone else, but then, apart from his sisters he came into contact with so few outsiders nowadays, apart from occasional visits to the hospital. After all, even his everyday medical needs were served by his sister Mary, even though he was sure that wasn't quite ethical. But then again, no-one knew him or his medical history better than his eldest sister and she'd always done what was best for him, hadn't she? She was at her surgery now and he knew that when she came home Angela and she would confer, and they'd agree with each other and his concerns would be noted and then dismissed. After all, what did he know? He was just the crippled brother!

He nodded once more in Angela's direction, he knew when to shut up, and his sister appeared satisfied with his acquiescence as she then asked:

"Cup of tea then Mikey, and some of your biscuits?"

"Mm, yes please Sis," he replied. Further discussion of the subject was thus terminated and Angela Stride walked out of the room and into the kitchen where the sound of the boiling kettle soon reached Michael's ears. He heard the sound of biscuits being placed on a plate, his hearing having been far more acute since the day when the blindness had struck him all those years ago and within minutes, his sister returned to the sitting room and placed the plate of biscuits within Michael's easy reach on the side table. She gently took his hand and guided his fingers to the handle of the mug.

"Be careful won't you Mikey? It's hot."

As he sat back with the tea in his hand Michael Stride concluded that he wouldn't mention the subject of the murders again unless his sisters talked of it when Mary returned home. Angela soon turned their conversation around to the subject of his next hospital appointment, still a full month away, but for now, certainly as far as his sister was concerned life in the Stride household had to all intents and purposes 'returned to normal'.

# Chapter 14
# Death by Chocolate?

The handshake that accompanied the first meeting between Sean Connor and Charles Carrick was one more suited to that of two old friends meeting after a long separation. It was firm and warm, and with the physical connection between them made, it was as if the two detective inspectors had also established a mutual psychological bond from that briefest of contacts.

Sergeants Cole and Clay were also included in the joint introductions and without too much in the way of informal preamble, the meeting began.

"Bad business, the judge," said Carrick, "yet another one to add to the list eh?"

"I'll say," Connor replied. "We haven't a single concrete lead yet. Anything from your end?"

"Well, all I can tell you is what we found out yesterday afternoon. I despatched Sergeant Cole here to Liverpool to interview David Arnold's widow and, well, look, it'd be better coming straight from you Lewis," said Carrick, nodding to his sergeant.

"Right Sir," said Cole, clearing his throat before beginning. "The lady lives just outside Liverpool in a place called Prescot. She was distraught, as we might expect when I got there. It seems her husband drove the Penzance express regularly. It was one of his favourite runs apparently. He wasn't just a locomotive driver; he was a railway fanatic, in love with trains since he was a boy. Anyway, the day before he'd died, he'd left home in the morning, driven the Liverpool to Manchester local, then taken the Manchester to Truro down to the South Coast. That would have taken him to the end of his shift, so he'd then caught a train himself from Truro to Penzance where he'd stayed the night in a guest house he always used when he did this particular run. It's called 'The Crooked House' and I've got the local boys down there checking it out. He'd have gone straight from there on the morning of his death to the station at Penzance where he'd have signed on for work and then taken the express out. The wife spoke to him the night before he died. He was in his room at the guesthouse apparently and all was well according to her account. Now Sir," Cole crooked his head to one side a little as he leaned forward towards Connor, as though about to reveal something important, which in fact, he was. "This is where we might just have something."

Cole paused for effect.

"Get on with it man, for God's sake," said Carrick firmly but jovially.

"Yes Sir, sorry Sir," said Cole.

"Well, as I was saying, when David Arnold got to the station he spoke to the staff supervisor who was on duty in the office. He said that he was surprised to find someone outside the station so early in the morning giving away free samples of luxury chocolate. He thought that the woman would have been better off waiting until later when there'd be more folk around on the station concourse. He didn't say whether he'd taken or eaten any of the chocolates, but, and this is why I think it might be significant Sir, when he'd left the office the supervisor sent his assistant, a young clerk called Deborah Vale to go and see this woman. It was normal practice after all for any company wishing to use the station for marketing purposes to obtain permission from the station master. The supervisor, a Mr Beattie had been given no such paperwork from the station master's office. The woman was obviously not authorised to be there. Anyway when Miss Vale got there, the woman was gone. She searched around the station for five minutes but there was no sign of anyone giving away free chocolates. Deborah Vale, being an enterprising girl even checked the streets all around the station. Perhaps she fancied some freebies for herself, but anyway there was no woman. Conceivably the woman gave the driver something sir, and then legged it quickly away from the scene of the crime, so to speak."

"Bloody hell, Sergeant," said Connor. "And you got all of this from the widow?"

"Yes Sir, seems the supervisor was an old friend of David Arnold's, known him for years. They used to exchange Christmas cards and so on, and anyway, he phoned Mrs Arnold to offer his condolences and he told her all of this. Before you ask, we've got the Penzance police talking to Mr Beattie even as we sit here. There may be more he can tell us, though I doubt it."

"Well done Sergeant," said Connor, who then turned and looked at Charles Carrick.

"I'd say, Charles that you and Sergeant Cole here have found out more in one afternoon than we've managed to glean between us down here from day one. A woman, I knew it! My own pathologist even suggested that poison was traditionally a woman's weapon."

"We don't know for certain that this 'chocolate woman' was the killer though do we?" asked Carrick, erring on the side of caution.

"No," said Connor, "but I'll bet a year of my pension that she's got something to do with it, even if she isn't the actual killer. It just seems strange, a woman handing out free chocolates at the station so early in the morning and then just disappearing before the morning rush hour crowds start arriving."

"And," said Lucy Clay, joining in the conversation, "the mere fact that Arnold spoke of the woman to the station supervisor leads me to think that the driver *did* take one or maybe more of her free samples, or why bother mentioning it?"

"My thoughts exactly Sergeant," said Carrick.

"Shame there's no description," said Connor.

"True," Carrick agreed, "but at least it's a place to start."

"It most certainly is," Connor concurred with his colleague from the West Midlands. "Now, if only we knew where to start looking for this woman."

"Well," said Carrick. "Sergeant Cole here has asked the Penzance police to help us out by following up their interview with the Station Supervisor and his clerk with a tour of some of the local guesthouses and bed and breakfast hotels. Working on the theory that the killer must have been from out of town, if the case is linked to those here in Richmond, we can probably assume that this woman, if she is the killer, or at the very least an accomplice, would have stayed overnight somewhere, and if she didn't have friends or relatives in town then a hotel would have been her only option. Single women staying on their own in a hotel room for just one night can't be too thick on the ground, so if we have to we'll check out everyone who was registered at any of the hotels in town on the night before David Arnold died."

"There could still be quite a few," Connor cautioned his colleague.

"I know, but we'll check them out just the same."

"I just hope we get somewhere with this case before the bastard strikes again," said Lucy Clay.

"You really think he, or she will strike again then Sergeant?" Carrick asked of Connor's assistant.

"I hope not of course Sir," Clay replied, "but I just have this awful gut feeling that whoever is doing this isn't finished yet, that's all"

"I hope you're wrong Sergeant," said Charles Carrick, "I really hope you're wrong."

"Excuse me Sir," said Lucy Clay to Charles Carrick, a thoughtful expression on her face.

"Yes Sergeant?"

"We seem to be assuming that this woman, whoever she was, wasn't local to Penzance, is that right?"

"I think that's a safe assumption Sergeant, he replied. "Bearing in mind the killings here in Richmond, I think she would have been a visitor to Penzance, there for the sole reason of administering the poison to David Arnold. I doubt she'd be a local to the town, though I admit I could be wrong. Only time will tell."

"So," Lucy went on, "even if she did check into a hotel or B & B in Penzance, the chances are that she used a false name and address. She wouldn't want to take a chance on being traced if the police did latch on to her, as we seem to have done."

"I take your point Sergeant," said Carrick, "and there's also the possibility that this woman, whoever she is, had nothing to do with the killing of David Arnold, though I find that a remote prospect."

As the detectives continued their conference in the office of Sean Connor, the sun streamed through the window and Connor himself couldn't help but feel that although they hadn't moved forward to any great degree, there was a small glimmer of sunlight creeping into the investigation. As with all such cases success or failure in apprehending the perpetrator often hinged upon the smallest insignificant clues or occurrences. Connor thought that perhaps this sighting by the dead man of a potentially bogus sales representative giving away chocolates so early in the morning could yet prove to be the key to unlocking the case. There was a long way to go, he knew that, but he felt that now they had something, he and the others would soon find more links that would eventually tie the case together.

A ringing sound began to emanate from the jacket pocket of Charles Carrick. He removed the phone from its home in his jacket, flicked the clamshell open, peered at the screen and then excused himself, rose from his chair and walked over to the window, where he continued his conversation in a low voice. Connor and the others lowered their own voices as Carrick alternated between talking and listening, mostly the latter, until, a couple of minutes later he closed the phone and returned to his seat, from where he addressed the others, who sat waiting in anticipation of an announcement from the detective inspector. When he spoke, they weren't disappointed.

"That was Doctor Gary Hudson, the chief pathologist back home in Birmingham," he said, giving Hudson's full title for the benefit of Connor and Clay. Based on what we found out about the chocolate woman I asked him to check Arnold's stomach contents again and guess what?"

"Chocolate?" asked Connor.

"Chocolate!" said Carrick, triumphantly. "Microscopic traces to be sure, but chocolate nonetheless. Arnold had vomited in the cab, and any traces contained in that would have been contaminated by the oil, dust and grease on the floor, from the soles of his boots, but the stomach definitely showed the smallest traces. At first Hudson thought it must have been ingested the night or the day before the victim died due to the trace amount but now he realises it could have been eaten on the morning of the victim's death, and the rest of it would have been expelled when Arnold vomited.

"We've got our murder weapon, at least in one case" said Connor.

"Death by chocolate," Lucy Clay volunteered, the use of the name of the popular chocolate dessert not being lost on the men.

"Very apt Lucy," said Connor.

"And very true by the sounds of it," said Carrick.

"There's still one big question we need to answer of course," said Lewis Cole, who'd been quietly thinking as the others spoke.

"And what's that Sergeant," asked Connor.

"Well Sir, we might have an idea how the engine driver was killed, and we think we know that this 'chocolate woman' was involved, but, bearing in mind the fact that three of the four victims lived here in Richmond and that David Arnold was possibly poisoned before he left Penzance even though he lived in Liverpool, then we still have the problem of identifying just where the killer lives. Is it here in Richmond, in Liverpool perhaps, or Penzance as we said but dismissed as improbable? Of course, there's the possibility that the killer lives somewhere else altogether and visited Richmond in the same way that she visited Penzance."

"Good God, Cole, you could be right!"

The exclamation came from Sean Connor.

"Lucy," he turned to Clay. "Get some uniforms out on the streets. I want the local hotels and B & B's checked for lone women staying for one or two nights immediately preceding the killings here. There's a chance that the killer delivered her death doses here in the same way as in Penzance, if 'chocolate woman' was indeed the killer."

Without another word, Lucy Clay rose and left the office. She'd have a team of officers making inquiries within fifteen minutes.

"A useful first conference, eh Sean?" asked Charles Carrick as the meeting drew to a close.

"Definitely Charles, thanks for bringing us the first piece of really useful information," Connor replied.

He'd given the West Midlands detectives a copy of the files on the Richmond killings. It included all that he and Clay had learned of the victims so far, and also a copy of the interview Lucy Clay had conducted with Professor Medwin. As Connor had said to Carrick, there wasn't much in the way of concrete information contained in the Richmond file, but perhaps as time went by and the two teams of detectives worked together, something might suddenly take on a new importance that had so far eluded them. Carrick and Cole promised to read and digest every word of the file after lunch, and then it would be time for the Birmingham police officers to return to their own patch. From then onwards however, the two inspectors would work closely together, both on the telephone, and with regular get-togethers, until the case was solved.

Both Connor and Carrick knew that it was now only a matter of time before they began to piece this case together. In the case of David Arnold, they now felt that they had the 'how?' now all they needed was the 'who?' and the 'why?'

If and when they could answer those questions in relation to the Richmond victims as well, they'd have their killer but as they both knew, for the time being 'chocolate woman' was still out there somewhere, perhaps with a deadly supply of tasty treats, so, until they could put a name and face to the lady and until she could be brought in to face her just deserts no-one on her list, if indeed she had one, could be considered safe.

For now though it was time for lunch, and whether by design or not, Connor noticed that not one of the four of the officers who'd met around the desk in his office that morning ordered the tasty chocolate dessert that was offered on the police canteen menu.

# Chapter 15
# After Dinner Speaking

Lunch over, the four detectives gathered once more in the office of Sean Connor. It would be a short meeting as Carrick and Cole had to leave for their return journey to Birmingham by mid-afternoon. They still had their own independent investigation to continue in the West Midlands and their own investigative team would be awaiting their return in order to find out what the two men had learned from their counterparts on the Richmond end of the investigation.

As they took their seats around Sean Connor's desk it was Connor himself who voiced the one point that had been on all of their minds since the morning meeting and which now needed discussing before the two teams separated.

"There is of course one scenario that we must seriously consider," he began; "and that is that there is more than one killer involved here. After all, the deaths of Sam Gabriel, Virginia Remick and David Arnold all took place on the same day and all within a couple of hours of each other so it's almost impossible that one killer could have been in two or three places at once in order to administer the lethal doses of poison. If we assume that this 'chocolate woman' was the one who gave David Arnold a poisoned chocolate then, unless she'd given Gabriel and Remick similar doses the day before with a very clever and very long time-delayed action, we have to assume that someone else was in Richmond in order to give them the poison."

Lucy Clay stopped twiddling the lock of her short blonde fringe that Connor knew to be his sergeant's trademark when deep in thought. She had been silent almost from the moment they'd re-entered the office. Now, having deliberated in her own mind for what seemed an age, she spoke:

"Actually Sir, if you'll all take a look at the notes of my interview with Professor Medwin, he did in fact raise the possibility of the killer having used a time-delay mechanism to deliver the poison. If the killer has sufficient medical and pharmaceutical knowledge and the professor believes that everything so far points to that possibility, then he or she could have refined the aconite down to small dissolvable pellets and sealed them into the kind of capsules you often get your prescription medicines in. He or she could even have obtained slow dissolving capsules of over the counter medicines such as ibuprofen, emptied the original contents, and placed the poison inside, together with a catalyst that would delay the release of the contents or at least allow for a slow release of the aconite over a period of hours. If small enough they could have been hidden in a fair sized chocolate and the victim might not have even known they'd swallowed it."

"I see," said Carrick, "and of course, if that is the case, then we could be looking for more than two people here. The killer could be like a spider sitting in the centre of a web, and this woman, and others perhaps are his 'angels of death', lets call them; being sent out to deliver his packages of poison to targets anywhere he directs them."

"So we could be looking for someone who isn't even in Richmond, Liverpool, or Penzance," added Sergeant Lewis Cole.

"Bloody Hell," said Connor, "how much worse can this damned case get? We're already getting nowhere fast and now we're raising more questions than we have answers for."

The others all knew that Sean Connor was right. The deeper they dug into this case, the more the options for confusion were arising. Were they looking for multiple killers, or one killer with a host of accomplices willing to do his or her bidding in delivering the poison to the victims?

"Another thing," Charles Carrick volunteered, "is the method of delivery to the victims. In the case of David Arnold and Sam Gabriel, it's highly likely that they would have been susceptible to accepting a chocolate from a pretty woman. The same applies to Mrs Remick. After all most ladies of my acquaintance are partial to chocolates, but what about Judge Tolliver? From what we know he rarely left his home, and his manservant would have known if anyone had delivered anything to the old man on the day of his death."

"Wait a minute," said Connor then directed his next words to his sergeant.

"Lucy, did anyone ask DeVere if there'd been any callers at the house on the day of Judge Tolliver's death?"

"Yes Sir, I asked him myself, but I've just realised, bearing in mind what we've been discussing, that I didn't ask if there'd been any visitors the day *before* he died. How could I have been so stupid as to fail to ask him that? Oh, he did leave the house for an hour to go to the shops, so there was a small window of opportunity for the killer then, but I'll speak to DeVere again as soon as we finish here"

"It's not your fault," said Connor. "We didn't know at that stage about the possibility of the time-delay capsules. Tell me, did Professor Medwin say anything more about the capsule theory? For instance, why didn't they show up in the post-mortem examinations?"

"That's easy to answer," she replied. "Usually the capsules themselves are made from a totally dissolvable granulated gelatine substance that disappears without trace once digested. In the trade they're apparently known as hard-shell capsules, and they are manufactured to a very high degree of tolerances and accuracy according to the final end use of the individual capsule. Once digested they'd be almost untraceable. We wouldn't have known what to look for it hadn't been for the professor."

"Very clever," said Carrick. "So I think it's safe to assume that we're looking for someone with specialist knowledge then."

"Without a doubt," Connor agreed.

The telephone on Connor's desk began to ring. He answered it with a gruff, "I thought I asked not to be disturbed," to the unfortunate telephonist on the switchboard.

"Sorry Inspector," came the poor woman's disembodied voice. "It's Doctor Nickels. She said it was vitally important that she speak to you right away."

"OK, put her through," said Connor, instantly calming down and actually thinking that the woman had used a fair bit of initiative in disturbing his conference. Most of the switchboard staff would have obeyed his instructions to the letter. This girl, whoever she was, had realised the importance of the call and risked his wrath in order to help him. He'd seek her out later and thank her personally.

"Catherine," he said as the connection was made.

Catherine Nickels spoke to Sean Connor for about two minutes, with the inspector hardly saying a word, just nodding from time to time and making noises of assent to whatever the pathologist was relating to him.

At last, he replaced the phone on the cradle, having wished the doctor a good afternoon and thanking her for the information. He turned to the others and announced:

"Doctor Nickels just told me that Judge Tolliver had enough aconite in his system to have killed a horse, no, in fact, two horses. The other victims all received a lethal dose but nothing in the vicinity of this amount apparently. Whoever did this made sure that there was no chance whatsoever of Judge Tolliver surviving the attack. According to Catherine Nickels this was definitely a case of overkill."

Carrick sat dissembling this latest piece of information for a moment then responded;

"You know Sean, I have a feeling that the judge might be the key to all this. He was a high court judge for years wasn't he? Perhaps we should be looking for someone with a grudge against the old boy."

"Yes," added Cole, "and maybe the other victims are linked to the judge through a case he sat in judgement on."

"That's the best theory we've come up with so far," Connor seemed pleased. "It would certainly fit with what we know so far, and would perhaps explain why the judge received such a terrifyingly high dose of the poison, if he was the one responsible for putting someone away who felt hard done to or aggrieved enough to commit murder. We need to look into the judge's case files, find out what he was involved in over the last, I don't know, maybe the last ten or fifteen years of his career. That would mean going back at least twenty years or so as I think he'd been retired for at least five years."

"I'll get some men on it right away Sir," said Lucy Clay determinedly.

"Good, and make sure they look into the criminals, the criminals' families, and the victims," Connor replied. "It might sound stupid, but this killer could even be a victim who felt let down by the judge letting some evil bastard get off lightly with a crime and who feels that justice wasn't properly served."

"Could be a long list," said Clay.

"Got any better ideas Sergeant?" Connor asked.

"No Sir, leave it to me. I'll get some good men on it," Lucy replied.

As the meeting broke up soon afterwards and Connor, Carrick, Clay and Cole shook hands all round, the Birmingham detective spoke to Connor one last time before leaving.

"You know Sean; I really think we might be on to something with the Tolliver link. Maybe the killer was sending us a twisted message with the over the top dose of poison administered to the judge, you know, like making us sit up and take notice. Perhaps we were supposed to make the link about the judge and a past case. Maybe the killer is playing us along, and leading us to where he or she wants us to go."

"Maybe Charles, but the only place that bastard is going is straight to jail when we lay hands on him, or her, along with the chocolate woman and any more of these 'angels of death' if they exist."

Carrick and Cole took their leave of the Richmond detectives and Lucy Clay went to organise the search through Judge Tolliver's files and also to speak to his manservant about possible callers the day before the judge's death.

Sean Connor sat back in his office chair and reflected on the day's events, and on the meeting with Carrick and Cole. He knew they were two good men, and could be relied on to treat the case with as much professionalism and diligence as he and Clay would apply to it here in Richmond. Connor also felt that they were getting somewhere, and that the investigation into the cases of Judge Tolliver could be the key to solving the case. He was a man who trusted his instincts, and at that moment all of those instincts told him that he and the others had, by diligent detective work, arrived at the one feasible theory for the deaths of the four victims. He just hoped that they would be able to find the link between the judge and the killer before anyone else fell victim to the deadly poison that, even at that moment could be waiting in an innocent looking capsule, disguised as a tempting chocolate or some other equally tasty food trap for the next victim to unknowingly ingest.

Only time would tell in the case of the last scenario, and time, as Sean Connor knew was most definitely not on his side. The theory was sound, that he knew, but so far he had no flesh to put on the bones of that theory. Had he known what was yet to unfold in the case of the aconite poisoner Sean Connor might not have felt quite as confident in his ability to bring the case to a successful conclusion, but then, as he knew from bitter experience, knowing the how and the why still wouldn't necessarily lead him to the who?

For now though he would have to proceed slowly, one tentative step at a time. A short while ago they had had questions, but no answers. Now at least, they were on the verge of at least answering some of the more basic of those questions. At any rate, that's what he thought at the time. Looking out of his window at the sun-drenched car park below, he allowed himself a moment of relaxation, closed his eyes and breathed deeply. Then, with his resolve set at maximum Sean Connor rose from his chair, departed from his office and made his way out of the building without speaking to anyone on the way. He had work to do, and he knew just where he was going.

# Chapter 16
# Afternoon Tea with the Strides

"I said no, and I mean no, and that's my last word on the subject Mikey. Now, will you please drop it?"

Michael Stride was quite taken aback by his eldest sister's tirade. He was used to a more refined tone from Mary, what with her being a doctor and all. She was normally so laid back and as a rule would never raise her voice, particularly towards Mikey. Now however, his sister appeared to be angry with him, though he couldn't quite make out why she needed to be so aggressive towards him.

"Look Mary," he began, only for his sister to interrupt him;

"No, you look Mikey. I've had a long hard day and then I come home and Angela tells me you want to go raking up the past all over again and bringing more hurt and shame on this family. Well, I'm telling you now, I just will not allow it. Do you understand?"

Michael certainly didn't need his sight to imagine his sister going red in the face with anger at that moment. He felt he had little choice but to acquiesce to her demands that he give up his quest, at least for the time being.

"O.K. Mary, I'm sorry. I just thought we might be able to offer some useful information, something that might help, that's all."

"Like what Mikey? Go on, tell me what we could possibly do that would help the police? It was *thirty years* ago Mikey, and we all know what happened back then don't we? Shit, it was bad enough that you had the misfortune to be born with only one leg, and that not much use as it is, but then to lose your sight through the sheer shock of what happened back then. Well, no I will not let it happen again. The past is the past and it can remain buried forever as far as you're concerned. Now, is that clear? I'll tolerate no more talk of us going to or even talking to the police."

"I think you've made it very clear, thank you Mary," he replied, feeling more useless at that moment than he could remember in a long time. Michael certainly didn't need his sister to remind him of his incapacity, or his day to day dependency on her and Angela. He was only too aware of his disabilities and though he would have wished his life to have taken a very different path, Michael had no choice other than to go along with his sister's wishes if he wished to continue his relatively peaceful and well cared for existence.

Mary seemed to calm down. She was also aware that she had perhaps spoken a little too harshly to her brother, who had no idea how much she and Angela had sacrificed over the years in order that they could look after him, in Mary's mind at least. Then again, she knew it wasn't his fault and her compassion for her brother now slowly began to overtake her anger. Mary moved across the room and sat beside her brother on the sofa, gently placing her right arm around his shoulder.

"I'm sorry Mikey," she said softly in his ear. "I shouldn't have said those things. They were cruel and hurtful and uncalled for. Please forgive me little brother."

Michael reached out his hand across his sister's lap and took hold of her left hand.

"It's OK Mary, really," he said. "I know it's hard for you, and you do so much to look after me. I don't want to make things difficult; for you or for Angela. You should know that. I was only thinking of our civic duty, but you're right of course. What bearing could what happened when we were kids have on what's happening today? I won't mention it again, honest."

Mary squeezed his hand and rose from the sofa. In reality, although she loved her brother dearly she often felt uncomfortable when she sat in very close proximity to him as she just had. She knew she shouldn't feel like that of course, but she couldn't help it, it always affected her that way. The fact that she experienced those feelings always gave Mary a feeling of guilt, a hatred of her own self for feeling like that towards her crippled brother, and that in itself made her try to keep such moments to a minimum.

"Angela," she called, knowing that her sister would be in earshot, just along the hall in the kitchen. "I think Mikey is ready for his meal now."

Angela came rushing busily into the room, carrying a tray containing Mikey's afternoon meal. He always had a sandwich and a cold drink about this time of day, and Angela had had it all prepared and ready when Mary arrived home. She'd told her sister of Mikey's conversation with her that morning, and Mary had made her hold the meal back until she'd spoken with their brother. Now that the argument was over and done with, the household could get back to normal, if any day in the Stride household

could really be described as such.

"Here you are Mikey," said Angela as she placed the tray in his lap. "Everything just the way you like it."

"Thanks Sis," he replied as his hand reached out to pick up the chicken sandwich she'd placed before him. There was nothing else to be said, at least for the present.

# Chapter 17
# A Burial of the Past

Sean Connor returned to his home on the outskirts of town shortly before seven that evening. Between them, he and Lucy Clay had set in motion the various threads that he hoped would provide them with a springboard from which to advance the investigation. Detective Chief Inspector Lewis had given his blessing to an extra three detectives being assigned to work with Connor and Clay, so in addition to the number of uniformed officers already working flat out on various tasks connected with the investigation, Sean Connor now had a team of over thirty officers working virtually full-time on the case. By six o'clock, he'd exhausted the amount of productive work achievable for the day, so Connor had taken the decision to call it a day and head for home.

Now, he sat in his kitchen with a glass of iced malt whisky in his hand, his shoes kicked off and lying in the corner of the room and his feet raised and resting on one kitchen chair as he sat on another.

Barely two sips into his drink Connor was disturbed by the sound of his doorbell ringing. At first he was tempted to leave it, to ignore whoever had decided to invade this little bit of personal space and freedom he'd allowed himself in the middle of an increasingly frustrating investigation. When the bell rang again however, this time for far longer than the first time he cursed his ill-luck and placed his feet back on the floor they'd so recently left, and, ignoring the shoes which were scattered at two differing sides of the room he padded towards his front door and in a mood of increasing cantankerousness he opened it to reveal, standing on his doorstep, none other than the smiling face of pathologist Catherine Nickels.

"Catherine," he spoke in genuine surprise.

"Hello Sean, I phoned the station and they said you'd left for home. I thought if I came straight round I'd catch you before you got too settled for the night. You don't mind do you?"

"Of course not," he replied, and Connor was genuinely pleased to see the attractive doctor standing on his doorstep. His earlier grumpiness seemed to be dispelled in an instant as he motioned for her to come in and follow him, which she did, until the two of them were seated comfortably in Sean Connor's living room, he in an armchair, Catherine on the sofa just across from him.

It had been a while since her last visit, and Connor wondered whether this time she was visiting him on business or for personal reasons. In truth he hoped it might be the latter. Since his divorce, Catherine Nickels had been the only woman who had set foot in his house on a social level and that had been for too short a time. Now, hoping that his question would be answered in the negative, Sean asked the doctor;

"Is this about the case Catherine? Have you found out something that couldn't wait?"

"Don't be silly Sean. If it had been I'd have telephoned. No, I just thought that you looked a little weary, a bit worse for wear the other day when you came to the morgue. I thought you might need a bit of cheering up that's all, so, here I am. I'm sorry if I'm intruding on your evening, and you can tell me to go away if you want, but I thought you might like some company. We could have a chat, maybe a drink or two and if you feel like it I'll treat us to a take-away, Indian or Chinese, you name it; I'm easy."

"We'll go Dutch," said Connor, "and let's make it a Chinese." He realised he was smiling broadly for the first time in a long while. He was delighted that Catherine had turned up out of the blue. The prospect of sharing his evening with a pretty woman, with a meal and drinks thrown in, was the brightest chink of light that had crept into his dull and increasingly boring life for some time.

With that, Catherine seemed to relax into her place on the sofa a little more, crossing her legs and leaning back against the comfortable cushions scattered randomly across it as she gratefully received the brandy that Connor passed across to her. He'd remembered her favourite tipple as well, she liked that.

Connor was used to seeing her in her white coat or worse still in her scrubs, her arms and hands invariably covered in the various fluids and such that were part and parcel of her job. To see her sitting on his sofa in her smart business suit, her hair neatly brushed and hanging loose rather than in it's usual position of being tied back so as not to interfere with her examination of the bodily remains associated with her everyday life, and sans the white coat of course, made him realise what a beautiful woman she really was. He just managed to stop himself from passing a highly flattering remark concerning her legs, which moved with a lithe suppleness as she uncrossed and recrossed them, her skirt riding up to reveal a little more leg, then transferring her opposite foot to the floor. Maybe now wasn't the right time for such compliments.

He allowed himself to think about the last time she'd been in this very room, but that had been six months ago, and Connor had been hit by an almost schoolboyish nervousness on that occasion, being tongue-tied and very gauche, until Catherine had beaten a hasty retreat from the house after less than an hour. Perhaps this time would be different. He hoped so.

Three hours later he felt that the evening was proving something of a success. He hadn't scared the pretty pathologist away, and they'd managed to studiously avoid the pitfalls of discussing the case he was working on, or his ex-wife. Catherine knew, almost by instinct as well as reports from mutual acquaintances, that Sean found it very difficult to talk about what had happened between Marilyn and himself and Catherine had no desire to open up old wounds that might spoil their time together. The two of them had found much in common between them and Connor had even managed, after they'd shared a sizzling repast of Chinese food to find the courage to place himself on the sofa, next to Catherine.

At last, the detective felt that it was time for a case of 'fortune favours the brave,' and, with a little hesitation, he reached across and took Catherine's hand in his own. To his intense relief, she didn't make any attempt to snatch it back. Instead, she allowed him to squeeze her hand, and she squeezed back, giving him the signal that he was waiting for. Turning his head to stare into her eyes, he used his free hand to turn her head until they were looking directly at each other. Seeing no sign of resistance in Catherine's eyes Sean Connor took his life in his hands, and leaned forwards towards her. Still she didn't pull back and then, their lips met. Sean Connor hadn't touched a woman since his divorce and Catherine had already told him there'd been no-one special in her life for some time, and now it showed. They kissed with a passion born almost of desperation in a kiss that they would both probably remember for a long time, even if nothing more came of that night.

Neither of them spoke one single word for what seemed an age. After the kissing stopped they simply sat staring into one another's eyes for some time, until Sean again took the initiative and allowed his hand to fall and rest on Catherine's lap. When he reached down to touch her knee, she froze for a second, then, as he felt her relax again, he allowed his hand to slowly work its way up her leg, beneath the skirt of her smart business suit which was beginning to lose some of its pristine appearance by then.

"No Sean, please, not here," her voice suddenly breaking into the heavy silence that had developed.

"I'm sorry," said Connor, rapidly pulling his hand away and sitting back, looking extremely contrite. "I thought…"

"It's OK, really," she said, "I only meant that we might be more comfortable if we went upstairs, that's all. You do have a bed up there don't you Detective Inspector?"

"I certainly do," said Connor, relief pouring into his voice, "or at least, I did the last time I looked.

Little more was said as Sean Connor took the hand of the beautiful pathologist and the two of them walked slowly from the sitting room, up the stairs and into the bedroom that Sean had once shared with his now forgotten ex-wife. As the two of them fell into each others arms and as the hours of darkness fell, Sean Connor and Catherine Nickels found the togetherness that both had been missing in their lives for a long time and as the dark of night gave way to the light of the following morning they came together once more, and then, before they knew it, the sun had taken the place of the moon and a day's work lay ahead for both of them.

Sean made breakfast while Catherine showered. Soon after, the two of them stood together on the doorstep where she'd arrived less than twelve hours ago, though now that seemed a long, long time ago.

"We really will have to do this again sometime," said Catherine.

"And soon, if you don't have any objections," Connor replied a little formally, his earlier clumsiness creeping back into the relationship with the cold light of day.

"You can bet on it," she went on. "I'll call you after work tonight if you like."

"Yes, please, do that Catherine."

"OK, now I really have to go. My clothes are all rumpled from our evening on the sofa, and I need to rush home and change. My staff would have a fit if they saw me in this state," she laughed.

"Go then, quickly," he laughed, "before I arrest you for loitering on my doorstep."

As she drove away from his house, Sean Connor's heart felt lighter than at any time since Marilyn had deserted him. The day ahead beckoned, and he approached it with a new gleam in his eye.

# Chapter 18
# Elementary, Inspector Connor

Lucy Clay was the first to see the difference in her superior officer that morning. Something in the way he carried himself as he walked through the open plan sector of the department on the way to his office gave him away, and she was a detective after all.

"You look like the cat that got the cream this morning Boss," she smiled at him. "Is there something I should know?"

"Morning Lucy," he replied. "If you must know I had a very enjoyable evening in the company of a very fine lady, and I'm feeling on top of the world."

"That's great Sir, and about time too if you don't mind me saying. Who's the lucky lady then, or is it a state secret?"

"As you say Sergeant, a state secret, or at least, my little secret for the time being. Out of respect for the lady, I'll keep my love life private for the time being if that's ok with you."

"Whatever you say Sir," Clay responded, smiling at her boss, and feeling secretly pleased that he had something else to occupy his time apart from work. She, perhaps more than anyone was aware of the workaholic tendencies that had virtually taken over Connor's life since his divorce. She knew it would do him good to develop a new social life, and if he'd managed to find a little romance along the way then Lucy Clay was delighted for him.

The rest of the morning was spent in going through interminable paperwork as the two officers tried to decipher some shred of a clue from the statements they and the team had so far managed to accrue. There was little that could be called useful and frustration and exasperation were beginning to creep into their day. There'd been no further word from Charles Carrick in Birmingham so Connor had to conclude that the investigation in the West Midlands had reached a similar hiatus as his own. As he and Clay were devouring their third cup of coffee of the morning a knock on the door brought some welcome relief from the paperwork.

Detective Constable Tim Kelly almost fell through the door, such was his enthusiasm to communicate the information he'd obtained.

"Yes Constable, where's the fire?" Connor joked with the young detective.

"Sorry Sir, it's just that I thought you'd want this information straight away."

"OK man, spit it out," said Connor.

"Well, I've been on the detail checking out the local hotels for this 'chocolate woman' we've been told about, and I called in at the Regency Hotel near the station and the receptionist there remembered a woman who stayed there the night before Sam Gabriel and Mrs Remick died."

Connor's ears pricked up. The young detective had got his full attention now.

"Go on man," he encouraged.

"Right Sir. Well, the receptionist, a Miss Reynolds, told me that a woman checked in at about seven in the evening. Miss Reynolds remembers her well because she was the only single person to check in during her shift that night. The only other rooms she let were to an elderly couple and a pair of sales reps from a tyre manufacturer who shared a room to save money. Anyway, she was able to give me a pretty good description of the woman and I've asked her to come down to the station after work today to help the police artist put together an impression of the woman."

Connor was impressed but said nothing. He knew that Kelly hadn't finished.

"The other thing is, she also remembers that the woman was quite agitated, as though she was scared or nervous abut something. She was a little furtive, that's my word, not Miss Reynolds' and kept looking over her shoulder as if she was being followed, or as if she expected someone to come up from behind her."

This was the best news Connor had received so far in respect of the investigation. He also knew instinctively that there was yet more vital information that Kelly was holding back until the end of his report.

"Do we have a name, Kelly?" he asked, unable to contain himself any longer.

"We do Sir. It may have been a false name and address of course, but Miss Reynolds allowed me a look at the register. The room was registered in the name of Miss Shirley Holmes, and the address," Kelly paused to check in his notebook,

"Don't tell me Kelly, the address was Baker Street, London?"

"That's right Sir, but how did you know?"

"Whoever she is, she's got a sense of humour, I'll give her that," said Connor. "Think about it man. Shirley Holmes? Think 'Sherlock', then put that together with an address in Baker Street and you have the great fictional detective himself. She's playing games with us Kelly, that's what she's doing."

"Damn, I'm sorry Sir, I should have thought… "

"Don't worry about it Kelly. Why should you have thought it? You got a name and that was what we needed. How about a description?"

"About forty-ish, smartly dressed in a two piece blue skirt suit, sort of ash-blonde hair Miss Reynolds said, though she did say she thought it was dyed. She couldn't remember the colour of the woman's eyes, but she did say that she was about the same height as she is, which would make her about five feet two."

"That's great Constable, it gives us something to be going on with, and narrows the investigation down a wee bit. She really was very clever, and if I'm not much mistaken the false name and address was left there deliberately. She knew we'd check the hotels, and this could be her way of taunting us."

"I know Sir. I just wish I'd thought of the Holmes and Baker Street connection myself. It's so bloody obvious when you think about it."

"I said forget it. At least when this receptionist comes in we might get some idea of who we're looking for. You've done well, really. You've maybe brought us our first major lead in the case. So, you get a big pat on the back Kelly. Honestly, you've done a good job. The hotel check by the police in Penzance yielded nothing, so you've gone one better than the boys down there."

Tim Kelly blushed. He wasn't used to receiving such effusive praise from the normally dour Detective Inspector. Obviously, Connor's good humour from his night with Catherine Nickels was spreading to his attitude towards the squad's junior officers. They were used to him being polite but a little distant at times. Kelly couldn't remember the last time he'd seen the D.I. look this relaxed, especially considering the heavy burden of the current multiple murder investigation.

"Thank you Sir," was all he could think of to say as Connor smiled at him, and then went on to say:

"I'll leave it up to you to supervise the receptionist's session with the artist when she gets here Kelly. Just make sure you get the picture to me as soon as she's finished, OK? And ask her if she remembers anything else that might be of help. I'm not insinuating that you didn't conduct the first interview thoroughly but you know as well as I do that witnesses often remember things later, when they've had a chance to think. Try to make sure she hasn't missed anything out that might be useful to the investigation."

"Will do, Sir," Kelly replied, and he took his leave of the inspector and Lucy Clay.

As the door closed on D.C.Kelly, Lucy Clay broke her silence, having patiently listened to his report to Connor without butting in or making any comment.

"D'you think he's found her then sir?"

"This woman certainly fits what little of a profile we've got for the 'chocolate woman' Lucy. A false name and address, furtive and suspicious behaviour, she really could be the one we're looking for. I only hope that the receptionist can tell us more."

"So, maybe we've got lucky."

"Maybe Sergeant, maybe," Connor mused. Then again, like I've said before, she could be just a courier for the poison, a delivery agent. The real killer could be her boss; someone who we don't even know exists yet. The whole thing is like a complicated jigsaw puzzle with some of the most important pieces still missing."

"At least we've got a few of the starter pieces now though Sir," Lucy said optimistically.

"We have indeed, Sergeant, we have indeed," Connor repeated, actually allowing himself to share in his sergeant's air of optimism.

His evening and night with Catherine had obviously had a very positive effect on him, and he knew it. He made a mental note to ring her as soon as he was free and try and make arrangements to see her again that evening. In the meantime he had work to do, lots of it, and as Lucy Clay left to continue her own avenues of inquiry Connor made his way to the outer office where his team of officers were still wading through the past cases of the late Judge Tolliver. Connor had the strongest feeling yet that the answer to the present day string of murders was rooted firmly in the past and that Tolliver's court records held the clues that would lead to the apprehension of 'The Chocolate Woman' as Connor now officially named her, at least in his own mind. There was still the possibility that she was a mere pawn operating under the control of the real mastermind behind the killings, but for now she was the only option he had to go on, and something was, after all, better than nothing.

The room was a hive of activity and Connor made a point of speaking to each of the officers present. He knew that by making them feel personally involved in the case and letting them know that they had his full confidence in their abilities, they'd work twice as hard in their efforts to find that elusive clue, or clues.

After half an hour amongst the team of detectives and uniformed officers and being satisfied that no stone was being left unturned in the attempt to find a connection between the judge and the poisoner Connor returned to his office, loosened his tie, and picked up the phone, hoping that Catherine wouldn't be up to her arms in blood and human entrails. He was lucky, and after a brief but intense conversation with the pathologist Connor found himself eagerly anticipating dinner at the town's foremost Italian restaurant that evening.

He considered that things were looking up, at least in one area of his life. Now, if only that luck would apply itself to the investigation...

# Chapter 19
# A Note of Concern

The woman whom the police had come to refer to as 'The Chocolate Woman' sank back in her armchair, raised the glass of chilled white chardonnay to her lips, took a long cool sip of the refreshing wine and allowed herself to relax. It had been an eventful few days, with of course the successful conclusion of the first part of the plan. She allowed herself a small moment of satisfaction as she tried to picture the frustration and consternation that must be exhibiting itself in the minds of those charged with tracking her down. She was totally confident that she'd covered her tracks sufficiently well that, even if they did have some idea of her involvement in the killings of Gabriel, Remick and Tolliver, they would equally have absolutely no idea who she was or how to connect the victims to her.

In a way she felt sorry for them. They must be tearing their hair out trying to discover her motive for the murders, and that of course, was the beauty of the entire thing. As far as the world and the police were concerned she couldn't possibly have any connection with and therefore any motive to harm any of the victims.

She uncrossed her legs and realised she'd been sitting in one position for too long. Her right leg was red where her left one had rested on it for the last twenty minutes. She'd been daydreaming and reliving the killings, the moments when she'd delivered the fatal doses to the poor unsuspecting idiots who had been her targets. They'd been so happy when she'd approached each of them, and so very accommodating in accepting her gifts. After all, as she'd explained to each of them, she was new at the job and needed to make an impression on her bosses or she'd find herself unemployed again, and she had her little boy to take of and... oh yes, so easy.

The jangling of the telephone on the hall table made her snap out of her thoughtful reminiscences and she rose from her chair and made her way to answer the infernal thing. She was angry for not bringing the phone into the room with her. The handset was cordless after all and she could have placed it next to the chair and wouldn't have had to rise and disturb her relaxation in order to answer it. The thought that she could have left it, just let it ring until the caller hung up never entered her mind for one simple reason. She knew who would be on the end of the phone when she answered it.

Sure enough the caller was exactly who she'd anticipated and The Chocolate Woman listened intently to her instructions as the voice at the other end of the telephone spoke quickly and concisely to her, allowing little time for her to respond apart from the odd, "Yes" or "Uh huh.." She did however make sure that she made a few notes on the pad beside the phone. She wouldn't want to get anything wrong or forget something important.

The value of her actions was amply demonstrated when, at the end of the rather one-sided conversation, the caller asked her to repeat the instructions she'd just received. Referring to her notes, The Chocolate Woman repeated her instructions back to the caller virtually word for word. Satisfied, the caller said a simple "Good, I'll be back in town the day after tomorrow", and hung up.

Picking up the notepad from the hall stand she returned to her comfortable armchair. She soon relaxed back into its cushions and crossed her legs once more, this time right over left, not wanting the red mark to return, and read and reread her handwritten notes of the telephone call she'd just concluded. Taking another sip of the wine she realised that she'd neglected it for too long, the contents of the glass were warm, too warm to drink. If there was one thing she despised it was warm white wine. She placed her notes on the wine table beside her and quickly made her way to the kitchen. As she walked back to the sitting room she stopped to listen at the foot of the stairs. All was silent in the house apart from the gentle ticking of the grandfather clock that stood just inside the front door. Not a sound came from upstairs, which was just as well. She wouldn't want him to have heard anything, better he remained ignorant of the call, and her involvement in the killings. She'd let him sleep for another hour before waking him, if he hadn't already woken up by himself.

Returning to her notes she read them one more time. Her instructions were clear and concise. Prominent among the words she'd written on the page were a name, and two places. The first of those towns was the location of her next supply of chocolates, left post-restante at the central post office, and the second gave the location of her next 'client', as she'd come to describe the victims to herself.

With a deep sigh of contentment The Chocolate Woman leaned back in her chair, took a larger than usual sip of her fresh cool glass of chardonnay, and began to make mental preparations for the next two days. There was much to do, and she was now operating on a strict timetable that must be adhered to if all was to go well.

As Charles Carrick returned to his wife and two children that evening in Birmingham and as Sean Connor and Catherine Nickels sat down to enjoy their meal at 'La Ristorante Italiano' at roughly the same time, they were unaware that whilst they continued to search for the killer of the first four victims, The Chocolate Woman, acting on the instruction she'd just received, was preparing to strike again.

The second phase of the case was about to begin!

# Chapter 20
# Alternative Therapies

Oblivious to the goings on in the home of The Chocolate Woman, Sean Connor and Catherine Nickels sat across from each other at a corner table in La Ristorante Italiano. The evening had been a great success as far as Connor was concerned, the meal superb, *he loved Spaghetti Bolognaise*, and Catherine had gone to a lot of trouble to look her best. She looked resplendent in a brand new, *he supposed,* little black dress, tailored at the waist and with a hem that ended just above the knee, it showed off her figure to perfection. Connor had been quite taken aback by her obvious attempt to impress him when they'd met at the door to the restaurant, and Catherine had been gracious enough to compliment him back on his casual open-necked shirt and smart blue trousers. They weren't new of course, but it had been a while since he'd worn them and putting them on for a date with a pretty woman had been a big thing for him.

Now, as they sat feeling replete after a dessert of fresh cream-filled profiteroles and sipping cappuccinos, and with the single candle in the centre of the table having almost burned down to its base their conversation turned to the things they'd both studiously avoided during the meal.

Despite being two professionals who'd known each other for some years and despite their respective ages, they'd been like a pair of fumbling teenagers on a first date as the evening had begun. Well, of the three at least the first date bit had been accurate. They had studiously avoided mentioning either the previous night that they'd shared together or the prospect of the remainder of this one. In short, after the passion of the night before, they were both a little unsure of exactly how fast and how far either of them wanted this new phase of their relationship to progress.

"Last night; you know, it was great for me," said Connor, hesitantly.

"Me too, Sean," Catherine replied, smiling at him in return.

"I wasn't sure if perhaps you might have had some regrets this morning, you know; when you got to work and thought it through a bit."

"Why on Earth would I have done that? We're both grown-ups Sean Connor, and we can do what the hell we like. At least, I know I can, can you say the same? You're not still hung up on your past are you?"

Connor felt stung by that last remark although he knew Catherine had meant no malice in the comment.

"I'm not hung up at all" he replied. "I just thought that you might not have meant last night to happen the way it did and I didn't want you to think I'd taken advantage of you in any way."

"Honestly Sean, you are a fool. You didn't take advantage of me at all. If anything it might have been a little of the other way around. Listen to me. You might be the great detective, but you don't seem to know too much about women or about the way relationships work. There are two of us in this, and I for one am quite happy with how things stand. I enjoy your company, and I think you enjoy mine so don't go trying to analyze how I feel or whether I want to be with you or not. Believe me Detective Inspector, if I didn't want to be here I wouldn't be, and that's all there is to it."

He reached across the table and Catherine reached back and allowed him to take a firm but gentle grip on her left hand. The candle on the table at last flickered and died, and in the faded light of the dimly lit restaurant, in a hushed voice, Sean Connor spoke softly and uttered the simple words:

"Right then, that's all cleared up. Now, your place or mine?"

As Connor and Catherine Nickels were leaving the restaurant in Richmond, Charles Carrick and his wife Lizzy were in the kitchen of their modest three-bedroomed home in Solihull on the outskirts of the city of Birmingham. Lizzy had had lots of questions for Charles that evening; she always took a great interest in his cases and would always offer to help with a personal opinion if she felt it might help her husband to solve whatever crime he might be working on. This time however, even she was baffled by the events that had taken place in both Richmond-on-Thames and at New Street Station. Carrick was always careful not to divulge anything confidential to his wife, herself an ex-police constable, but he hadn't had to hide much from her on this occasion as there was so little information available to impart. He had however given her the information about The Chocolate Woman and the hotel as told to him by Sean Connor on the phone earlier that afternoon. The receptionist, it seemed had been asked to work a double shift by the hotel manager and wouldn't be able to visit the police station until the next day in order to help the police artist put together an impression of the woman.

"I can't see the wood for the trees here, Charles," she said to her husband.

"Eh?" he asked, a little distracted.

"Well," she went on, "You seem to have a killer or killers who use a particularly nasty strain of poison to despatch the victims. What you don't have is a clear motive or anything at present to connect the victims together. You say that this judge might have something to do with it, but as yet you don't know how, right?"

"Right so far," said Carrick.

"Then you have this woman in the hotel. She might or might not be the one you're after, have you thought of that?"

"Of course Lizzy."

"I thought so. Well, it seems to me you have to dig as deep as you can into the victims' pasts, not just the judges."

"Eh?" Carrick was intrigued by the way his wife's mind worked at times. She could be as direct and incisive as a ballistic missile homing in on its target when she got going.

"Look Charles, I'm not criticising you or this Inspector Connor in Richmond, but like I said, wood and trees."

Carrick still looked perplexed. He couldn't see where his wife was going with her theory. Lizzy went on:

"Look, you and Mr Connor seem to be putting all your eggs in one basket by going after the judge's previous cases. Surely you must see, Charles my darling, that he wasn't the only one with a past. All of the victims had a history and it could be that something in their pasts connects them to the killer and to the judge or just to the judge or whatever. All I'm saying is that the judge himself needn't have been the reason, or the catalyst for the killings to begin with."

"You're right as usual Lizzy," her husband responded," but you know as well as anyone that we have to start somewhere. I'm sure Connor has thought along the same lines, but the judge is as good a starting point as we've got for now."

"I know Charles. Just remember though that he needn't necessarily be the key you need to unlock the case."

Charles Carrick sighed and looked lovingly at his wife of fifteen years, and the mother of his children. She'd given up her own career in the police force to marry him when he'd been a uniformed sergeant, not long before his promotion to the detective ranks and she'd never lost the intuition of the investigator. She loved helping him theorise over his cases and it never failed to amaze him at how accurate her insights could be from time to time.

Now he looked her in the eye, smiling as he did so and tried to bring the current 'case conference' to a close. He felt an overwhelming sense of love and longing for his beautiful wife, and he had other things on his mind than aconite and chocolate poisoning.

"Right then Miss Marple," he replied. "I'm sure you have a point, and we will I'm sure be looking into all the victims' pasts as a matter of course, but you are right my darling girl, that one of them may be the real reason behind all this, rather than the judge as we all tend to think at present. I'll be sure to pass your comments on to my esteemed colleague Mr Connor in Richmond in the morning, but now, my dear girl, the kids are fast asleep and it's dark outside, and I'm fed up with police work for the night."

Without saying another word, or allowing her to speak in return, Charles Carrick took his wife by the hand, led her from the kitchen into the hallway, turning off the lights as they went and then with a playful push on her behind he guided his wife up the stairs.

Miles away from Birmingham, the Chocolate Woman put the romance novel she'd been reading down on her bedside table, listened for a minute to make sure all was quiet in the house and then, satisfied that there was no movement from the next room she turned off the light, pulled the quilt up close to her chin, and allowed her head to sink into the comfort of her pillow. She was asleep in seconds.

# Chapter 21
# Thoughts Over Breakfast

Angela Stride woke from her deep sleep to hear the unmistakeable sound of her brother coughing. His bedroom was next door to hers and she always kept his door open at night so that she'd be able hear him if he called out to her. The sunlight breaking through the crack in her curtains told her it was already daylight outside, and that at least Mikey had slept through the night. One of his problems was that, minus one leg, the prosthetic one being removed at night for comfort, and with his blindness to contend with, he often had difficulty turning over in bed, having fallen out on numerous occasions in the past and thus an in-built self-preservation instinct often left him lying in one position on his side for too long and his lungs became congested, leading to the coughing fits such as he was now in the throes of.

Angela rose, threw on her dressing gown and quickly made her way to her brother's room. It took her less than five minutes to ease his coughing, with a drink of water and a tonic mixture that Mary recommended for the purpose. She helped Mikey to dress and then assisted him into the seat of the stair lift that she and Mary had paid to be installed to make his passage up and down the stairs more comfortable and dignified.

At the bottom, she placed his walking sticks in his hands and he made his way with surefooted knowledge of his surroundings into the living room and to his usual position on the sofa.

"You just relax now Mikey. I'll be in the kitchen for a few minutes and then I'll have your breakfast ready before you know it."

"Thanks Sis, you do work hard at looking after me and I do appreciate it you know."

"Hey, that's what we do isn't it Mikey? We all look after each other."

"Well, you and Mary do anyway," he replied. "There's not a lot I can do to help the two of you is there? Speaking of Mary, when is she due back? Is it today or tomorrow?"

"Now, Michael Stride, just you stop talking like that. You help us just by being here, and where would we be without your help with all those tricky crossword clues? You're the man Mikey when it comes to those things. Without your help, Mary and I would be left with blank spaces every time we do a puzzle. As for Mary, she'll be back from the medical conference tomorrow and then we'll all have a slap up meal to celebrate her success. It's not every day your sister gets to deliver a lecture to a load of other doctors you know. It's a real honour for her."

"Of course it is," said Michael, who was proud of his eldest sister but who was still a little angry with her for being so nasty with him the other day. As Angela disappeared into the kitchen and busied herself with the business of preparing breakfast for her and her brother Michael Stride sat harbouring his own secret thoughts of what he'd like to do if he got the chance. He still felt that he should say something to somebody. It might be worthless information he was imparting, then again it might not. The trouble was, his sisters were invariably right about everything and he would have to devise a way of doing the right thing without arousing their suspicions. It was at times like these that Michael Stride really despised his own infirmities. Being blind and restricted to the use of only one good leg made his options seem deeply limited, so, for the time being, he did the only thing he could do. He sat, thinking, biding his time, until a means presented itself.

Angela came into the room ten minutes later with a tray loaded with freshly buttered toast, strawberry jam on a plate with a knife for spreading it, and a pot of steaming hot coffee. She poured for both of them, put two teaspoonfuls of sugar in Mikey's mug, one in her own and then spread two slices of toast with the jam and placed them on a plate which she passed to Mikey.

"Here we are, Mikey," she said with a cheery smile on her face that Mikey would never see.

"Thanks Sis," Mikey replied.

As he bit into the toast and tasted the sticky sweetness of the strawberry jam on his tongue his mind was only half concentrating on the breakfast that his sister had prepared for him. The other half was racing with the thought that had just come to him. There *was* a way to do what he thought needed to be done, but the big question was; could he do it in the time he had available to himself without giving himself away and thus compromising his promise to Mary, and, more importantly, giving her cause to lose her temper with him once again?

Angela stared at her brother; he seemed to be a million miles away.

"Is everything alright Mikey?" She asked with a hint of worry in her voice.

"Is there something wrong with the toast?"

"No, everything's fine," Michael replied, snapping back to the reality of the moment.

"I was only thinking Sis, just thinking, that's all."

# Chapter 22
# The Face of a Killer?

"I've got it Sir!" Tim Kelly literally burst into Connor's office without hesitating to knock.

"Kelly?" said Connor, a look of surprise on his face as the young officer, realising his lack of decorum, stood a little sheepishly just inside the door, a piece of paper in his hand. Connor had been daydreaming a little, reliving yet another night of warmth and loving in the arms of Catherine Nickels. He could hardly believe his luck.

Kelly regained his composure quickly and advanced towards the inspector, proffering the piece of paper as he did so.

"The composite Sir, the picture photofit of The Chocolate Woman, here it is. Miss Reynolds was most helpful. She came in first thing this morning knowing how important it was to get this done for us."

Connor took the sheet of paper from Kelly's hand and stared long and hard at the image produced by the police artist in response to the receptionist's description. The face that stared back at him was of a woman of around forty years of age with shoulder-length hair of indeterminate colour, though Kelly had earlier stated that the receptionist had described it as ash-blonde, and with what seemed to Connor to be deeply sad eyes, peering out from beneath a fringe that touched upon her eyebrows. The mouth was soft, almost kindly in its appearance and the nose was small and added to the feeling that this was a friendly, warm and caring person, rather than the cold blooded killer they were seeking. If this was an image of the Chocolate Woman, and she was indeed the killer of at least three and maybe all four victims they knew about so far, then her looks certainly belied her ability to be ruthless and calculating in the delivery of her lethal cargoes.

As Connor continued to stare at the image, Kelly spoke.

"I particularly asked Miss Reynolds if she remembered anything else, as you requested, and she did recall one thing. It seems that the woman insisted on paying in advance for the room when she checked in, which is unusual, and she paid by cash. Miss Reynolds found that a little odd as most of the hotel's clients pay by credit card nowadays. Anyway, that wasn't really the big thing she remembered. She told me that when she asked the woman if she'd like an early morning call or if she wanted to place her breakfast order there and then, the woman said that she wouldn't be staying for breakfast because she had a train to catch and would be leaving very early. I know it's not much Sir, but I thought it might be significant. Oh yes, one more thing. I asked Miss Reynolds if she saw the woman leave the hotel but her own shift ended at midnight so she wasn't there in the morning. She'd taken the initiative and asked the receptionist who'd replaced her if she remembered seeing the woman in Room 14 leave and the answer was no."

"Well done Kelly. Seems like a clever and resourceful girl. It might be worth noting the train angle, it might even be an attempt to throw any trailing hounds like us off the scent if we got this close, but it's something to go on. We can check with the local station and see if anyone remembers a woman matching this description boarding a train on the morning of the deaths but it doesn't explain how she delivered the lethal doses of aconite to Gabriel, Remick and Tolliver if she'd already left town. You've done well though young Kelly. Now, off with you and see what else you can dig up for me."

"Yes sir. Thank you sir," said Kelly as he departed from the office leaving Connor deep in thought.

A short time later, Connor was joined by Lucy Clay and the two of them discussed the implications of the information Kelly had obtained from the hotel receptionist.

"It's not a lot to go on Sir is it?"

"Hardly anything at all Sergeant' Connor agreed. "But, for the time being, it's yet another very slender and tenuous lead, and so far that's all we've had to go on in this infernal bloody case. I don't mind telling you Lucy, I'm getting bloody frustrated at every turn with this one. We just don't seem to be getting anywhere."

"What about the receptionist Sir? Do you think her information is accurate and reliable?"

"Well Lucy, let's face it. She hasn't really been able to tell us much at all, so I don't think she's been lying to us or making it up if that's what you mean. Kelly seems to have done a good job with her. I doubt there's much more she could have told us, and yes, I think she's probably as good a witness as we'll get. She's used to seeing people over the reception desk, and is probably quite good at reading body language and gestures if my own experience of hotel receptionists is anything to go by. I just hope her facial recognition skills are up to scratch and that this picture she's dictated to the artist is a relatively accurate representation of the woman we're after."

Lucy Clay thought for a moment, going over in her own mind the information Kelly had obtained and as related to her by Connor. Finally, a question that was also niggling at Connor came into her head and she asked her boss;

"Do you really think she left town that morning sir?"

"No Sergeant, I don't. I believe we're dealing with a very clever, very dubious character who knew that sooner or later we'd track her to that hotel, and who set up a convincing story with the hotel staff in order to throw us off the scent. I also believe that the woman in this picture had every intention of visiting the victims one by one to administer the aconite poison, and that she probably lives locally. This hotel prank was a clever blind to confuse us, that's what I believe. Listen Lucy, I want you to get a forensics team down to the hotel. I know it's probably too late to find anything of use but I want Room 14 at The Regency gone over with a fine tooth comb. There will certainly have been other guests in that room since The Chocolate Woman, but we can take steps to eliminate them from our inquiries if the search throws up any sort of trace evidence."

"I'm on my way Sir," said Lucy, rising from her chair.

"Another thing before you go," said Connor

"Yes Sir?"

"On your way out send a couple of uniformed officers along to the railway station. We'd better check out the 'train to catch' story just in case there's anything in it. Have them interview as many of the railway staff they can find who were on duty that morning. Get them to show copies of the photofit to them and let's see if anyone there *does* remember seeing the woman. It's a long shot, and I don't think it'll throw anything up, but we'd best not leave any stone unturned, if you know what I mean."

"Right you are Sir. I'll send Harcourt and Stoner, they're good men. They've been putting in lots of hours on this one sir. They really want to see the bastard caught."

"As do we all Sergeant," said Connor as she made a move to depart.

As she reached the door, she turned and addressed the inspector before leaving.

"Sir? We'll get him, I know we will."

Connor nodded.

"You can bet your life on that Sergeant Clay."

"Oh, and Sir?"

"Yes?"

"I do believe that's a trace of lipstick on your collar Sir. I thought you should know, you know Sir, just in case…"

Connor blushed.

# Chapter 23
# The Mechanics of Murder

Stopping only at the pre-arranged collection point to pick up her lethal box of aconite- laced treats, the Chocolate Woman made her way to the designated address in Guildford as per her instructions. As a believable representative of a major confectionery manufacturer complete with wig and fake identity card she had no trouble in convincing newsagent Arminder Patel of her credentials. When she explained that she was in the area to promote a new line in luxury chocolates, Mr Patel was at first dismissive of her sales pitch, assuming that the cost of the product would be too high in order for him to make a profit on the goods. He suggested that she try some of the larger independent retailers as she had explained that the large supermarket chains were already 'on board' as she put it.

When she informed him however that she was authorised to give him a month's supply of the new line completely free of charge, followed by a further month at half the normal wholesale price, his ears pricked up. He was almost hooked, but there was one final hurdle to overcome. Arminder Patel would never dream of accepting a new product without testing the goods for himself.

"Of course, you must try them anyway, they're absolutely delicious," said the woman, reaching into her briefcase and extracting what she described as her 'sample box'.

She offered the box to the newsagent, who saw that there were only three chocolates in the container.

"I've had a busy morning," she explained.

The Chocolate Woman knew of course that all three of the chocolates were laced with a deadly infusion of aconite. It hardly mattered which one he took.

"Mmm, excellent," said Patel as the chocolate melted in his mouth, and he reached out and took another.

Satisfied that her task had been completed successfully the woman now played out the last act of her impersonation, getting Patel to sign a 'contract' for the supply of the new product. Arminder Patel signed on the dotted line and she took her leave of the doomed man with a cheery wave and a "Thank you so much, have a nice day Mr. Patel."

Driving at a steady pace so as not to draw any undue attention to herself she stopped only to follow her instructions and dispose of the one remaining chocolate. It was easy to melt the poisoned confection by simply opening the hood of the car and placing the chocolate on top of the hot engine block. A stroke of simple genius and the murder weapon was rendered instantly untraceable! Less than an hour after leaving Patel's Newsagents the Chocolate Woman pulled up on the drive outside her quiet suburban apartment home, switched off the engine of the old Volvo she'd owned for as long as she could remember and made her way into the house. A sound from above caused her head to turn and her eyes to cast their glance upwards. There in the lower branches of the birch tree that stood outside the front door of her home a blackbird was singing its cheerful song. She smiled, and she felt as though all was right with the world.

Once inside the house she hung her coat on the hall stand and made her way upstairs to quickly change out of the pseudo sales reps' uniform and into something that would make her more recognisable as being herself. She could hear the sound of the radio or television coming from the sitting room, and new that he'd be sitting waiting for her when she came downstairs. She had no worries about him disturbing her. He'd never move from his chair until hunger got the better of him, and it was too early for lunch. She'd go in and see him when she'd changed but for now, she had her own priorities.

In her bedroom she quickly divested herself of the jacket, blouse and skirt that had been her disguise for the morning, hung them neatly in her wardrobe and then she dressed in a simple lightweight grey polo-neck sweater and black sports pants. She looked at herself in the mirror. She thought she looked quite attractive, but there was one last job that had to be done in order to eradicate the visual persona of the killer who had visited Mr Patel that morning. It took less than five minutes to remove the make-up and to return to being what she usually appeared to be; ordinary and anonymous, just the way she wanted it to look.

She padded down the stars in her stocking feet and pushed the door to the sitting room open. He was listening to the radio, his back towards her and the volume of the music turned up quite loud. She doubted that he'd even heard her come back into the house. She walked up close behind him and reached out to touch him on the shoulder. He jumped at her touch, then realised it was her and turned down the volume on his hand-held radio.

"I'm sorry. I didn't hear you come in." *She already knew that.*

"That's ok, I'm home now. Can I get you anything?"

"A cup of tea would be nice."

"Right then, a cup of teas it is," she said cheerfully.

"Did your shopping trip go well? Did you get everything you wanted?" he asked.

"Oh yes," she replied. "I got everything I wanted."

As the kettle began to sing as it came to the boil in the tidy suburban apartment in the tree lined avenue and the chink of spoons on crockery signalled the making of the traditional English pick-me-up, thirty miles away the sound of sirens signalled the arrival of the police and ambulance services at the premises owned by Arminder Patel. They'd been summoned by a customer of the newsagent's who'd discovered the unfortunate owner gasping for breath and writhing in agony on the floor of his shop. The police were the first to arrive, and the paramedics were only a minute or so behind them in screeching to a halt outside the shop.

They were both too late. Arminder Patel took his final breath as two uniformed police officers walked through the door to his shop. There was little or nothing for the paramedics to do though they tried everything at their disposal to try to facilitate a heartbeat from the hideously contorted body that now lay still, the throes of death having left Arminder Patel curled in a foetal position, his knees drawn up and almost touching his chin. As they placed his body in the back of the ambulance and left the scene of Patel's recent losing battle with the grim reaper, back in the home of the Chocolate Woman the door to the sitting room opened wide as she entered the room once again.

"Tea's ready," she trilled happily.

# Chapter 24
# New Plans

"In conclusion, the subject is a twenty-two year old male in good physical condition, no evidence of disease present. Giles Temple was the victim of a Road Traffic accident (RTA) and was pronounced dead at the scene by the attending emergency doctor. Cause of death was multiple traumas to the head and torso consistent with an RTA. There were four separate fractures of the skull evident and the subject had suffered a massive cerebral haemorrhage. There was also damage to the liver, spleen and multiple rib fractures, a fractured pelvis and both legs had suffered compound fractures both above and below the knee. Traces of a controlled Class A drug, namely heroin, were present in the body in ample amounts to have caused the subject to suffer from impairment of judgement and brain functions which in my opinion would in themselves be sufficient to have been a contributory cause of the accident in which the subject was reportedly the driver and only occupant of the vehicle"

Catherine Nickels clicked off the overhead microphone which recorded her words as she carried out her work from day to day. Assisted by Gunther she wheeled the remains of the unfortunate Giles Temple to the cold room and slid the body into its temporary resting place. After divesting herself of her 'scrubs', the green working gown that constituted her daily work apparel, she washed up and made her way back to her office.

Sitting at her desk she ruminated for a minute on the sheer wastefulness of life that she had to contend with every day. The young man she'd just autopsied had been in the prime of life, barely out of his teens and should have been looking forward to a long and productive life. Instead, thanks to the use of the drugs that were such an invidious blight on modern society his recently warm and vibrant body was now a cold and lifeless shell lying in a mortuary cold room and his parents would mourn forever the loss of their son.

As she shook herself from her thoughts on the folly of youth Catherine's thoughts turned to the subject that had occupied most of her morning before she'd paused them in order to carry out her examination of Giles Temple's remains. She knew that Sean Connor was becoming bogged down by the case of the aconite poisoner and she'd thought of a way that she might possibly help him in his search for answers. She made a decision and reached for the telephone.

Doctor Gary Hudson was surprised to receive the call from his counterpart in Richmond. Catherine had received a copy of his report on the examination of the body of David Arnold, which Charles Carrick had brought with him when he'd visited Connor, and Gary Hudson at first presumed that the report was the reason for her call. Perhaps she wanted to compare notes.

"No, actually Doctor Hudson, it's not that at all," she said, when he asked her if that was indeed the reason for her call.

"Please call me Gary," he replied. "You have me intrigued, Doctor. What can I do for you?"

"You'd better call me Catherine then Gary. Actually, I wanted to discuss the use of aconite with you in more detail."

"Go on," said Hudson, wondering just where Catherine was about to lead him.

"Well, I've been thinking. Whoever is behind this obviously has a degree of pharmaceutical knowledge, yes?"

"Agreed," said Hudson.

"OK. The police are working on the theory that one of the victims, possibly Judge Tolliver is the key to the solution of the case. They think he may have been involved in a case that left someone with a grudge against him though they've yet to find any connection between the judge and the other victims."

"So where do we come in Catherine?" asked Hudson.

"It's just this," said Catherine. "The use of aconite as a poison is rare, as we both know. The police are doing their best, but there's no certainty that any of the judge's cases actually involved aconite itself. It may simply be the chosen weapon of the killer."

"I see what you mean."

Hudson was beginning to follow Catherine's reasoning and he had a good idea where she was going with her theory. Her next words confirmed his thoughts.

"You and I have access to a vast database of medical records, both past and present. What if we could find any instance of the mention of aconite in the post-mortem records on either our own databases or in the recorded files of forensic history for the past, say, twenty or thirty years?"

"You're saying that the police might not be looking in the right place?"

"What I'm saying Gary, is that if we can find reference to aconite being present in any quantities whatsoever in the forensic records or in the historical files, we might be able to give the police a second line of inquiry to open up."

"And of course," said Hudson, "we have access not only to criminal files but to those involving accidental exposure to the poison,"

"Or suicides," she went on.

"But surely the police will be looking into all that anyway," said Hudson.

"The police," Catherine went on, "are looking for a connection between aconite and the murderer. What I'm saying Gary, is that there could be a connection between aconite and the victims, from a source and in a way that the police haven't even thought of yet."

"That's a wild theory if you ask me Catherine," he replied a little dubiously. He wasn't sure if Catherine was on the right track and whether he and she were the people to be looking into this new avenue she'd opened up.

"Why don't you just pass your idea along to the inspector in charge at your end and let him take it up?"

"I intend to do that as well Gary, but he's got enough on his plate just now trying to connect all the parts of the case together. I don't think he'd have the time or the manpower available to him to open up another line of inquiry until he's exhausted the current ones. As I've already said, you and I might just be able to access information that the police can't get to yet, and we can do it without breaking any ethical rules."

Gary Hudson knew that Catherine was right. Unlike a doctor-patient relationship there was no code of confidentiality between a pathologist and a corpse. Whatever findings someone like Catherine or Gary ascertained in the course of their work automatically became a matter of public record. Between them, they also had access to records and information that wouldn't appear on any police computer. Medical journals contained much that would be of interest to the medical community without ever being of the slightest use to the police, and that in itself suddenly gave Gary Hudson an idea, as his earlier scepticism towards Catherine's theory evaporated.

"I've thought of something we could do."

"Go on Gary," said Catherine, pleased that her colleague in Birmingham now appeared to be on board wither in the cause.

"Why don't we compile a sort of history of aconite and it's applications during the last, say fifty years?" he said. "It could throw up all sorts of things that we or the police might be able to connect to the victims, or their families, and might even lead to a clue as to the killer's identity. It needn't be as comprehensive as a full blown medical paper but I'm sure between us we could put something together in a short space of time."

"Excellent" Catherine exclaimed. "How do you want to do it?"

"Easy," Hudson replied. You start with medical journals and I'll start with case histories. Using our computers and the internet it shouldn't take too long; maybe two or three days to put a decent report together."

"You're on," Catherine replied enthusiastically.

"In the meantime if the police solve the case and catch the killer all well and good, and if not then we give them what we manage to find. It might be that one of us hits on something sooner rather than later and then we can go straight to the police with our findings."

The two pathologists spent another five minutes putting their plan together, then after agreeing to keep in touch at least twice a day with progress reports, they said their goodbyes and went about their daily business.

Gary Hudson was pleased that Catherine Nickels had called him. After all, she could have done this on her own but she'd taken the time and trouble to invite him 'on board' as she put it. He was glad to help. The task of autopsying David Arnold had left a bad taste in his mouth. No-one should have to die as that poor man had done and Hudson was now determined to do all he could to help both Catherine and the police, if he could, in any way he could. In addition, preparing the paper would be a good academic exercise, and he looked forward to seeing what they would discover together.

Catherine Nickels allowed herself a moment or two to bask in a brief moment of triumph. She was delighted that Doctor Hudson had joined her in her desire to help and assist the police case. She couldn't have told Hudson of course that she particularly wanted to help Connor because she was involved in a romantic entanglement with the detective, but anyway, that hadn't been necessary.

Although he didn't know it Sean Connor now had an additional team at work in his efforts to catch the aconite poisoner. Catherine wanted to keep it that way until she and Hudson found something worth reporting to the police.

Before she had time to access her computer in order to begin her search for information she was interrupted by a knock on her door.

Gunther entered with a worried expression on his face.

"What is it Gunther?" she asked seeing the lines on his forehead and realising that something bad must have happened.

"Catherine, please come. We have a new arrival, a local newsagent, and by the look of it we have another aconite poisoning to deal with."

Catherine nearly jumped up from behind her desk, scattering papers as she left the room, and less than five minutes later she found herself face to face with the mortal remains of Arminder Patel. For now, her research would have to wait. She had a post-mortem to perform.

# Chapter 25
# Slow Progress

Connor was becoming depressed. It had been four days since the series of murders had begun, and twenty four hours since Catherine Nickels had confirmed that Arminder Patel had become the latest victim of the poisoner and no real progress had been made.

The search of the room assumed to have been recently occupied by The Chocolate Woman at the Regency Hotel had thrown up nothing of forensic value. Apart from the fact that three other people had stayed in the room since the suspect, it had been cleaned on a daily basis by the staff and was therefore devoid of anything useful to the police. Any trace evidence that might have been present would have been totally corrupted by the time the police forensic squad got there.

Little or nothing had turned up from the Birmingham end of the investigation. Charles Carrick had been wholeheartedly apologetic during their last conversation. Connor wasn't surprised. After all, David Arnold had no actual connection with Birmingham. It was pure chance that he'd died as his train had pulled into the station there, or had it? That was something that Connor would ask Carrick to look into. Perhaps the killer wanted the engine driver to expire at exactly the time he had done. Maybe Birmingham held some significance for the killer. He didn't know how Carrick and Cole could establish such a link without greater knowledge of the killer's motives, but it would help to know if David Arnold or any of his family had any connection with the city, either currently or historically.

As for the checks on the judge's case histories, that was still an ongoing task for the team of uniformed and plain clothes officers at work just yards from where Connor sat contemplating the case in his office. He'd check with them in a minute or two, but before leaving his office he picked up the phone and called Catherine. He hadn't seen her off duty for two days. She'd been so busy at work that she'd been worn out by the time she'd got home and had apologised but had told him that she needed to rest. Connor understood and had noticed a worn and tired look on her face when he'd seen her at the mortuary the previous day. He didn't know of course about her joint investigation with Gary Hudson or that she was staying up late at night, her fingers dancing over the keys of her computer as she searched the internet and made copious notes of the results of her endeavours.

Pleased to find her available and delighted when she accepted his invitation to dine at his house that evening, Connor felt a little less depressed as he made his way into the main open-plan office and walked across to a computer terminal where Lucy Clay was standing huddled over the shoulder of an officer who was operating the mouse and scrolling information down the screen of his terminal.

Sensing his approach, Lucy turned and greeted him with a smile. "Hello Sir."

"Sergeant," he replied. "Anything yet?"

"No Sir, sorry. We've been through every case the judge was involved in for the last twenty years, and there's no mention of aconite in any of them. Not only that, but he didn't preside over a single case of poisoning of any kind during that time. We haven't been able to tie in any of the other victims or their families with any of those cases either."

"Like we agreed the other day Lucy, the connection may have nothing to do with aconite poisoning. That might just be the killer's own way of despatching his or her victims. What we have to look for is a case that somehow ties all the current events together. Now that we have Mr Patel on the list of victims the net is suddenly that much bigger. The killer may not realise it but the more people he or she kills the greater the chances are that we'll make the connection we need to nail this murdering bastard. I just hope we can do it before anyone else dies."

"So what do you suggest we do, Sir?"

"If you've exhausted the last twenty years without anything turning up or even looking promising then I suggest you go back another ten years, and then *another* ten and so on until we do find something. It's there somewhere Lucy, I know it is. We just need to find it, and soon"

"Right Sir. Come on John, you heard the Boss," she said to the constable seated at the computer."

"OK Sarge," replied the young officer as his fingers instantly began their incessant dance across the keyboard in search of the information that just might help to crack the case.

Lucy Clay turned to face Connor.

"What will you be doing while we're here sir?"

"I'm going to see the manservant at Judge Tolliver's house again Lucy. He was with the judge for a long time. It's just possible that he knows something that even he doesn't see as relevant or important in respect of the judge's murder. I need to know more about the judge's personal background as well as his legal one."

"Are you thinking this could be more of a private out of court personal vendetta rather than one to do with a trial case?"

"I don't know Lucy. I'm just not sure we're on the right track, and talking with DeVere might just convince me one way or the other. We've gone through all the papers at the judge's house. You and the others have checked God knows how many case histories here, and we're still no nearer to finding a connection between the judge, the other victims and the killer's possible motive. Unless this business relates to something that happened even further back in time then it has to be something unrelated to the court records. Maybe it's really focussed on one of the others and not on the judge. He could have been a peripheral figure in all this. I really don't know, and I bloody well want to know."

"It's a funny thing you know, Sir. You just mentioned going back even further in time. Well, when we interviewed his friends and neighbours following Mr Patel's murder, one of his neighbours told me that the Patel family moved to this country just over forty five years ago when Arminder Patel was a little boy. What could he possibly have been involved in that far back that would put him on some present day death list?"

"Unless it wasn't to do with him directly, Sergeant. Maybe it was his father, grandfather, or someone else from his family's past as could be the case with all of the victims, including the judge."

"Good Lord, Sir! That certainly doesn't help to narrow the field down does it?"

"No, I'm afraid it doesn't, but we have to start looking at this from every angle, no matter how unusual or unlikely."

"Right Sir, I'll get on it then. I hope you have a bit of success with Mr DeVere."

"Me too, Lucy. See you later."

Connor was gone before Lucy could say another word. She shrugged her shoulders, looked back into the room where the team were hard at work and called to the young officer with whom she'd been working before Connor's arrival.

"John, I want you to check into something for me."

# Chapter 26
# Mary's Homecoming

Mary Stride breezed through the front door of the house she shared with her brother and sister. Everything was quiet, unusually so, and Mary wondered where the others were.

"Hello there," she called out.

No answer. She tried again.

"Mikey? Angela? Anyone there?"

Mary was unnerved by the silence that greeted her calls. The house was normally a hive of activity whenever Angela was present and Mikey would invariably have the radio or television switched on if he was sitting alone. He couldn't see the TV screen but he enjoyed listening to a lot of the programmes, particularly the news and documentaries. Something was wrong. It had to be. All of Mary's good humour disappeared to be replaced by a sense of urgency and dread. What if something had happened to Mikey and Angela had had to take him to the hospital? No, it couldn't be that or Angela would have rung her to tell her.

Mary knew that Mikey had no scheduled medical appointments so there was no reason why both he and Angela should be missing from the house. Not only that but Angela was due to be at home all day and would never have gone out and left Mikey alone, so wherever the two of them were, they had to be together. For a moment Mary half believed that Mikey had convinced Angela to take him to the police station to reveal what he thought the police should know, but then

Mary thought better of that idea. No, Mikey had promised to drop the subject, they'd kissed and made up, it was over with. Despite her uncomfortable feeling when in close physical proximity to her brother, Mary loved him and she knew he loved her back and the Strides never went back on promises to each other

All of Mary's instincts told her that there was something very out of kilter in the neat but apparently deserted house. She walked into each of the downstairs rooms and then out into the back garden, again finding no sign of her brother and sister. She walked slowly back into the house and called out again, receiving only the sound of silence in return.

She paused with her hand on the wooden moulding at the bottom of the stair rail, her head slightly on one side, listening. Hearing no sound from upstairs she slowly began to make her way up the stairs, the creaking of the fourth step making her jump, even though she'd heard it so many times before.

"Get a grip on yourself, girl," she said aloud to herself, and carried on to the top until she reached the first floor landing. The rear bedroom was hers. She preferred the peace it afforded from the sounds of passing traffic and she popped her head round the door to confirm that it was empty. It was. By-passing the bathroom Mary next moved to the door of Mikey's room, the largest bedroom in the house, which she and Angela had made sure was specially adapted to help cope with his disabilities. As she pushed the door open slowly, she first sensed, and then saw the horrific sight that met her eyes.

Michael Stride lay on his bed, curled up into a grotesque parody of a foetal position. His eyes were open and betrayed the horror of his last moments. Michael couldn't see while he was alive but it was as if in death his eyes, having witnessed the final horror of those final painful moments, had left an imprint of terror on the useless pupils that would live with Mary for ever.

Close by, on the floor beside Michael's bed lay the body of her sister. Angela too was curled into that awful crouch, and Mary couldn't help but notice that her right arm and hand was extended as though she were reaching out to Mikey, trying even with her last breath perhaps, to help the brother she adored.

Mary's legs felt weak, she barely knew what she was doing as, almost as though she were an automaton, she shakily walked first to the bed where she reached out a trembling hand to check for a pulse in her brother's neck and, finding none, she repeated the procedure with her sister. They were both dead, which she'd already known of course just by looking at them both. She couldn't help herself. Suddenly she no longer felt any repulsion at being close to Mikey. Mary reached out again, this time with both arms and she tenderly took her brother's lifeless body in her arms and hugged him, sobbing as she did so, until her tears fell and splashed onto his face.

A full minute passed and Mary suddenly realised that she could be compromising any police investigation into Mikey's death. Knowing this, she simply replaced him as she'd found him and moved to Angela who she gently kissed on the forehead, her face now a mask of tears.

Unable to cope with the horror of her discovery Doctor Mary Stride ran from the room. She didn't need to examine the two of them closely to know that they had been dead for some time before she'd arrived home. She almost fell down the last five stairs and at the bottom she paused for a few seconds in the hallway, trying to gather her thoughts and her breath.

Her professional brain needed to kick in, to take charge of the situation and she knew she had to control her emotions. Touch nothing in the house; make sure nothing was missing, and call the police. Yes, of course, she must call the police! Pulling herself together Mary remembered not to touch anything, not even the telephone. Instead she reached into her handbag which still stood on the hallstand where she'd left it when she'd arrived home only a few minutes earlier and removed her mobile phone.

She dialled the emergency service and was quickly connected with the police operator who promised that someone would be with her within minutes. The operator would also arrange for an ambulance and paramedics to attend, though Mary knew that was simply routine procedure. There was nothing anyone could do for Mikey and Angela.

As she heard the sound of approaching sirens, Mary Stride reflected through her tears that perhaps she should have listened to Mikey after all. She knew what had killed her brother and sister and now she would have to explain to the police why they hadn't come forward sooner when they could have avoided all of this, and she knew, as the guilt built up like a rising tide inside her, that her brother and sister might still be alive if they had done.

The past had come back to haunt Mary Stride, and along with the tears, the guilt and the pain, for the first time in her life, she was not just afraid, but very, very afraid.

# Chapter 27
# A Sudden Twist

Lucy Clay was the lead detective as the two cars arrived at the Stride home. She'd automatically called Connor as soon as the emergency call had been routed to the murder squad's office. He would divert from his intended destination at Judge Tolliver's house and even now was on his way to the double murder scene. DeVere could wait.

Mary Stride was sitting on the bottom stair as Lucy walked into the house. The eldest of the Stride siblings was quietly sobbing, her shoulders hunched and her head sunk into her hands. She barely noticed the police officer's arrival and only looked up when Lucy tapped her very gently on the shoulder and spoke softly:

"Miss Stride?"

"Yes," sobbed Mary.

"You made an emergency call. Your brother and sister; where are they?"

"Upstairs," Mary replied, unable to get past one word sentences for the moment. Clay understood her reaction; the poor woman was in shock.

"Come with me," Clay called to Detective Constable Simon Fox, who'd responded quickly when she'd grabbed him on her way out of the office. Fox had had quite enough of being stuck indoors for the moment and he'd jumped at the chance to accompany the sergeant on the call.

As the two detectives slowly mounted the stairs Mary Stride at last found her voice, enough at any rate to call out to the detectives:

"It's all my fault. I should have done as Mikey said."

Lucy had heard such utterances before from the bereaved relatives of murder victims and now was not the time to either console or to deny Mary Stride's statement. That was for later. She needed to see the bodies. All she knew so far was that the emergency operator had told her that the caller had reported her brother and sister as having been murdered. She'd said she was a doctor and that she knew they'd been poisoned.

The scene that greeted Lucy and Constable Fox was little changed from the one that had at first assaulted the gaze of Mary stride upon her arrival home. Clay knew as soon as she saw the positions of the bodies that it wouldn't take much to confirm that these two unfortunates had just joined the ranks of those who already lay in the mortuary as a result of the work of the serial poisoner.

"Go back downstairs," she ordered Fox, "and bring the M.E. up here as soon as he arrives."

The medical officer was required to pronounce the victims officially dead before the detectives could have the body moved and get down to the 'nitty-gritty' of their investigation of the death scene.

Simon Fox was only too pleased to leave that room. The horror of seeing the state of the two recently deceased human beings in such horribly contorted positions was enough to make him wish he'd stayed in the office searching though the computer databases for clues.

Lucy Clay's initial inspection of the death scene produced nothing of value. She could of course ascertain that the victims had died horribly and in all likelihood from the effects of poison, but that was all. The forensic team, when they arrived would carry out a meticulous search for trace evidence and if the killer had left any tiny semblance of a clue or had left a trace of his or her DNA or other means of identification, they'd find it.

As Lucy Clay carried out her fruitless search, downstairs the occupants of the second car were going through the necessary procedures of taping the entrance to the garden, and the front door, identifying the house as a crime scene to any onlooker or passer-by. The yellow tape was soon in place and while Fox paced up and down the garden path waiting for the medical examiner and fighting back his own feelings of nausea and revulsion, the two constables from car two sat and attempted to console Mary Stride, whom they'd assisted into the kitchen of the house, allowing her to sit on one of the dining chairs that sat under the table. They felt safe in letting her do so, as there was little likelihood that the killer had been in that room, and the table and chairs appeared undisturbed.

By the time Sean Connor arrived on the scene less than fifteen minutes later, the two officers had heard the most incredible story told by Mary Stride and which one of them, Detective Constable Sue Rawson had had the presence of mind to record in her notebook as soon as she realised the significance of what the bereaved sister was relating to her.

Upon his arrival Connor had gone straight upstairs to where he'd been told by Fox that Lucy Clay was waiting for him. Also present in the bedroom was Doctor Sally Hawes, the on-duty medical officer who had immediately pronounced both Michael and Angela Stride dead, thus allowing the bodies to be moved as soon as the police had carried out their initial examination of the crime scene, and a forensic technician Connor hadn't met before.

"It's bad Sir," said Lucy as Connor approached the open doorway from the landing.

Connor nodded to his sergeant and walked past her into the room. The forensic technician was busy taking photographs of the death scene and his continually popping flashlight was disconcerting to Connor who felt as though he'd walked into a scene from a horror movie.

"I see what you mean Sergeant," he at last responded to Clay's earlier comment, as he took in the sight of the one-legged man, his false leg lying unattached on the floor, and the woman, both lying in the hideously contorted positions that reflected their death agonies.

"What d'you think Doc?" he asked of Sally Hawes.

"We won't know until we've completed the post-mortem of course, but I think you'll find that we have another case of poisoning here Inspector. I'd almost bet my career on it that once we dig a bit deeper we'll also find that it was aconite that was responsible."

"No Doctor. Aconite wasn't responsible," said Connor, a mean expression crossing his face as he spoke. "No, some crazy screwed-up bastard of a human being is responsible for this. The aconite is just a tool, like a gun or a knife. Just because it's organic doesn't make aconite any less of a weapon than either of those."

"Yes, well, I know that of course, I just meant…"

"I know what you mean Doctor, and I'm sorry. I didn't mean to snap. It's this bloody case. It's getting to me. Whatever we do we just can't seem to get a grip on what the damn motive for these killings is, or who's behind it all. Every time we get a lead it just runs up against a brick wall. It's driving me nuts!"

A voice from behind broke into the conversation.

"Alright to move the bodies now Inspector?" asked one of the newly arrived paramedics.

"Yes, right, no problem," he replied.

"Where's the sister, Lucy?"

"Downstairs Sir, with a couple of constables. She's in a state of shock."

"Yes, well I think anyone would be after coming home to find what she found. Come on, let's go have a word. We'll have another look around up here after they've removed the bodies and the forensic boys have finished with the place"

Connor and Clay made their way down the stairs and along the hall to the kitchen. As they approached the door they found their way blocked by the diminutive figure of Detective Constable Rawson.

"Hello Constable. Is there a problem?" asked Connor.

"Well Sir," she replied. "Before you go in I think you should know what the lady in there has been saying."

Connor craned his neck a little to try and see past the officer who blocked his way, but the view was obscured by the back of the second constable in the room, D.C. Paul Bowers.

"I'm all ears Constable," Connor replied and he and Clay both leaned back against the wall of the hallway as Sue Rawson began to refer to her notes.

"Look Sir, I know you really want to get in there and speak to Miss Stride yourself, but while I've been with her she's been babbling on a bit. At first I just thought she was being a bit over the top and melodramatic, a shock thing if you know what I mean. Anyway, I suddenly realised she was saying some pretty scary stuff and I asked her to start again and I wrote it all down. To cut a long story short, she says that her brother and sister's deaths are her responsibility and that if she'd listened to Mikey, as she called him and called the police sooner she might have prevented the murders of her brother and sister. She says it's all her fault and that she just didn't want to dredge up the past. Apparently there's a very old skeleton in this family's cupboard Sir, and according to Mary Stride it's come back to haunt them. She refused to believe that there could be a connection between then and now at first you see, and she kept telling Mikey to drop the subject and in the end he agreed. She does seem a little confused and she was rambling a bit, but in the end she sort of just let it slip out."

"Let what slip out Constable?"

"Oh, yes Sir. She says she knows who the aconite killer is."

"Bloody Hell!" said both Connor and Clay simultaneously, and the two of them almost knocked Sue Rawson over as they pushed past her and into the kitchen to get their first view of and to hear the strange story of Mary Stride.

# Chapter 28
# Revisiting the Past

Connor and Clay sat at one side of the well-polished pine refectory table that took centre stage in the Stride's kitchen. At the other side of the table sat Mary Stride, looking pale and visibly shaking as she faced the two detectives. Constable Rawson sat beside Mary comforting her as necessary and Paul Bowers stood guard on the kitchen door with orders from Connor to admit no-one until they'd finished talking with the grieving doctor. Four cups of hot steaming tea stood on the table, made by Sue Rawson. After introducing himself and Lucy, Connor had asked Rawson to put the kettle on and make them all a drink in the hope that it would help to try and compose the grieving woman before asking her to relate her story. He could see the sorry state she was in and knew he'd get little of use from her until she was in a calmer frame of mind. Lucy Clay sat by his side, notebook and pen in hand, poised to record what just might be the words that would help them solve the case.

Mary Stride reached out with a trembling hand and took hold of the cup that Rawson had placed before her. It was all she could do to raise the cup to her lips and take a sip of the tea without it spilling over the lip of the cup and onto her clothes. She managed it, and the hot liquid seemed to have an instant calming effect on her; her hand trembling just a little less as she replaced the cup on the empty saucer.

Connor decided that the time was right to give Mary a little push.

"Doctor Stride? When you're ready I'd like you to repeat a little of what you've already related to Constable Rawson. I believe you seem to think that this is all your fault and that think you know who's responsible for all the recent deaths in and around the town. I need to hear your story for myself. When you're ready, please Doctor, in your own time."

Mary Stride took a deep breath in an effort to regain a little more of her normal professional composure. She sniffed, reached for a tissue from the box that had magically appeared on the table courtesy of Rawson's forethought, and wiped the tears from her face. She appeared to slump into her chair for a second and then with what was probably a supreme effort on her part, she pulled her shoulders upwards and backwards, raised herself to her full seated height, and began.

"I'm the one responsible for all of this Inspector, because if I'd listened to my poor brother Mikey we could have helped you put a stop to this before it got this far and both he and Angela would still be alive. You see, I stopped him from calling the police despite his fears and his desire to 'do the right thing' because I felt that our family had suffered enough and because I thought that there couldn't be a connection between what happened all those years ago and what's happening now. I know now that I was wrong. Inspector, my father was Terence Stride!"

She spoke the last sentence as though she expected Connor to know instantly to whom she was referring. If that was her hope, she was wrong.

"I'm sorry Doctor. I've never heard of him."

"Oh, yes, well perhaps it was a bit before your time I daresay. I was only thirteen myself when it all began. Anyway, as I said my father was Terence Stride and thirty three years ago he was accused of the murder of a man named William Prentice."

There was still no sign of recognition from the police officers.

"William Prentice was a private investigator who specialized in divorce cases; you know the sort of thing I mean. He'd get the dirty photographs that were popular in the courts in those days in order to prove infidelity and so on. Well, one day his body was discovered in the garden of a house on Fuller Road about two miles from here. It's gone now, all pulled down when they built the new industrial estate. Anyway, Prentice had a partner named Andrew Forbes who told the police that Prentice was investigating a case of adultery involving a woman who lived in Braintree Close, about half a mile from Fuller Road. Her husband was convinced that she was having an affair with a married man who lived on Watson Street. We of course live on Watson Street as you know. A witness later gave a statement to the effect that she saw a man following Prentice a few minutes after midnight on the night of his death. She gave the police a description of the man. That description matched the appearance of my father Inspector, and from that moment onwards our lives were turned upside down. The police came to interview everyone who lives on Watson Street and as soon as they saw my father I'm sure they thought they'd got their man. To make matters worse my father had no real alibi for the night of the murder. He was a taxi driver and according to his statement he was just sitting in his cab waiting for a call to his next fare by the side of a road at least three miles from the scene of the murder at the time the police said it had taken place. The radio controller at the taxi company who my father worked for confirmed that he wasn't on an actual call at the time but obviously couldn't confirm his exact whereabouts.

He was taken in for questioning and vehemently denied any involvement in the killing. He also denied having known the woman who was at the centre of the Prentice investigation, which she confirmed, but the police thought she was lying in order to try and save her marriage. It seems her husband was a violent man and the police assumed she'd deny the affair anyway to try to deflect the police from the belief that she herself could have been involved in the murder. Anyway, it was discovered that Prentice had gone out on the night of the murder with his camera, and the camera was missing. In fact, it was never found. Eventually, faced with a lack of any tangible evidence to link him with the murder, the police had no choice but to release my father, but the damage had already been done.

Almost as soon as he came home, the gossips started their character assassination. I'm sure you'll know what I mean. The previously happy family man that was my father became a figure of hate Inspector. Everywhere he went he'd hear comments about the murder, the women in the area began a campaign of innuendo and slander, calling him everything from a philanderer and an adulterer to a murderer. Of course my mother wasn't immune to all of this and she was only too aware of what was being said and the strain began to tell on their marriage.

Even when someone else was arrested for the murder and eventually convicted, the backstabbing and the innuendo and the whispering went on, until my mother couldn't stand it any more. She started to believe that my father had been unfaithful Inspector, can you believe that? After all his denials, and after someone else was convicted, she actually believed all the lies that were being circulated about him and, anyway, she threw him out. They were divorced soon afterwards and our lives went from bad to worse.

My father couldn't live without my mother Inspector Connor and three months after the divorce he drove his car into the middle of a level crossing late at night and stopped the engine. The driver of the express train that hit him never even saw him in the dark. He was killed instantly, so they said. My father had left a note back at the cheap little flat he'd rented when he left home in which he wrote of his love for my mother, of how he was innocent of everything that had been said about him and of his love for his children, but his mind was gone you see Inspector. He couldn't live either *with* the shame that the lies had heaped upon him or *without* my mother, who was without a doubt the love of his life. The inquest verdict was a simple 'suicide whilst the balance of his mind was disturbed' but in fact he was murdered Inspector; murdered by the campaign of nasty and vicious lies and innuendo that the wagging tongues of the day had directed at him. He was an innocent man who was driven to his death by gossip and tittle-tattle."

The tears welled up in Mary Stride's eyes again and Sue Rawson, moved by the story that the doctor had told them so far, reached out her hand and placed it reassuringly on Mary's left arm. Lucy Clay reached into the box of tissues on the table and extracted one which she passed to the tearful woman. Connor realised that this was a very stressful situation for Mary who, after all had just found her brother and sister dead upstairs a very short time ago and compassion dictated that he offer her a break to gather herself before continuing her story. She refused, wanting instead to go on and relate the rest of the tale to the inspector.

"My mother believed him at last Inspector Connor, but it was too late. She realised that he'd been telling her the truth all along and believed that she'd been partly responsible for his death. She felt as though she'd driven him to suicide and she couldn't live with that knowledge. She was an intelligent woman Inspector, she worked part-time for Jordan's Pharmaceuticals as a research and development assistant. She worked with highly dangerous poisons every day of her working life, and three weeks after my father's death she came home armed with a phial of refined aconite poison and took the lot in a goblet of brandy."

Mary Stride paused for effect as the significance of the word 'aconite' sank in to the police officers' brains, and then continued.

"Unfortunately for her my brother, who was sadly born with only one leg, was sent home from school early that day as he was unwell, and as he was pushed, in his wheelchair, into the house by the teacher who'd brought him home they heard the sounds of my mother's death throes from the sitting room. As the teacher wheeled Mikey into the room to see what was happening they came face to face with my mother in her agonised contortions and her final and terrible fight for breath as the poison did its dreadful work. My mother had chosen to die that way Inspector, probably as her own punishment for what she thought she'd driven my father to, but she never intended Mikey to see what he saw that day, I know she didn't. Mikey's brain just couldn't cope with it Inspector, he was only nine years old and his mind dealt with the trauma in the only way it could. It shut off his vision, his eyes. He was literally struck blind by what he'd seen and experienced. The doctors at the time said that the blindness might be temporary but it stayed with him for the rest of his life. That awful day was thirty three years ago. Do you understand now when I tell you that my family has suffered enough? Can't you see why I didn't want Mikey to call you?"

"I can see the suffering, yes," said Connor. "But I don't see what it has to do with today, or why your brother thought there was a connection between then and now."

"Of course, I haven't finished yet. You remember I told you that someone else was convicted of the murder of William Prentice. His name was Stanley Miller and he looked a lot like my father, so I know why the police at first thought my father might have been the murderer. Like my father, Miller always protested his innocence of the murder, but he never saw his name cleared. He was attacked and murdered himself by a fellow convict who thought to make a name for himself. His wife Fiona carried on the fight to clear him however, and she succeeded in getting the conviction overturned a year after his death."

"I still don't see…"

"Wait, please Inspector, I'm coming to it. After Miller was cleared the case was reopened but no-one was ever arrested or convicted for the murder of William Prentice. Thirty years ago his widow gave what was probably the last of a string of statements to the press in which she vowed to find justice for her dead husband. She told the reporter that she was convinced that either my father or Miller must have been the killer as the police surely wouldn't have pulled in two wrong men who both fitted the description of the witness. Of course she conveniently forgot that the witness didn't actually see the killing anyway, just a man following Prentice shortly before he was killed. Anyway, I suppose Mrs Prentice was just trying to earn a few pounds for herself by selling those ridiculous stories to the tabloids but soon after that last story I received a threatening letter, anonymous of course, in which the lives of my family were threatened. It said we were all the spawn of a murderer and that even if he had cheated justice, his sins would be visited upon us, and all those who had failed to bring his killer to justice. Those were pretty much the words the writer used, or some such quasi-religious sounding stuff. It was Elizabeth Prentice who sent it, I'm sure of it, and it wouldn't surprise me if she didn't send similar letters to the other people connected with the case.

Mikey saw it all when the deaths started occurring recently and I was the blind one who stopped him from telling anyone because I didn't believe she could possible have waited all this time to exact her revenge. Judge Tolliver was the one that clinched it for Mikey."

Connor was intrigued and horrified by the things he'd been hearing and now asked the question.

"What was the judge's connection to the case Doctor? Did he preside over the trial of Miller?"

"Oh no, that would probably have put him in the clear. Miller was found guilty at his trial remember. It was the appeal court that eventually cleared him. No Inspector, Judge Tolliver wasn't a judge back then. He was a rising star, a barrister destined for the bench without a doubt, and it was his clever legal arguments that secured the posthumous acquittal of Stanley Miller. As far as Mrs Prentice was concerned, that put Tolliver in clear league with the Devil and his minions and she said so quite vociferously in one of those ridiculous statements to the press. If you want to find your killer Inspector then I suggest you find Elizabeth Prentice. I don't know what the others have to do with it, I was only a teenager at the time, but it *has* to be her."

"But that was a long time ago Doctor Stride. Why would she suddenly decide to start killing people now? And why would you think she'd be using aconite to do so just because your mother used it to, er, to commit suicide?"

He said the last few words as compassionately as he could. This woman had suffered enough and he wasn't sure if she was on the right track even now.

"Oh yes, I'm sorry. There was just one more thing I forgot to mention. There was a strange coincidence in the case that I haven't mentioned before Inspector, I'm sorry. You see, Elizabeth Prentice was the head of the Research and Development laboratory at Jordan's. My mother worked for her, indirectly of course and like my mother, she was and I'm sure still is an expert in the preparation of and the use of poisons, including aconite. For some reason she's back and she wants us all dead!"

Mary stride slumped back in her chair, feeling that she'd said all she could. It was enough for Connor.

"Lucy, get on to headquarters. Get me the address of Elizabeth Prentice."

Connor's case had suddenly leapt into life. He had a name at last!

# Chapter 29
# Wrong Address

Leaving the forensic team to gather whatever trace evidence they could find at the scene of the double murder, and with Mary Stride being accompanied by Constable Rawson for treatment for shock at the hospital (and for protection against a possible attack by the poisoner), Connor and Clay sped through the traffic on their way back to the station fully expecting to find the latest address for Elizabeth Prentice waiting for them when they got there. It was, but not quite as Connor would have wanted or expected.

As he and Clay exited from their car in the police station car park, Connor could see that his immediate superior, D.C.I. Lewis was standing waiting expectantly on the steps that led up to the main entrance doors. Something told Connor that the Detective Chief Inspector was waiting for someone, and that same instinct told him that he and Clay were the objects of the D.C.I's doorstep vigil. He was right on both counts.

"Hello Sir," he called as he and Clay approached his boss. "You waiting for us by any chance?"

"Yes Sean, I am. Hello Sergeant," he nodded to Lucy Clay. "I'm afraid I've got some bad news for you. I was in the murder incident room when your call came in and the boys told me you'd got a hot lead on the aconite killer, so I waited around to see what they came up with. It took them less than five minutes to find out where your suspect is. Elizabeth Prentice is currently lying beneath the ground in the graveyard at Holy Trinity Church. She died three years ago."

Connor looked crestfallen, as did his sergeant, the two of them taking a full ten seconds to gather themselves before Connor spoke.

"How did she die Sir, do we know?"

"A heart attack Sean, nothing sinister I'm afraid. She can't possibly be your killer unfortunately."

"But Doctor Stride was so sure," said Lucy Clay. "Perhaps Mrs Prentice has a son or daughter who's carrying out her mother's vendetta against those she believed were responsible for William's death."

"You've lost me I'm afraid Sergeant," said Lewis. "Come on you two. Let's retire to my office and you can fill me in on what this new development is all about."

It took Connor and Clay about fifteen minutes to bring the D.C.I. up to date with the murders of Mikey and Angela Stride and with the statement made by Mary Stride which had clearly implicated the sadly deceased Elizabeth Prentice.

"Wait," Lewis ordered as he picked up the telephone and dialled the internal number for the incident room. He gave the officer who answered orders to check on the possibility of Elizabeth Prentice having had any children who, as Clay had cleverly deduced could be responsible for the killings in some warped revenge for the death of their father all those yeas ago.

While they waited Connor brought the D.C.I up to speed with everything they'd found out so far, which amounted to precious little as he readily admitted.

"We seem to take one step forward and then another two back, Sir. Every lead turns out to be a blind alley, and this time I really thought we'd got something. The connection was just so strong, though there is just the one weakness in Mary Stride's story."

"Which is?"

"She readily admits that she saw the connection between the deaths of her father, Stanley Miller and Judge Tolliver, but she couldn't give us an inkling of how the other victims were connected. I know she was young at the time that all she described took place but she seems to have a very good memory for details and I'm sure she would have at least remembered the family names of those involved."

"Unless the current victims are descended from the female side of whatever families were involved at the time, Sir," said Clay. "With marriages and so on through the years that would give them entirely different surnames and would certainly explain why Doctor Stride doesn't recognise their names in connection with the case."

"A very good point Sergeant," Lewis intoned. "Look into that will you when we've finished here?"

"Course I will Sir," Lucy replied, smiling, pleased that the D.C.I. saw some merit in her hypothesis.

The phone on Lewis's desk rang. Before it had chance to ring for a second time he snatched it up from its cradle.

"Lewis," he answered, and then listened without interruption as the caller spoke to him. Whatever else anyone might say about him, Detective Chief Inspector Lewis was a superb listener, one of the talents that made him such a good policeman. He never interrupted a speaker, preferring to hear the entirety of anyone's speech before delivering his own reply. Now, he listened for at least a full minute as his caller spoke, until he simply said:

"Right, well, thank you," and hung up.

"Elizabeth Prentice had a son and a daughter, James and Laura. Unfortunately they were both killed ten years ago when the light aircraft they were flying in, piloted I might add by James Prentice, crashed into a hillside on its way over the Pennines on its way to Scotland. There were no survivors. I'm sorry to say it looks like Mrs Prentice is yet another one of your blind alleys Sean."

Connor sat quietly thinking for a minute. No-one disturbed him. Both his boss and his assistant were equally aware of Connor's habit of thinking deeply abut a problem before making an utterance on the subject. When he did speak, it was hardly a speech of reassurance.

"You're right Sir. It is a blind alley, and do you know what? I think this whole bloody case is a blind alley and that we've been approaching it in the wrong way."

Lewis and Clay were taken aback as Connor continued.

"Look Sir, we've approached this case from the beginning using the assumption first of all that use of aconite is in some way connected with the killer or with one of the victims. Perhaps it isn't. Then we assumed that the victims were connected, either to each other, or to the killer or to something that happened in the past. Perhaps they're not! What if, and I admit it's a big if; but what if there's no connection at all between the victims and that the killer is simply doing this for kicks? The connection with the unhappy past of the Strides may be just a coincidence, a bloody big one I'll grant you, but it's a possibility. Then again, there might be a connection that we just haven't found yet and it might have nothing at all to do with Judge Tolliver's past cases or anything to do with the law at all. It may be something personal and that we simply don't know about. It could be something that simple and we can't see it even though it might be there right in front of our eyes, and the killer could be sitting there mocking us while we go around chasing shadows from the past that simply aren't there anymore."

Connor stopped, aware that both Lewis and Clay were staring at him.

"Sean," said his boss." If you don't mind me saying so, it sounds as if you've just opened every door in the asylum and let the inmates out to run wild. As for the use of aconite, what about the Strides' family history?"

"That could be a coincidence Sir, or just another blind to throw us off the real scent."

"You look tired Sean. Why don't you take a couple of hours off, have an early lunch perhaps?"

"Listen Sir, I'm not cracking up. I really think we should rethink the whole approach to this case. Someone is making fools of us and I don't like being made a bloody fool of."

"Look Sean, it's your case. You do what you think is right OK? Just try and get some results, because we sure as hell need them and I meant what I said about you looking tired."

Connor and Clay left Lewis's office and as soon as the door closed behind them Clay turned to Connor, grabbed him by the arm and said,

"You know Sir, I think you could be right. Maybe we have been going about this in the wrong way."

"Bloody Hell Lucy, I'm glad about that; for one horrible minute I actually believed that I was going round the bend in there, and that Lewis was right about me cracking up."

Lucy Clay looked into his eyes, and the two detectives couldn't help themselves. They burst out laughing, and every eye in the office turned to watch them as they entered Connor's office and closed the door where they continued to laugh for at least another full minute.

# Chapter 30
# A Tactical Shift?

"It was stress Sean, that's all. You both needed to let it out and laughter was the best outlet for both of you in order to relieve the situation."

Connor and Catherine were lying in his bed after another romantically comfortable evening together. He'd waited until now to tell her of the fit of giggles that had overtaken both he and Lucy Clay after they'd left Lewis's office.

"Not very professional of me though was it?"

"Don't be too hard on yourself Sean. You've been under a lot of pressure during this case, both you and Lucy. It can't be easy when every clue you think you've found turns out to be meaningless."

"I know Catherine. I was so sure that Mary Stride had given us something to go on when she told us the story of her family's history. In fact I still can't shake the nagging thought that there is still some connection between the Strides and what's been happening."

Catherine thought for couple of seconds then, realising how strung out Connor was becoming over the case she decided that the time was right to inform Connor of the out-of-hours investigations she and Gary Hudson had been carrying out.

Connor was amazed and extremely gratified when she explained the whole thing to him. Now he understood why she hadn't been available for a couple of nights, and there was him thinking she'd gone off him!

"Why didn't you tell me sooner?" he asked when she'd finished.

"I didn't want to make you think that we working behind your back, or that Gary and I were trying to solve your case without you. We wanted to find something concrete to hand over to you before we let both you and Charles Carrick in Birmingham know about what we've been doing."

"And have you?"

"Not yet I'm afraid. What we've done is to ask the computers to collate every single recorded mention of aconite for as far back as the records go this century. They're still working on it. We think we might be able to find a link between aconite and a situation that wouldn't necessarily come into the realms of any police investigation. Someone may have been carrying out research using the poison for example, and that would perhaps be listed in medical journals or essays and not in any police records. Whoever was involved in any such research may or may not be connected with your case. We don't know. It may be a wild goose chase but we thought it might help. I know you've said that the use of aconite may be coincidental or just the choice of the killer without any historical connections, but even so there has to be a way somewhere to connect that person to the aconite. Maybe this is the way to do it. I wouldn't have told you about it yet, but you seemed so down and…"

"No need to say any more," said Connor, taking hold of Catherine's hand in his own. His arm went around her neck and shoulders and he pulled her close to him. They kissed, his head swimming pleasantly as he held her close, smelling the sweet aroma of her perfume, and Connor felt an instant release of much of the tension that had taken hold of him.

"Thank you," he whispered softly in her ear. "That really is one of the nicest things anyone's ever done for me, really. I appreciate it more than you know."

"So you don't think that Gary and I have been going behind your back, and treading where we perhaps shouldn't have?"

"Hell, no. You're both involved in the case at a professional level aren't you? That gives you every right to look into what caused the deaths of the victims sent to you for autopsy. As far as I'm concerned you're doing us all a favour by extending the scope of the investigation further than we could do on our own. As you say, you and Doctor Hudson have access to sources of information that we don't, and it is just possible that you might find something that will be useful to us in solving this bloody enigma of a case. Like I told Lewis, we're missing something, and once we find out what that something is we'll be halfway to finding the killer."

"Sean, have you thought of the possibility that the killer might be selecting the victims at random?"

"I've thought of it, yes, but it seems incredulous that someone would go to all this trouble to murder a number of strangers who he or she has just picked out from the crowd. If that were the case, why kill all except one of the victims here in the Richmond area and then one on the other side of the country as in the case of David Arnold?"

Suddenly a thought struck Connor like a bolt from the blue and he jerked up into a sitting position.

"Sean, what it is?" Catherine was startled by his sudden movement.

"Sorry. Listen. What if we've been approaching the whole case not only from the wrong angle, but from the wrong *place*?

"I'm sorry, you've lost me."

"Look, so far we've assumed that the killer is based in this area and that that accounted for the fact that the majority of the victims also lived in or around Richmond, right?"

Catherine nodded. Connor went on.

"Now, how about we turn the case on its head? What if the real or main target of the killer was actually David Arnold?"

"The train driver?"

"Yes. For some reason, the killer goes to Penzance, slips Arnold the lethal chocolate or chocolates then hightails it back to Richmond and carries out a series of random killings to throw us off the scent of his real motive, and therefore his real target?"

"Under normal circumstances you might have a point Sean, but you have to remember that the killer couldn't be in two places at once. We know for a fact that someone gave David Arnold the aconite on the morning of his death and whoever that person was, they couldn't possibly have got back to Richmond in time to poison Sam Gabriel and Mrs Remick that same morning."

"True," said Connor, "Unless we return to my earlier supposition that there are two of them. Two killers working together Catherine. It has to be. Or at least one mastermind and an accomplice, carrying out the orders of the brains behind the killings. You see, we've been working on the assumption that there was a connection between all of the victims that would lead to someone or something that happened in or around Richmond in the past. What I'm suggesting is that the killings might still be connected, but that the connection lies not in Richmond, but in Liverpool!"

"Liverpool?"

"Yes, Liverpool. David Arnold was poisoned in Penzance, died as his train pulled into Birmingham, but his home was in Liverpool. From Charles Carrick's inquiries it appears that Arnold had lived there all his life, so it's safe to assume that if he was the central target then it would have to be connected to something that happened there and not in Richmond. It would also explain why Charles has found nothing of any use in his investigation, which for obvious reasons has been quite limited. He's in Birmingham, the victim came from Liverpool and the Merseyside Police have been helpful enough to Charles, but both he and they have been working on the assumption that Arnold was in some way connected with Richmond. What if he wasn't, that's what I'm saying? What if the connection should be reversed, and that there's something that connects all of our Richmond victims to him, or to the city of Liverpool?"

"Sean; that hypothesis is so far-fetched and stretches the believable imagination so far that it's positively brilliant! As crazy as it all sounds, you might actually have something there. That could be why nothing fits and why you keep running up those blind alleys you talk about. The reason could quite possibly be that the alleys you should be looking up are over a hundred miles away."

"Catherine, do me a favour. When you next look into the history of aconite and its applications please try cross-referencing it with the city of Liverpool and see what the computer throws up."

"I'll do it in the morning, and ask Gary to do what he can from Birmingham too."

"Thanks." Connor relaxed, a visible relaxation that saw him suddenly sag back against his pillows, his head coming to rest on the bed's pine headboard. Catherine reached out to him and he allowed his head to loll to one side until it came to rest on her shoulder.

"Well, it looks like we're both going to have a very busy day tomorrow Detective Inspector," she grinned at him. "But until then, tell me, do you have any other plans for the rest of this evening?"

"But of course," he replied, pulling her close to him with one hand and at the same time reaching across to the side table and turning out the light.

# Chapter 31
# Alex Gregson – A Breath of Fresh Air

Sean Connor slept badly. His usual talent for switching off from work and getting a good night's sleep had deserted him; somehow this was one case that he couldn't simply put to bed at night. As he tossed and turned beside the sleeping figure of Catherine Nickels he realised how preposterous his hypotheses of the previous evening would sound to his boss, as indeed it was beginning to sound to him. Surely no-one would go to the extent of murdering someone from Liverpool and then murder another five people all the way down in Surrey just to create a false trail for the police. It was too stupid for words and though he would put it to Charles Carrick in Birmingham the following day, he began to see it as a 'clutching at straws' theory. No, the answer had to be somewhere in Richmond; he just had to look harder and deeper into the victims and their respective histories.

On arriving at his office in the morning he reflected that summer was coming to an end. The warm sunshine of the past few days had been replaced by a heavy, cooler atmosphere that he'd been only too aware of as he'd driven to work. The overcast skies and gathering clouds of autumn lent themselves well to Connor's mood, which was becoming as deep as the atmospheric depression that had settled over southern England.

He called Charles Carrick, who agreed that Connor's Liverpool theory was a long shot but who nevertheless generously agreed to despatch Sergeant Cole to the city to liaise with his counterpart there in exploring David Arnold's past to a deeper extent than they had done so previously. It wasn't that far away, Carrick agreed, and Cole would enjoy the drive and the chance of another 'day out' as he put it.

As he sat ruminating over the seemingly endless notes that had begun to build up with each passing day, he found himself staring at the e-photo that the police artist had produced with the help of the receptionist from the Regency Hotel.

"Who are you?" he asked himself, speaking aloud.

"Talking to yourself, Sir?" came a question from the doorway. He hadn't heard Lucy Clay as she'd quietly opened his door.

"Sergeant, come in," he replied, and it was then that he noticed a figure lurking in the background behind Clay.

"Who's that you've got with you?"

The pocket-sized figure of a very small uniformed woman police constable appeared from behind Lucy Clay. Connor had to admit to himself that he didn't recognise the young officer. Perhaps she was new?

"Sir, this is Constable Gregson, Alexandra Gregson. She has some information that I think you ought to hear. I suggested that as she'd discovered it herself she should be the one to tell you about it."

Connor smiled at Alex Gregson, trying to put her at ease. It was obvious that she was a little in awe at being in the presence of the D.I. in the close proximity of his office.

"Please come in Gregson, and tell me what you've discovered."

Alex Gregson stepped forward with a clipboard in her hand, obviously containing the precious information she'd brought to Clay's attention. She seemed to hesitate for a minute and Lucy Clay gave her a verbal prod.

"Go on Alex, tell him!"

"Yes, right. Well, yesterday Sergeant Clay asked us to delve deeper into the past histories of everyone involved either directly or indirectly with the case. I was given the job of looking into the records of the old

Prentice case and I checked and rechecked all the information we'd found so far. I went through everything we had and I realised that there was one area we hadn't explored."

She paused to draw breath.

"Go on Constable," urged Connor.

"Well, we'd found out that William and Elizabeth Prentice had given birth to a son and a daughter who had both been killed in that light aircraft crash, but having discovered that, the first check was sort of closed as it was obviously thought that there couldn't be any further connections in that direction. Anyway, I went a little further this time, and I found out that James Prentice, the son, had been married a few months before the air crash. His widow is still alive Sir, and here's the point of greatest significance, as I hope you'll agree. Margaret Alice Prentice is the owner of a specialist chocolate and sweet shop in Penzance!"

Sean Connor almost leaped from his chair in excitement. He grabbed the clipboard from Gregson, looked at it, then quickly turned and placed it on his desk. Sean Connor then took the highly unusual step of gently taking hold of Police Constable Alex Gregson by the arms, and in a wholly politically incorrect gesture he kissed the young officer on the forehead.

"Constable Gregson, you are without a doubt the brightest star in this station. Well done!"

An elated Constable Gregson quickly recovered from the shock of her superior's sudden show of emotion, and showing great wisdom she accepted Connor's kiss in the spirit in which it had been delivered.

"I'm glad I could help Sir, and thank you."

Connor once more took hold of the clipboard from his desk, grabbed his jacket which rested on the back of his char and gestured to Lucy Clay to follow him.

As the two officers surged at top speed through the incident room to the surprise of the officers who sat at their desks and computer terminals carrying out their allotted tasks, he shouted to Lucy Clay who followed in his wake.

"How far is it to bloody Penzance?"

Five minutes later they were in the car heading out of the town, and three hundred miles and just over five hours later, he and Lucy Clay arrived in the picturesque seaside resort town of Penzance in Cornwall where they soon located the police station that was the workplace of Inspector Harry Sefton, who Lucy had been connected to as she called from the car on their approach to the town.

Sefton greeted them warmly as they sat in the small but modern office he called his own. Now, thought Connor, they were about to get somewhere with this so far God-forsaken case.

# Chapter 32
# Interview Room 2

Margaret (known locally as Maggie) Prentice sat looking frightened and forlorn in the interview room provided by Harry Sefton. He, Connor and Clay now stood watching the suspect through the one-way plate glass mirror that afforded a view into the room beyond. The brightly lit interview room was a stark contrast to the darkened room in which the officers now stood; part of the secret of the workings of the one-way mirror.

"She doesn't look like a killer, does she?"

The words came from Inspector Sefton after he'd observed the woman for almost twenty minutes.

"They rarely do, do they?" Connor responded.

"No, I suppose you're right Mr Connor. Are you going to talk to her yet?"

"No. We'll leave her to sweat for another ten minutes or so. Perhaps if she's scared enough she'll tell us the whole story without too much prompting."

"According to the two officers who picked her up at her shop she came along quietly enough. Seems she was really surprised when they walked in and asked her to accompany them to the station. It wasn't 'til you met her at the door and told her what she was here to be questioned about that she started to panic a bit."

"Which just goes to show how cool she can be," said Lucy Clay. "She had no idea we were on to her and probably thought you wanted her for something unconnected with this case."

"That's possible," Sefton replied, "though that would imply that she might have something else to hide apart from information about this poisoning case of yours."

"Maybe she does," Connor intervened in the conversation. "At this stage we can't be sure just how much she knows or how deeply she's involved, but I intend to find out, and quickly. Funny thing is that she doesn't look anything like the e-photo we had produced back in Richmond. Maybe that proves my theory that there are two of them."

"Or maybe it proves she's innocent Sir," said Clay, and Connor glowered at her. She said no more.

When the door to the interview room finally opened to allow Connor and Clay to enter, Maggie Prentice turned sharply to see who was coming into the room. Her chair had been strategically placed so that she would have to twist right round in order to do just that, thus increasing her discomfiture with her current situation. She was smaller than Connor had expected, maybe only a shred over five feet tall, with short mousey brown hair cut in a bob. He judged her age at between fifty and fifty five, which would have made her about twenty when the Prentice killing took place all those years ago. She'd been a widow for some time, and it kind of showed in the slightly unkempt appearance she portrayed. There probably wasn't another man in her life, and probably never would be.

The two detectives sat in chairs directly opposite the suspect. Just when Maggie Prentice thought the interview was about to begin, the door opened once more. She wasn't sure this time whether to turn and look at the new arrival or to concentrate on the two officers who sat facing her. She continued to look at Clay, refusing to look Connor in the eye, probably believing she would get a more sympathetic response from a woman. She was wrong, as she would soon discover. The two Richmond detectives were now joined by Inspector Sefton, who pulled up a chair from the side of the room and joined them in facing Maggie.

If she'd felt uncomfortable and intimidated by the sight of the two detectives sitting opposite her, she now felt even more so with the addition of yet another policeman on the other side of the table.

The detectives were silent for as long as they could be in a premeditated attempt to put pressure on the woman.

"Wh…what am I doing here? Why have you had me brought here?" she suddenly blurted out, her voice trembling and displaying the fear she was obviously feeling.

"I think you know very well why you're here Mrs Prentice," Lucy Clay began. She and Connor used a well-practised interview technique, with the sergeant beginning the questioning and Connor stepping in when he felt it necessary to do so. This always served to increase the pressure on the suspect by making them aware that Connor was the superior officer and that when he spoke, it was on matters of greater importance than the routine questions posed by his sergeant.

"You're here to answer questions relating to the murder of David Arnold."

"Murder? No, never, I never killed anyone. I didn't do it."

"Oh, but I think you did Mrs Prentice. You approached him early on the morning of his death as he walked to work and somehow convinced him to take and eat a chocolate laced with aconite. You killed him as sure as if you'd pointed a gun at him and pulled the trigger. We'll find out whether you admit it or not. There's team of police officers and forensic technicians crawling all over your shop even as we speak, so if there's anything there we'll find it."

"They won't find anything, I mean, there's nothing there, I…"

"You destroyed the evidence, is that it?" asked Clay in a voice that totally dispelled any thoughts Maggie Prentice might have had that she would get an easier ride from the female officer.

"No, of course not, there was never anything…"

"Never anything on your premises. Is that what you mean Mrs Prentice?"

This question came from Connor, who saw a chance to go for the jugular early in the interview. This woman obviously wasn't a career criminal and he judged that she would be relatively easy to break down. She was already tripping herself up in response to Lucy Clay's questions, which of course were specifically worded to encourage the suspect to do just that.

"No, that's not what I mean."

"So they were on your premises then?"

"Yes, no, I don't know. You're confusing me. You're trying to trick me."

"I've no need to trick you Mrs Prentice. None at all. All I want is the truth and that shouldn't be so hard for you should it? If you have nothing to hide why would you think I'd even need to try and trip you up, as you put it?"

Connor knew she was close to cracking, to revealing whatever she knew about the killing of the train driver.

"All I meant was that you've brought me here and accused me of murder, and you don't know the first thing about me."

"Oh but we do Maggie." Clay rejoined the interview. "We know you were married to James Prentice, who was the son of William and Elizabeth Prentice We know that your husband died in tragic circumstances, and we also know that your mother-in-law had vowed vengeance on those she thought were in some way responsible for her husbands, and your father-in-law's death. We know that she was an expert on poisons and that she headed up the research lab where the wife of one those accused of the murder lived. He was cleared and never charged, but that didn't stop your mother-in-law believing him guilty did it?"

"I don't know I tell you. I don't know what you're talking about."

"Yes you do." This was Connor. "You cold-bloodedly administered a lethal poison to a man who was about to take out an express train loaded with over a hundred passengers. Didn't you stop to think for one minute that he could have died while that train was travelling at over a hundred miles per hour? Your bloody revenge killing could have killed all the people on that train but for a stroke of luck in that the poison didn't hit him until he'd slowed down to stop at Birmingham."

"I didn't know it would kill him... I,"

He'd got her!

"Yes Mrs Prentice? You what?"

Maggie Prentice was beaten, and she knew it. Connor's last verbal assault on her had forced her to reveal her involvement. She knew there was no going back and that she would have to try a damage limitation exercise if she was to avoid a very long prison sentence.

"I thought it would just make him poorly for a while. At least that was what he said."

"Who Maggie? Who said it would make him ill?"

"I don't know," she sobbed.

"You must know Maggie," said Clay. "You don't go out and kill someone on the say so of a complete stranger. Do you really expect us to believe that for more than a second, or do you want me to think you did this all on your own. If you want to take the blame and go to prison for the rest of your life then so be it?"

"It's true, honestly. I don't know who he is. That is, I..."

Maggie Prentice was becoming lost for words. She was incriminating herself further with almost every sentence that came from her mouth. That was in part due to the practised interview technique of the officers carrying out the interview, and partly due to her own ignorance of the criminal way of life and her inability to keep quiet. Luckily for the detectives she hadn't asked for a solicitor so far. When she did the interview would have to be halted to allow her to consult with her legal counsel before continuing. Connor was determined to get all the information he could from the woman before that happened. As yet of course, this was strictly an informal interview and as yet Maggie Prentice had not been cautioned, so technically the question of legal representation hadn't actually arisen.

Connor decided to go in for the kill.

"Listen, Mrs Prentice, I'm going to make you a one time offer. Turn it down and I won't give you another chance. If you tell me all you know about the man who's behind this, I'll make sure you're charged as an accessory and not with the actual murder itself, as long as you tell me the truth. If you don't then I guarantee you'll be charged not only with this murder but also the five in Richmond."

"But, you can't," she shouted, panic in her voice. "I've never even been to Richmond, let alone killed anyone there. I thought it was a joke, honestly. Well, not strictly a joke perhaps but just a way of making him ill, so that he'd know it was all to do with the past."

"So tell me the truth," urged Connor, "and why and how killing David Arnold has got anything to do with happened to William Prentice all those years ago."

Maggie Prentice was by now clearly on the verge of breaking down completely. Tears were streaming down her face, she sniffed, and Lucy Clay passed her a tissue from a box that lay on the table between them. Prentice took a moment or two to wipe her eyes, blew her nose, then took a deep breath before continuing.

"James was a good man," she went on, referring to her late husband. "He was going to carry on his mother's fight for justice for his father when he got back from Scotland. He'd read everything to do with the case and he agreed with his mother that the Stride man or Stanley Miller must have killed his father. The law wouldn't make them pay, so he was determined to do it himself. Whichever one of them was responsible would be brought to justice. He was determined to do it."

"So that justifies killing innocent people does it?" asked Connor.

"James wouldn't have killed anyone Inspector. He just wanted the truth to come out, that's all. When he died I sort of took on the mantle of trying to get at that truth for a while, but I wasn't any good at tracking down clues or evidence or stuff like that. I forgot all about it until a few weeks ago when I got a telephone call out of the blue from a man who sad he knew who'd killed my father-in-law and that he could help me get even. He said I owed it to the family, to my husband, my mother-in-law, and most of all to my father-in-law."

"Ok, but where does David Arnold fit in to all this?"

"It wasn't David Arnold himself Inspector, that's why I believed the man when he said he just wanted to make him sick for a while. I didn't really think he wanted to kill anyone. David Arnold's grandfather was one the men who gave Terence Stride an alibi for the night of the murder. He was a travelling salesman who was in town that night and when he came forward to say that he'd been drinking in a pub with a man who matched Stride's description and later picked him out from photographs the police had no choice but to release him as they said he couldn't have got from the pub he was supposedly in and get to the murder scene in time to kill my father-in-law. Thomas Arnold went back to Liverpool and probably never gave the case another thought, even though he'd probably given a murderer an alibi. He died a year later, and David Arnold's father passed away last year, so the trappings of guilt had to fall on David."

"This is madness," said Sefton, breaking his silence at last. "You can't go around killing or even trying to maim people just because you think they're related to someone who gave an alibi to the man who you think killed your father-in-law. The law cleared Terence Stride, so you have no right to become judge, jury and executioner."

"The law let him go free, and that gave me and my family the right."

The officers looked at each other, as the realisation hit them that Margaret Prentice might just be delusional, and the prospect of an insanity defence became a possibility.

Suddenly Prentice fell silent, and before Connor, Clay or Sefton could ask her the name of the man who had telephoned her and set the whole ball rolling, she took a deep breath, leaned back in her chair and said:

"Excuse me, but should I be saying all this to you on my own? I mean, shouldn't I have a solicitor or someone present to help me? I think I'd rather not say any more for the moment thank you."

The moment was gone. Connor had gambled and lost, for the time being. He'd return to Margaret Prentice shortly. She seemed to have forgotten his offer of a few minutes earlier. He would try again with her solicitor present. A good lawyer would surely advise her to cooperate in order to lessen the charge again this client. He spoke into the recording machine that stood at the side of the room.

"Interview terminated at two-forty. Inspectors Connor and Sefton and Sergeant Clay are leaving the room, awaiting arrival of suspect's solicitor."

The three officers rose and left Maggie Prentice sitting in the interview room alone with her thoughts. She could wait. They knew they'd got her. It was only a matter of time before the truth began to unravel.

# Chapter 33
# Another Brick in the Wall?

Giles Evans-Bailey looked to be exactly what he was; a young and ambitious country solicitor with aspirations to greatness that were as yet unmatched by his legal abilities. Just starting out on the long road that would constitute his legal career; he'd sat talking with Maggie Prentice for over an hour before leaving the interview room to consult with the detectives.

"My client is prepared to speak with you again," he said to Connor, who'd been impatiently pacing up and down the corridor of the police station while the client/solicitor conference had taken place. "She has appraised me of your offer to her before I became involved in the case and despite my disquiet at your having conducted such a lengthy interview without my client having access to legal representation, I have informed her that it would be in her best interests to co-operate with your enquiries."

"Mr Evans-Bailey, first of all, your client was merely helping us with our enquiries in an informal situation. She was not under caution and it wasn't until she incriminated herself by her own admissions that we became factually aware of her direct involvement in the murder of an innocent man. My offer to her still holds strong. A long as she is honest and open with us and tells us what we need to know in order to apprehend the person behind the killing of David Arnold and other victims in Richmond I will ask that she be charged with a lesser offence than she might otherwise have been charged with."

"Thank you Inspector. I'm sure my client is grateful for your consideration. Now, if you wish, Mrs Prentice is waiting?"

Maggie Prentice appeared to have shrunk when the detectives re-entered the room. She had sunk into her chair and looked every inch a beaten woman. Whatever psychological dysfunctions might be at work in her brain she was fully aware of the gravity of her situation, that much was certain.

Connor, Clay and Sefton retook their seats and this time Giles Evans-Bailey was present sitting at the side of his client. His inexperience made him no less a threat to the police investigation as he could quite easily advise his client to say no more at any time during the interview and that would do little to help catch whoever was behind the killings. This time round Connor took the initiative and began the questioning of his one and only suspect.

"Now Mrs Prentice, I'm sure your solicitor has told you that co-operation is in your best interests"

The woman nodded.

"All I want from you at this stage is a name; the name of the man you say called you and who got you to deliver the fatal chocolate to David Arnold. You can tell me later how he got the aconite chocolates to you and exactly how you got David Arnold to eat one or more of them, though I think I already know the answer to that one. For now, I just want that name. If you aren't prepared to give it to me then the deal is off, and you'll be charged with the murder of David Arnold and with complicity in the five murders that have taken place in Richmond. It's your choice Maggie. Take your time before you answer."

Maggie Prentice sighed and seemed to lose herself in thought for a minute. She leaned close to Evans-Bailey and whispered something in his ear. The detectives, though sitting just across the table from the pair were unable to her what she said. The solicitor was the next to speak.

"My client will give you the name you request on condition that after she has done so you will ensure that she is afforded protection."

"Protection?" asked Sefton.

"Yes, she fears that the man in question might try to arrange for some harm to come to her if he becomes aware that she has divulged his identity. She considers the man to be highly mentally unstable."

*That's rich, coming from her,* thought Connor to himself.

"Don't you worry, Mr Evans-Bailey. We'll make sure that no harm comes to your client while she's in our custody. I can assure you of that.

"Thank you Inspector Sefton."

The solicitor turned to his client, looked her in the eye and nodded.

Maggie Prentice took a deep breath and allowed herself one last pause for thought before revealing to the detectives the one thing they wanted above all else at that moment.

"He wouldn't tell me his name at first Inspector. He told me he knew everything that there was to know about the case and that it was high time someone was made to pay for what'd happened to William Prentice. The law had done nothing to find his killer, and now the killer's family were free to go about their business with no stain on their family names. Not only that but the people who'd ensured that the guilty went free were also free to go about their daily lives as though nothing had ever happened. He said that the witnesses and the legal professionals had lied and cheated in order to let the killer go free and that whether it was Stride or Miller who did the actual killing they were just as guilty in his eyes. I agreed with him because that was exactly the way my mother-in-law and my husband had thought, so I suppose it was easy enough for him to convince me. He told me that he had a way that we could use to make them all pay, so that William Prentice would at last be avenged. I replied that I wouldn't even listen to him if he didn't tell me his name. He could have been anybody after all, trying to trap me or playing some sick joke on me and the memory of a dead man. Eventually I convinced him that if he wanted my help, then he had to tell me who he was. That's when he finally gave me his name. You must understand that I've never once set eyes on him since this all began. I received my instructions by phone, and he made sure the chocolates were delivered to my shop just like any ordinary stock delivery. He always used a payphone so I couldn't call him back, and he said he would always call from a different place. He said he lived far from Richmond, though he didn't say where. Because of that he said that no-one would ever know where to find him. I never knew where or how to contact him. He would always call me. It was all so easy really."

"The name, Mrs Prentice, give us his name," Connor demanded.

"Oh yes," she went on. "His name, Inspector is Andrew Forbes."

The name rang a bell with both Connor and Clay though they couldn't place it immediately.

"The name is familiar," was all Connor could say.

"It should be, Inspector Connor," Maggie Prentice said with an evil, leering grin that spread across her face. The madness was creeping back into her personality. Connor could almost see and feel it.

"Andrew Forbes was the business partner of my late father-in-law William Prentice, and guess what? He was in love with my mother-in-law too!"

Connor said nothing for a minute then nodded his head at the woman, rose from his chair and motioned for Clay to follow him. He turned to Inspector Sefton.

"Please do me the favour of placing this woman under official caution," he said. "The charge is accessory to murder."

Sefton nodded.

Connor then turned once more to the woman sitting at the table.

"Sergeant Clay and I are leaving for now Mrs Prentice. We'll check out what you've told us and believe me, if I find out you've lied to me, that charge will quickly be upgraded to one of murder in its own right, do you understand?"

"I've told you the truth, Inspector. What you do with it is up to you."

"I have one last question," said Connor. "Do you know the identity of the other Chocolate Woman?"

"I'm sorry?"

"The woman who delivered the poison to the victims in Richmond; do you know who she is?"

"I have no idea at all Inspector. He never told me anything about what he was doing in Richmond, much less who was helping him."

They left her sitting there. In a few minutes Sefton would escort her to the charge room where the duty sergeant would begin the task of logging Maggie Prentice into the system and the long process of the legal machinery that would end in her trial and conviction would begin.

Connor returned to Sefton's office, from where he called Charles Carrick in Birmingham to advise him of the latest breakthrough.

"At last," said Carrick into the phone. "Well done Sean. Now we're getting somewhere."

"I thought that as David Arnold died on your patch and that as this side of the investigation is very much yours, you might want to come down here and talk to her yourself."

"I think I might just do that Sean."

"I'm sure Sefton here will be only too pleased to transfer her into your custody if you want to get her up to Birmingham to be further questioned and where I would think she'll stand trial anyway."

"Yes, I think that would be a good idea. I'll speak to this Inspector Sefton in a few minutes after I've been and told my boss the good news. I presume you'll be heading back to Richmond now and going after this Forbes character?"

"Too right we will," said Connor enthusiastically.

"Right, well I'll let you go then, and well done once again Sean. Now, is there anything else I can do at the moment?"

Connor thought for a moment before answering, and then with a hint of levity in his voice he delivered his reply to Charles Carrick's question.

"I think you should get your Sergeant Cole back from Liverpool, before his expenses get too high."

With Carrick's laughter ringing in his ears he replaced the phone on its cradle and within half an hour he and Clay were on the road once more, beginning the long journey back to Richmond, leaving Maggie Prentice in the capable hands of Inspector Sefton.

# Chapter 34
# Traffic Jams and Dead Ends

The return journey to Richmond became an interminable grind for Connor. With Lucy Clay at the wheel of the Mondeo he had little to do but think about the case that at last seemed to be opening up before him. Soon after leaving the picturesque resort town behind he'd phoned the station and instructed Fox to search for the last known address of Andrew Forbes. There was nothing else he could do for now but wait, and his mood wasn't helped by the volume of traffic on the roads. Despite the time of year it seemed that every day tripper in the Southwest had converged on Penzance that very day and were now all heading home at the same time as he and Clay needed to get back to town. Caravans, tourers, even slow moving tractors all appeared to be queuing up to create a log jam of hold up after hold up that even had the usually mild tempered Lucy Clay gritting her teeth with the frustration of having to keep slowing down and, finding scarce few opportunities for overtaking, the journey rapidly became one of agonising frustration.

Connor turned his mind to thinking about the interview he'd just conducted with Maggie Prentice. They had what appeared to be some answers, but there were still many questions that remained. The local police in Penzance, having cautioned and arrested the Prentice woman, would keep her 'on ice' until the following day when Carrick and Cole would arrive from Birmingham to conduct a far more intense and searching interview with the woman. Connor had to admit though, that he didn't think that Maggie Prentice knew much more than she'd already revealed. True, they would need to find out more of the intricate details of how she'd carried out the poisoning of David Arnold but that in itself would throw little light on the overall mantra of the case. Many things still bothered Connor. He could scarcely believe that someone had gone to all this trouble in order to murder what in most cases were distant or at least one or two generations removed relations of the original participants in the events that surrounded the death of William Prentice. Either the man behind the murders was seriously deranged, or there was a hidden meaning to the killings that had escaped the police so far.

Lucy said little in reply to Connor's occasional grunt or short comments on the interview. She preferred to keep her eyes on the road and her mind on the business of avoiding piling into the back of an articulated wagon or a long stream of vehicles that would suddenly behave like a kamikaze snake as fifty sets of brake lights snapped on at the same time. Someone way up front had probably encountered another tractor!

As they entered the third hour of the interminable trek home Connor's phone began to vibrate and ring in his pocket.

"Connor," he said as he snapped the flip phone open.

It was Simon Fox.

"Sir, I've found that address you asked me to get."

"Good work Fox. That was quick. Where does he live?"

"Well Sir, it was easy really. Mr Forbes lives right here in Richmond, in Henley Close, less than three miles from your own address actually."

Connor's immediate thought was that Maggie Prentice had been misdirected by Forbes to make sure she didn't try to find him in Richmond. She'd been adamant that he'd told her he lived a long way from the town these days. He didn't trust her, of course, and why should he?

Fox continued.

"Do you want me to go round there and see him Sir? Is he connected to the investigation?"

"Yes, he most definitely is," Connor replied.

He thought for a moment. By his reckoning Forbes would be in his seventies or eighties now, and even if he were the mastermind behind the murders it was unlikely that he'd pose much of a physical threat to the physically fit and muscular young police detective. The decision made, he spoke into the phone again.

"Listen Fox, I want you to take two uniformed officers with you and get round to that address. I have to warn you that Andrew Forbes is our chief suspect for the aconite poisonings. I doubt he'll put up much resistance, but be on your guard. Try to convince him that you want him to accompany you to the station on some routine matter relating to a complaint received from a neighbour, or something like that. If you can think of a better pretext to get him to go with you then feel free to use your initiative."

"Yes Sir," Fox replied, eager to be on his way and pleased that Connor trusted him to go out and bring in the suspect on his own.

"Go on then, get on with it man," said Connor, almost able to feel his young subordinate champing at the bit.

"Right Sir, I'll be off then."

"OK, Fox, and just be careful. If you get him to come in quietly, or even if you don't, give me a call and let me know. I should be back at the station in a couple of hours if this infernal traffic eases up a bit. Hopefully you'll have him there by then"

Connor clicked the phone off to enable Fox to go about his task.

"Was that wise, Sir?" came the voice of Lucy Clay from the drivers' seat. "He's very young and inexperienced."

"He's old enough to have made it to the detective ranks Sergeant. That makes him old enough in my book. He's also a damned fine officer and I think we should have a little faith in the men in our team to get the job done, don't you?"

"Yes of course, I'd just hate to think of him getting into trouble out there that's all."

"Oh come on Lucy," Connor softened a little. "He's going to see an old-age pensioner who might be the killer of at least six people but who probably walks with a Zimmer frame when he's not mixing his deadly concoctions. Fox will also have two uniforms for back-up as well so I don't think he'll come to any harm, do you?"

"Of course he won't Sir. I suppose I'm just tired from this incessant traffic we've had to contend with."

"Not for much longer I hope Lucy. They all seem to be moving a bit faster now than for the past half hour."

It was true. The nearer they got to London and its environs the thinner the stream of traffic became as drivers turned off towards their final destinations. When he saw a sign that said 'Richmond-on-Thames 30' he at last began to feel that he was nearing home.

"Nearly there Lucy. Only thirty miles to go. Just over half an hour at this speed, eh?"

"Definitely won't be long now Sir."

The vibration in his pocket was followed by the ring tone of his phone once again.

He answered quickly, knowing it was probably young Fox with news. It was.

"Sir, I'm at the home of Andrew Forbes, and I hate to have to tell you this but..."

"But what, Fox? Don't prevaricate, just tell me."

"Well Sir, we got here a short while ago and couldn't get an answer from knocking at the door or from ringing the doorbell. We began to take a look through the downstairs windows and that's when we saw him, just lying there."

Connor's heart began to sink as Fox continued.

"We managed to find a window that was only half shut and believing that the occupant of the house might be in some distress we entered the property without a warrant..."

"Yes alright. We don't need the legalese Fox. You were quite justified to enter under those circumstances. Just tell me what you found."

"Yes Sir, I'm sorry. Anyway, Mr Forbes was lying on the floor of what appeared to be his study. I doubt very much that he could have been the aconite poisoner Inspector, because he seems to have been dead for a number of days. I'm no forensic expert of course but the body was in a bit of a state if you know what I mean Sir, not fresh, like, and from what I could make out it looks like he could be another victim of the poisoner himself. He was all curled up and it looked as if he'd died in great agony. His face was all contorted and..."

"Ok, Ok, I get the picture. Look, whatever you do don't touch anything. I suppose you've called it in to the station?"

"Yes Sir, forensics are on their way, and D.C.I. Lewis is coming over as well."

"Give me the exact address Fox. We'll be in town soon and we'll join you there."

Connor hung up on Fox and turned to Lucy Clay.

"Bloody hell Lucy. We've missed one. Forbes wasn't the killer and in fact it looks like he might've been the first bloody victim. Either Maggie Prentice was lying to us about the killer's name or the sick son of a bitch used Forbes's name in order to throw her, us and everyone else off the scent. If we don't find this bastard fast the trail is going to go stone cold. Oh yes, and by the way, the Boss is going to be waiting for us when we get there and I can promise you he isn't going to be a happy man. Put your foot down if you please Sergeant, and switch the bloody siren on. It's time to get these buggers out of the way. This is an emergency call after all, right?"

"Right Sir," she replied, and the unmarked car suddenly accelerated in response to the pressure of her right foot, and Connor and Clay completed their journey to the accompanying sound of the siren that ensured a smooth passage for the final twenty miles of their drive.

# Chapter 35
# 22 Henley Close

Number twenty two Henley Close, Richmond-on-Thames needed no finding once Lucy Clay turned into the leafy, tree-lined cul-de-sac. Three police cars stood outside the property, lights flashing, and a team of paramedics were unloading a stretcher and other equipment from an ambulance, its twin blue flashing lights joining those of the police vehicles in giving the late afternoon gloom a surreal 'twilight zone' effect.

Nearby another official looking vehicle stood, though this one was devoid of the roof lights that identified the rapid response emergency vehicles. On its side was the simple and unobtrusive emblem of the Constabulary with the words 'Forensics Unit' appended just below the police force's coat of arms. It looked empty and deserted which meant that the forensics team had already begun their examination of the death scene.

Three unmarked cars stood slightly to the side of the emergency vehicles. One was easily identified as the grey jaguar that was the preferred means of transportation of Connor's boss D.C.I. Harry Lewis, one was immediately recognisable to Connor as being Catherine's and the other was without a doubt the vehicle used by Simon Fox to drive to Forbes's house. Lucy Clay pulled her Mondeo up close to Lewis's jaguar and she and Connor were out of the car in seconds, pausing only to stretch their muscles after the long drive from Cornwall before making their way up the driveway towards the front door.

As they neared the door a figure stepped out from behind the heavy oak door of number twenty two. Detective Constable Harry Drew looked pale and shocked. Lewis had brought Drew with him when he'd decided to visit the scene in Connor's absence and of the two Harrys it was obvious that Drew was the more sensitive to whatever he'd seen in the house. Lewis was more than experienced when it came to dealing with dead bodies, and Connor knew it. Unlike some D.C.I.s who were little more than 'glorified desk jockeys with degrees' as Connor often described them Lewis was one of the 'old school'. He'd worked his way up to his current rank, having started his career in the police force as a beat constable and stopping along the way at all ranks on the way to his present position. Connor respected him and Lewis was well-liked by everyone at the station.

"Are you alright Drew?" Connor now asked the young detective.

"You look a bit pale if you don't mind me saying so, Harry," added Lucy Clay.

"It's a bit bad in there Sir. The body looks as if it's being lying there for a week or more I would say. I've seen bodies before Mr. Connor, but not when they've been ripening for so long. The doctor and the forensics people have made a start, on Mr Lewis's instructions but I never realised it would smell that bad Sir, really I didn't."

"I know what you mean Drew. Get some air and don't come back in until you're ready. We can take care of everything now, anyway."

"Thanks Mr Connor. I appreciate it."

"Take your time Harry," came from Clay as the two officers walked past Drew and into the house of death.

The smell of decomposing human flesh was recognisable as soon as Connor and Clay passed over the threshold from the fresh air of the outside world into the fetid atmosphere of a house that had contained its dead occupant for many days. The smell ranked at number one in Connor's all time list of things to avoid, but he knew that in his job it was something he couldn't evade. The air in the hallway was filled with flies, and the two officers had little doubt as to what had been the insects' food source for the past few days. The pungent smell of death reached out to grip their nostrils as they moved along the passageway towards the study, the room easily identified by the sounds of their fellow officers and the other specialists in the room as they went about their unenviable business.

D.C.I. Lewis was in conversation with Catherine Nickels as Connor and Clay made their entry into the room. They stopped upon seeing the two newcomers and Catherine smiled as she caught sight of Connor.

"Hello Sean."

"Hello Catherine. You caught the call this time, eh? Hello Sir," he directed the last to Lewis.

The chief inspector nodded in greeting.

"A bad business Sean," he said.

"I could have left it to one of the others but thought it best to come along myself," said Catherine in response to Connor's question.

"We got here as soon as we could Sir," Connor aid to Lewis, aware that he was involved in two separate conversations.

"I know. You seem to have done well in Penzance from what I've heard. We've been here for a while. Before I say anything else I think I'll let the good doctor here fill you in on what she thinks from her preliminary examination of the body."

Catherine led Connor and Clay to the far side of what had obviously been a working study until recently. As they crossed the room Connor took in the rows of books that lined the purpose-built shelves along the wall opposite the window. Novels by authors such Conan-Doyle, Poe, Patterson and Christie stood on one shelf, with the lower tier taken up by books on forensic science, legal procedures and one, 'Investigation Procedures and The Art of Covert Surveillance' was an obvious 'How To' guide for private investigators and served to remind Connor that the victim, like himself, had been in the same business; different tracks perhaps, but at least for the most part, on the side of the angels.

Two forensic technicians were at work gathering whatever trace evidence might be present, and dusting the room for prints. So far the killer had left no real evidence to distinguish his or her presence at any of the previous crime scenes. Perhaps this time the police would get lucky.

Catherine led them around the heavy old-fashioned mahogany desk to where the remains of Andrew Forbes lay on the floor, just below the wide expanse of the room's expansive bay window. From the position of the body it was evident to Connor that the victim had probably been sitting in his leather office chair when he'd been hit by the effects of the aconite. He'd fallen to the floor in his agony and panic and must have rolled around for some time in his death throes before coming to a final stop in the curled-up foetal position so common in the victims. His chair was slightly to one side of the desk, where it had rolled on its casters as Forbes had hit the floor.

"I don't think there's any doubt about the cause of death Sean," Catherine began. "I'll be able to confirm it after the autopsy of course, but you can take it that I'm ninety nine percent certain that death was due to aconite poisoning."

"Turning his nose up again at the sight and the stench that pervaded the room, Connor asked,

"Any idea how long he'd been here before we found him?"

"A week, maybe a little longer? Again, I'll be able to find out with a bit more certainty when I get him back to the lab for examination. There's been significant insect activity on and in the body, so that will help to give us a more definite timeline to when he died."

Connor shuddered. Lucy Clay, fighting back the urge to heave, was the next to speak.

"It proves that we're on the right track though, Sir. Whoever is doing this is somehow connected to the Prentice case. They have to be, surely. Maggie Prentice thought that Forbes was the man behind it all; I think she firmly believed that. You said in the car that the killer used Forbes's name to fool her and us, and I agree, so I think it points to the killer being connected with the original case in some way. He's being very clever in his efforts to cover his tracks and his identity, but we're closing in on him, I'm sure of it."

"Listen Sean." It was D.C.I. Lewis. "I've sent a couple of officers around the Close to see if anyone saw or heard anything suspicious in the last week or so. If we're lucky someone might have seen The Chocolate Woman or whoever it was when they came to visit Forbes."

"I don't think it was her Sir."

"You don't?"

"No. I also don't think it was her who delivered the aconite to Judge Tolliver. Both he and Forbes here were directly connected to the original Prentice investigation, and I have a feeling that they knew their killer personally. He would have wanted to make sure they died. Remember how Tolliver had a large enough dose to kill a horse in his body? I could be wrong of course but I think the killer stayed and watched Tolliver and Forbes die out of a sense of gruesome satisfaction."

"And the others?"

"Sam Gabriel, Virginia Remick, Arminder Patel, David Arnold and the Strides were different. They were, I assume, the offspring of others who were connected to the case. We know the Strides and Arnold's connection, tenuous though it was but we still don't know how Patel, Remick or Gabriel were involved. We need to concentrate on that and try to establish what their or their family's links to the case were. Once we find those links we're going to be even closer to tracking this evil bastard down."

At that moment the paramedics asked for and were given permission by Catherine Nickels to remove the body if the police were finished with it for now.

Lewis looked questioningly at Connor, who nodded to his superior. There was little more he could discover from the body here at the scene and to be honest, he'd be glad to get the rank-smelling remains of the ex-private investigator out of the house. As soon as the body had gone and the forensic people gave their assent Clay followed Connor's order to open the windows of the study. The fresh air was a welcome intrusion into the foul stench of putrescence that would pervade their lungs for some time to come. It would be days before the smell of death left that room, but for now, just the touch of the lightest breeze from outside was a relief to those present at the death scene.

Catherine exited the room behind the paramedics and would follow the body to the mortuary where she would begin her detailed examination of Forbes's remains without delay. As the forensics team continued their minute investigation of every inch of the dead man's study Connor gestured for Clay to follow him out of the room, which the sergeant did with haste and with relief.

"Your thoughts, Sergeant?" he asked as the two of them stood just outside the front door gulping in lungfulls of sweet tasting fresh air for the first time in over half-an-hour.

"I have a feeling that Mr Forbes was the first victim Sir. I think the killer made sure of his death before he commenced with the other killings. We didn't know of course because no-one came and found the body until today. That would mean, if my theory is correct that Forbes not only knew his killer as you suggested in there, but that he could also in some way be the key to all that's happened so far."

"Good thinking Lucy," Connor grinned. "Those are my thoughts exactly. Let's go back in there and take a closer look at that study. Forbes had a computer, it's on his desk, and there's a bloody great filing cabinet just waiting to be searched in the corner of the room."

An hour later, the detectives emerged once more from the house to take the air and relieve their lungs of the odour of decomp. They'd found nothing, but that in itself had told them something. Andrew Forbes had kept scrupulous records on his computer of every case he had ever been involved in. When it came to the case of his partner's death however, there was no trace of a single file relating to it. That meant that either he had never recorded the details on his hard drive, *unlikely*, or that the killer had stayed long enough in the house to access the files and delete them, *highly likely*. The filing cabinet had produced similar results. In this case it was obvious to the searchers that files had been removed. There was a huge gap in one of the filing cabinet drawers that indicated a number of missing files. Connor would bet his life on the fact that they were the Prentice files, particularly as the missing papers all appeared to be from the master file under the heading 'P'.

Connor had ordered the forensic technicians to remove the computer and have it sent to the specialists at headquarters for closer analysis. The killer may not have been aware that although he'd deleted the files, modern police technology would allow their computer analysts to retrieve and recreate them from somewhere deep within the computer's hard drive. Connor neither knew nor understood the technology involved in the process, but he knew it could be done.

"If there was something on those files that would lead us to the killer, and I suspect there is, or why would he have taken the time to delete them, then we're going to find it Lucy, and when we do…"

"When we do Sir, we'll have the sod."

The two detectives were joined by D.C.I. Lewis who had remained studying the scene while the forensics team worked.

"Well Sean, what d'you think? Does this bring you any closer to solving the case? We can't take much more of this you know, bodies turning up all over town and the police appearing incapable of finding out who's responsible."

"I won't know that Sir until we find out what was on that computer. I just hope the computer techs can retrieve the missing files. Then we might just have a chance of tracking the killer down."

Detective Constable Simon Fox took that moment to come running up the driveway with an elated look on his face.

"Sir!" he called out as he ran, the delivery being directed at neither senior officer in particular. "I think I may have found us a witness. One of the neighbours, a Mr Vetchinsky, remembers seeing a car parked on Mr Forbes's drive about a week ago. He can't tell us the make of the car unfortunately, as he says it was mostly hidden by the trees on the driveway. It was unusual because Mr Forbes didn't get many visitors apparently. Not only that, but the witness says that the driver of the car was a man, not a woman. He doesn't know if he can give us a detailed description, as he was in his garden at the time and didn't pay too much attention to the man when he went into the house. He just saw him in passing so to speak, but he says he'll do his best with the police artist if we want him to."

"Vetchinsky? Is he Polish or something Fox?"

"Russian by birth Sir. Full name is Vladimir Nikolai Vetchinsky. Says he's lived in this country for over forty years. Seems he was a refugee from the communists and we gave him asylum a long time ago."

"I take it his English is good then?"

"Perfect Sir, apart from a slight accent. Why?"

"Just wondered if he'll make a good witness in court if we need him. As long as he's fluent he'll come across as a stronger witness, that's all."

Connor's boss had seen Fox's approach and had been listening to the conversation.

"Looks like you were right Sean," said D.C.I. Lewis.

"A man! Yes Sir, it does doesn't it? There's something else I've had niggling at the back of my brain as well. We know about Maggie Prentice in Penzance but, apart from the fact that we got a description of a woman who was a little furtive from the hotel receptionist at The Regency we don't have any real evidence to suggest that The Chocolate Woman, or rather, another Chocolate Woman, has actually been at work here in Richmond. What if we've been barking up the wrong tree all along? We could be looking for a man, rather than a woman, for all of the local killings."

Connor was of course as yet unaware of the visit by the woman to Arminder Patel's shop. Had he been so, he might not have been as confident as he now sounded. For now though he had hope, real hope that he was close to discovering the identity of the man, as he now believed the killer to be, who was the real influence behind the woman or women who had been the delivery system for his vengeance, if indeed vengeance were the true motive for the murders.

Perhaps Connor thought that the eye of the storm had passed. If he did, then unfortunately he was to be proved wrong.

# Chapter 36
# Bedtime Story

"That was a pretty gruesome scene this afternoon, Catherine don't you think?"

"I've rarely seen worse, I must admit, Sean."

Catherine Nickels had joined Connor at his home after what had been a gruelling day for both of them.

Connor's long trip to and from Cornwall had left him drained and worn out and he'd been surprised when Catherine had called from her office just after ten at night to ask if he fancied some company.

He'd readily agreed to her driving over to his house. He needed the diversion that another human being would provide. He was getting too bogged down by death and too preoccupied with tracing the aconite killer. In short Sean Connor needed a touch of human warmth and Catherine was just the person to provide it.

"I don't really want to talk shop at this time of night, but has your preliminary examination of the body revealed anything we don't already know?"

"Not yet, Sean. I think I was right in saying that the victim died seven or eight days ago, I'll be more precise tomorrow, and there's little doubt about aconite having been used once again. So no, nothing new I'm afraid, not yet, at least not in that area anyway."

"Are you by any chance saying you have news in another area?"

"Actually Sean, yes I am. You remember the little study that Gary Hudson and I put together to track down incidences of the use of aconite?"

"Of course I do, but when you hadn't mentioned it for a day or two I thought you'd hit a dead end."

"At first, so did we. I'd spoken to our local expert Professor Medwin, who'd given me plenty of advice to follow and I'd contacted various medical and scientific journals who were all happy to release any articles they'd previously published going back almost a hundred years, but nothing seemed to have any relevance to this case. Then, Gary Hudson phoned me just this evening. He's very lucky because, being based in Birmingham he has certain contacts who allowed him access to the files of the UK Forensic Science Services laboratories who are located in the city. The FSS have a state-of-the-art database that contains references to a million and one items of medical and forensic trivia that probably wouldn't mean a thing to anyone who wasn't specifically looking for that exact item. Anyway when Gary's contact checked out what Gary had asked for, he was surprised to find that someone else had been looking into the same thing just a few weeks ago. It appears that one of his colleagues in the historical archive section had been approached by a man who said he was studying the historical uses of aconite as a poison and that he needed the information for an article he was writing. The man identified himself as a free-lance journalist who was preparing a piece for one of the big Sunday newspapers."

"Did he give a name Catherine, come on now; don't hold out on me."

"Yes Sean, he did. He gave his name as Roger Cahill, and Sean wanted to find out if the name was genuine and just before I came here this evening he called me back with the news."

"Catherine. *Tell me!*"

"The name is genuine Sean. Not only that, but Roger Cahill was a reporter for the Richmond Echo at the time of the Prentice murders and he was a reporter who obtained at least two interviews with Elizabeth Prentice before her death. His paper carried her accusations against the police, Stride, and Miller"

"And just how did you find all this out in so short a time my dear Doctor?" asked Connor with a smile on his face.

"I didn't Sean. Gary did. He asked his friend at the FSS if his colleague had checked out Cahill's credentials and he had done just that, and he'd recorded Cahill's details on the system. They don't just give out that kind of information to just anybody you know. He wanted to be sure that Cahill was genuine, so ran a background check on his bona-fides before releasing the information to him. When Gary ran a cross-check using aconite as his search key he found some articles Cahill had written for the Echo about the Stride woman's suicide all those years ago. Simple!"

Connor was more than impressed.

"So, if Cahill was trying to find out about aconite and its uses, he may be the man we're looking for. After all, if he just wanted background information on the Prentice case, he should have had all he needed from his previous work on the story. If he wanted to use aconite himself however, he'd need that kind of information in order to obtain the stuff or to at least work out how best to use it as a murder weapon. Catherine, you're a bloody genius; and your friend Gary of course."

Connor pulled Catherine Nickels close to his body. He looked down at her face, his eyes peering softly into her own. Their lips met, and they dissolved into each other. A long minute passed before they pulled away from each other and Catherine grinned at Connor.

"Well, Detective Inspector, I hope you're satisfied with my efforts to assist you in your inquiries."

"I must say that I am truly impressed Doctor. First thing in the morning I shall start tracking down our friend Cahill. That gentleman has a lot of questions to answer."

"Oh, he won't need much tracking down Sean. The address he gave to the FSS lab is recorded on their files. He still lives right here in Richmond. Would you like it?"

"Would I…? Come here young lady!"

Connor gave Catherine a playful slap on the rear and the two began a game of 'chase' through Connor's house until the two of them fell laughing and giggling like a pair of teenagers onto the sitting room sofa.

After a pause for breath Connor sat up and looked into Catherine's eyes once again, this time with a more serious expression on his face.

"You know, laughter apart, this could be exactly the breakthrough we've been looking for. Between the pair of you, you and Gary Hudson could just have given us the killer on a plate. I don't know why this reporter would want to suddenly begin killing people with a connection to the old Prentice case, but sometimes a killer doesn't need what you or I would see as a logical reason to do what they do. Tomorrow we'll see just what Roger Cahill has to tell us about his own aconite investigations and what it has to do with our murders."

"You really think he could be the one?"

"There's only one other reason, well, perhaps two, that would have him researching aconite at this time."

"Which are?"

"One, he is genuinely trying to write a piece on the uses of aconite as a poison, perhaps inspired by his previous connection with a case of a similar nature and in response to what's been happening lately. It could be a profitable exercise for him if one of the major Sunday papers were to pick up his story."

"And two?"

"Ah yes, two. Well, suppose he has an idea about who the killer is, and thinks that he can crack the case himself? Journalists often think that they make better investigators than the official police force even though they usually end up hindering rather than helping any investigation they get involved in. That could be his angle. Tell me, just how long ago did he request the information from the FSS lab? Was it before the killings began, or after they'd started?"

"It was well before the killings started Sean. Three weeks before in fact, giving him plenty of time to put to good use any information he'd gleaned on how to produce the poison himself."

"Right," said Connor. "That knocks out option two straight away and also leaves option one looking shaky. Why would he dredge up an article on aconite poisoning when the subject wasn't even topical at the time he dug up the information? No, Mr. Roger Cahill is smelling a little fishier by the minute as far as I'm concerned. I can't believe that you've managed to find all this out so quickly Catherine. You and Doctor Hudson have done more than well. You're a pair of geniuses if you ask me."

"That's a bit strong Sean, though I appreciate the compliment. It was nothing you and your people couldn't have discovered in time though. I'm sure you'd have got there eventually."

"Maybe, but time doesn't appear to be something we have on our side at the moment. Every time we turn around or think we've got a lead we're faced with another corpse to add to the body count. If it wasn't so late at night I'd assemble the whole team and raid Cahill's house right now."

"So why don't you?"

"Because I don't think he'll be killing anyone tonight, if he is our man. He probably thinks he's safe from detection and by this time of night he's probably tucked up in his bed. I will make a couple of calls and have Sergeant Clay and a couple of constables meet me outside his address very early in the morning, if you don't mind me leaving you to lock up when I go."

"Do I take that as an invitation to stay the night Sean Connor?"

"Er, yes of course it is. Unless of course you have somewhere else you'd rather be?" he teased.

"Well, it's hardly the most romantic invitation I've ever received, but it is quite late at night I suppose."

Now it was her turn to tease Connor.

"Hold on," said Connor as he picked up the telephone. It took him less than two minutes to set up his 'assault team' for the following morning's visit to Cahill's house, and then he returned his attention to Catherine.

"Now, where were we?"

"Something about me driving home alone in the dark was it, Detective Inspector?"

"Oh shut up and come here," said Connor as he took Catherine Nickels firmly by the arm and led her from the room, turning out the lights as they went.

"It's very dark Sean; do you think you can find the bedroom in the dark?"

"I said shut up, and stop teasing."

"Yes Sir, Detective Inspector. Shall I set the alarm clock when we get up there?"

"Catherine!"

She laughed once, then 'shut up' as instructed. The top stair creaked, but neither of them noticed. They had other things on their minds.

# Chapter 37
# The Art of Misdirection

Sean Connor rose early, just after five thirty a.m. and true to his promise he left Catherine sleeping peacefully. She stirred only once, when he left the house just before six after a quick breakfast of coffee and toast. After dressing Connor padded his way upstairs to the bedroom and leant over the bed, kissing her gently on the forehead. Her eyes flickered open for a second or two as she kissed him back, then he was gone, and Catherine slept on for another hour.

At the very moment that Catherine's feet touched the bedroom floor, Lucy Clay was knocking on the door of the home of Roger Cahill, Connor by her side. The neat three bedroomed semi-detached house was in the middle of Acton Road, and was flanked by a row of very similar, nineteen thirties-built houses which all bore the marks of time. Built in the style typical of the era, the whole street appeared a little rundown, though the bay-windowed houses retained something of an air of faded art-deco elegance in their exterior decorations and gateposts. Elm trees were spaced at equal intervals along the pavements on both sides of the street, planted in open patches of well tended and weed-free earth and Acton Road looked the epitome of everyday suburbia. Was this the kind of place that a killer might live? Connor knew better than most that killers are not some set-apart breed or sub-species of the human race. They are for the most part ordinary people who live ordinary lives; their friends, relatives and neighbours so often unaware of the dark secrets that they harbour. So, the answer to the question was yes, it was just the sort of place that a killer might live.

On the third knock a voice from somewhere inside the house shouted;

"Yes, yes, I'm coming. Just a minute whoever you are. Do you know what time it is?"

Connor knew very well what time it was. The crack of dawn was always the best time to take down a suspect, when the sleep was still in their eyes and their brains still befuddled by slumber.

The door opened and a man wearing a well-worn velvet dressing gown stood staring at the entourage of police officers gathered at his door and on the driveway of his home. Connor had the instant thought that the man who was looking at him as though he were a creature from another planet couldn't possibly be Roger Cahill. Cahill had to be at least seventy years of age, and this man was probably no more than forty, though his dishevelled hair and unshaven visage probably made him look older than he was. Thirty-five then, perhaps.

"Who the hell are you, and what do want at this time of the bloody morning?" asked the man.

"Police officers, sir. I'm Detective Inspector Connor, and this is Sergeant Clay. We're looking for a man named Roger Cahill."

"I'm Roger Cahill. Now what am I supposed to have done that merits so much attention before the sun has risen Detective Inspector?"

"I'm sorry," said Connor. "I was under the impression that Roger Cahill the former journalist lived here. Our information must be incorrect. The man we want is at least…"

"My father."

"Pardon?"

"You want my father. You were about to say that the man you're looking for is at least seventy five years old, weren't you? Well, that's how old Dad is. I'm afraid you're out of luck though Inspector. He's not here."

Somehow, that information didn't surprise Connor too much. He'd gotten used to disappointments in the course of this investigation.

"Look Mr Cahill, it's very important that we find your father. We think he can help us with an important inquiry we're conducting and it's a matter of urgency that we speak with him."

"You'd better come in," said the younger Roger Cahill, beckoning Connor and Clay through the door. Connor gestured to the waiting officers to stay where they were while he and Clay accompanied the man into the house.

"Can I get you some tea or coffee?" Cahill asked the two officers as he led them into the kitchen. "I need some coffee. I just can't function in a morning until I've had at least two shots of caffeine."

"Yes please," Connor answered for the two of them, hoping that the familiarity of drinking together at the breakfast table might make the man more receptive to his questions, as was often the case.

They waited until Cahill had boiled the kettle and made the coffee before taking seats opposite him at the table. The coffee was strong, but tasted good to Connor and Clay. Obviously the Cahill's, or at least this younger one, liked quality in the delivery system for their daily caffeine intake.

"Now Mr Cahill, about your father?"

"Yes Inspector. I presume you want to speak to him about these murders that've been taking place?"

"We do indeed Mr Cahill, but why would you assume such a thing?"

"I'm not a fool Inspector. The police don't make house calls at six thirty in the morning just to discuss a parking ticket now do they? Also, I'm aware that my father was involved in reporting on a case years ago that had some sort of connection with the poison that's being used today. Am I correct?"

"Quite correct Mr. Cahill. Now, about your father?"

"I've already told you, he's not here."

"Yes, I know that, but where is he? That's what we need to know."

"I'm afraid I'm not at liberty to tell you that Inspector. Dad doesn't want anyone to know where he is for the time being."

"I'll bet he doesn't," said Lucy Clay with more than a hint of sarcasm in her voice.

"Why use that tone Sergeant?" asked Cahill. "Oh, I get it. Wait a minute. You don't think Dad has anything to do with these murders do you?"

"The thought had crossed our minds Mr Cahill.

"You're mad. He's never harmed a soul in his life!"

"Then why has he disappeared?"

"Look Sergeant, Inspector, I'm not sure just what you've been told or what you think Dad's done, but the only reason he's gone away is because he was scared out of his wits when the killings started and believed that he was the next one on the killer's list."

"Then why did he contact the Forensic Science Services laboratory a few weeks ago and make certain inquiries relating to the use of aconite as a poison?" The question came from Connor, taking over from Clay once more.

"What? No, you're mistaken. He never did such a thing. Look, if I tell you what I know will you promise to leave Dad alone until all this is over?"

"I can't make any promises Mr Cahill, but if your father has got nothing to do with the killings then we won't have to bring him in for questioning, though if he's in danger he might be better to make contact us so that we can offer him police protection."

Connor's comment seemed to go unnoticed as Roger Cahill junior took a deep breath and began his story.

"Look, it was about six weeks ago. The phone rang and Dad was just ages talking to whoever was on the other end. Afterwards, I asked him who'd been on the phone. He said it as an old colleague from his days as a newspaper reporter, someone who'd worked for another paper but who he once knew quite well. Anyway, this man had told Dad some disquieting news about an old case and said that there was a chance that it was about to become headline news again. He wanted to know if Dad had kept his old records of the interviews and his investigative research from the old days. Dad had told him that he had of course. They were in a filing cabinet in his office across the hall there." Cahill pointed to the doorway, indicating the office as being across the hall.

"This man then told Dad that he thought that someone was after anyone who was involved in the case though he hadn't explained to Dad why that should be. Dad thought it was all something and nothing, and told me that he thought the man might be becoming deranged or at least a little senile in his old age. That told me that he was about the same age as Dad, though he is far from senile, let me assure you. Anyway, this man had told Dad that he should be careful, and that was about all. Dad told me that there was nothing to worry about. All he'd done was to report on a case that happened over thirty years ago and done a couple of interviews with someone's widow and that would hardly put him on some crazy person's death list. He told me to forget about it.

I thought no more of it until a couple of days later. Dad was in town on his way to the library when he was mugged. You can check that with your own people Inspector. He wasn't badly hurt, just a few bumps and bruises, but his wallet was stolen and he lost fifty pounds or so in cash, his credit cards and driver's licence. Two young men were responsible, though the police never found them or Dad's wallet and documents. The same night as the mugging we were robbed here at the house. Well, when I say we, I mean Dad was. Someone broke into the house and ransacked his study, but the only things taken were his papers relating to the old case that the man had called about. Dad was convinced it had something to do with the case but the police constable who came round the next day said it was probably the lads who'd mugged Dad who had broken in. They would have got the address from the driver's licence of course, and probably just broke in to cause mischief. Dad had no proof of anything otherwise so though he was getting a bit worried there was nothing else he could do."

Cahill paused for breath. Connor and Clay said nothing. They waited instead for the man to continue. Certain fragments of the case seemed to be joining themselves together as Cahill spoke and they were content to listen to his narrative and mentally join those pieces to what they already knew.

"Anyway, Dad became very nervous over the next couple of days and he tried to call his old colleague on a couple of occasions, but he told me that he couldn't reach him. He was never at home apparently. The phone just kept ringing. I told Dad that the number he had for this old acquaintance might be out of date but he insisted it was current. I suppose he'd checked with directory enquiries. When the news came in some time later about the poisonings in town, Dad very nearly had a stroke on the spot. He was terrified Inspector. He made numerous further attempts to contact the man who'd called him, without success. Dad told me that he and this other man were probably in great danger from whoever was killing these people. After all, that was what the man had said wasn't it? That someone was out to get anyone involved in the old case? That day he made arrangements to disappear from town, and he's been in hiding ever since. He calls me every day Inspector just to let me know he's ok, but he won't even tell me where he is. He says it's safer for me that way. That's about all I can tell you, but at least it shows that Dad isn't your murderer doesn't it?"

"Maybe," said Connor, "and maybe not. It could all be a blind of course, but I must say I tend to believe you Mr Cahill. However, I must agree that it's possible that your father is in great danger, and we must find him and speak to him as soon as possible. Please, when he calls you today tell him about our visit and tell him that it's imperative that he calls us. We will protect him, I promise you."

"I'll try Inspector, if you think it's that important."

"It is Mr Cahill, believe me."

Connor and Clay left the younger Cahill with his thoughts, and hoped that the man would be able to convince his father to get in touch with them when he next called. As they drove back to the station Connor and Clay reviewed their early morning expedition.

"What do you think then Sir?"

"What I think Sergeant, is that we're up against a very clever and a very devious killer. I believe that he was the man who called Cahill, and put the wind up him in the first place. Then I think he paid some thugs to mug the old man in order to get hold of his credentials, which he later used to obtain the information from the FSS lab using Cahill's identity. They do check identities at the lab you know. They don't just give out information to anyone who asks for it. This man whoever he is, was also responsible for the break-in at the Cahill house. There must have been something in Cahill's files on the case that would either incriminate the killer, or at least lead us to him. Cahill might not have realised the significance of what was in those files so he wouldn't have taken any special precautions to prevent their theft. As far as he was concerned they were probably just archives of his past career as a journalist. When the killings began, he ran in order to save himself from the killer."

"But why didn't he just call us, Sir?"

"Because Sergeant, he thought that this other man from his past was on his side. He'd tipped Cahill off that there was someone after them hadn't he? Cahill probably never thought that the man could be the killer himself. He ran because he thought he'd be safe, and also because the man who phoned him probably told him something that would make him afraid of going to the police, perhaps something to do with incriminating himself in some way. I'm afraid I'm in the dark as to that question Sergeant, but I think I'm pretty much on the spot with the rest."

"We're as close as we've come so far Sir, without actually having a name for the killer."

"Yes, like I said. He's a master at the art of misdirection He uses other people's identities the way I change my tie each day. Every time we think we've got him, it turns out he's using someone else's name. I also think he's connected with the original case as well. Cahill told his son that he was a reporter, like himself. That could be true or it could be that he was using a fake identity again. It would be easy to disguise his voice after all those years. Cahill couldn't be expected to remember the man's voice that well, because voices change with old age. We need to check out every news report and reporter who wrote in depth about the Prentice case. He's clever alright, very clever, but we're getting closer Sergeant, I know we are. He's going to run out of fake IDs soon, and when he does, he'll be like a rabbit trapped in the headlights of a car. We'll have the bastard, you can count on it!"

As they pulled into the police station car park, Connor allowed himself a small smile. He felt it was now only a matter of time before the killer made that vital slip-up that would lead to his capture. They might not know who he was, but they were rapidly discovering plenty of people that he wasn't!

As they got out of the car and walked towards the steps that led into the building Lucy Clay made one observation that might have had Connor questioning his most recent thoughts on the case.

"Sir, you know that bit where you said that the killer changes his identities the way you change you tie each day?"

"Yes, what of it?"

"Well, it's just that you've worn the same tie for three days now, Sir."

Clay ran up the steps, narrowly avoiding the playful slap that Connor directed at her head as she did so.

# Chapter 38
# In Conference

The conference that was called by Detective Chief Inspector Harry Lewis took place in a rather less than cheerful atmosphere. Charles Carrick and Sergeant Lewis Cole were there, invited as a courtesy along with Connor, Clay, and the D.C.I. himself.

"Since this case began we haven't exactly made startling progress have we?" asked the D.C.I.

"That's true Sir," Connor responded, "though we do seem to be narrowing things down a bit. We think we just might be on the verge of identifying a prime suspect."

"I know Sean, but you've said that before and it looks like you're only getting this far because all of your possible suspects are being killed themselves."

"I don't think that's quite fair Sir," Carrick interjected. "Sean has been working flat out trying to get a handle on the case, as have we in Birmingham. It's just that this character whoever he is a real slippery customer. We'll get him eventually though, I'm sure of it."

"I'm not making any personal accusations here Inspector Carrick. I'm simply pointing out the lack of tangible evidence and the fact that people continue to die while we stumble around in the dark. I mean, look at this e-photo of the so-called suspect as given to our police artist by this Vetchinsky character. It's so bland and relatively vague that this could be you, Sean or even me, God Forbid!"

Lewis passed the e-photo to Carrick who had to agree that it wasn't much to go on. The face could have belonged to almost anyone.

"Well, Sir, you must remember that the witness did say he didn't get a good look at the man. He was gardening at the time and only looked up for a moment when he saw the man get out of his car. Most of his view was from the back and the side. His vision was partially obscured by the trees in the street." Lucy Clay was obviously doing her best to back up her boss.

"Yes, of course Sergeant," said the D.C.I. "Now, what about this reporter who seems to have eluded you? Is he a suspect or a witness or what? Nobody seems to be too clear on his status at the moment and I don't like to be kept in the dark Sean, you should know that."

"You're not being kept in the dark Sir. Roger Cahill was a reporter on the Echo at the time of the original Prentice murder. He reported on the case itself and also conducted follow-up interviews with various family members. He's close enough to the case to be considered a suspect under normal circumstances, but his son has given us a pretty convincing argument to the effect that his father fled town because he was in fear of someone, possibly the real killer, and I tend to believe him."

"Hm," said Lewis thoughtfully. "Any idea where he is yet?"

"Not yet, but I've asked the son to let me know the minute he hears from his father, and begged him to get his father to come out of hiding and come and talk to us."

"I want to know the minute you find out where this man is Sean. He could be vital to our solving the case, do you understand?"

"Of course. I'd do that anyway, as a matter of course."

"Yes, I'm sorry, I know you would Sean. Now, what about the woman who was seen in the Regency Hotel? Are we any further along in determining who she is?"

"No, Sir." It was Lucy Clay who responded. "We not only have no idea as to her identity but the forensics people did find one thing that was of interest to us when they conducted a follow-up examination asked for by the Inspector."

"Oh yes? Didn't know about a follow-up examination."

"It was just an idea," said Connor. "I thought it wise to go over the place a second time with a fresh team, and I never thought they'd find anything, but they did."

"And?"

Lucy Clay came into the conversation once again.

"They found tiny traces of glue, adhering to the sides of the waste basket in the room. It was the type of glue commonly used in wig-making, and we think that it may have come from our Chocolate Woman when she removed her wig at the dressing table. The waste basket stood right beside it. If she wore a wig, then it might explain why she's been so hard to track down. She could have completely changed her appearance to become the Chocolate Woman and then changed back to her ordinary self when she'd left the Regency."

"You make her sound like Superman, Sergeant, switching identities at will"

"Yes, I know, but that seems to be what she did, and also seems to be something our killer is quite good at; assuming the identities of other people.

"Right, well, once again I insist that you keep me posted on developments. Now, how about you Inspector Carrick? Has your investigation been in any way more successful than ours here in Richmond?"

"No Sir, I'm afraid not. I'm convinced that the centre of the investigation has to lie here, and that the death of David Arnold in Birmingham was just pure chance. He could conceivably have died anywhere along the train's route, and you could now be having a conversation with a detective from Bristol, Worcester or any of the towns along the Penzance to Glasgow line for that matter."

"And the FSS lab in Birmingham. Did they give us anything that could help identify the killer?"

"No Sir." This was Connor. "They dealt with the man's application by e-mail, and he provided sufficient verifiable identification to convince them of his bona-fides. He then sent them a signed document to back-up his request for information and they were only too happy to help him it seems."

"I hope they're gong to do something about their checking procedures in future."

"They are sir. They're horrified that they might have unknowingly helped a serial killer by providing him with information."

"A bit late now," said Lewis.

The conference continued a while longer as the officers present exchanged scraps of information and ideas. When they eventually left the D.C.I.'s office that afternoon they were all quite subdued. Even the usually cheerful Charles Carrick and his sergeant declined the offer of tea or coffee, instead choosing to depart for Birmingham straight away. Connor and Clay returned to Connor's office where they sat quietly for a minute or two. It was Connor himself who broke the silence.

"I suppose Lewis is getting a lot of pressure from the Chief Super on this one. That's why he's getting a little tetchy."

Chief Superintendent David Hodges was the head of the local police division, and Lewis's boss. He would certainly be pressing the D.C.I. to come up with a solution to the case, as he himself would be coming under increasing pressure from his own superiors. It wasn't every day that a town like Richmond-on-Thames became the haunt of a serial killer, and it wouldn't be long before even more weight was brought to bear on him to resolve the case, Connor knew that.

"I know, but he didn't have to bite your head off like that," said Clay, sympathetically.

"Never mind Sergeant, it goes with the job."

There was a knock on Connor's door. It opened to reveal the face of D.C. Simon Fox.

"Sir, I've just taken a call from Roger Cahill."

"Has he heard from his father, Fox?"

"It *was* the father. Roger Cahill Senior himself. He said that he'd spoken to his son, and that he would call you personally in an hour to discuss meeting you somewhere to talk. He wouldn't tell me where he was, though I did try to get him to reveal his location. I wanted to put him straight through to you but he said he needed more time to put a rendezvous together that wouldn't compromise his safety."

Connor grinned from ear to ear.

"Thanks, Fox, well done for trying. Don't worry about it. I can wait a little longer. Close the door as you go, there's a good chap."

As the door snapped shut Connor turned to Lucy Clay, and for the fist time in days she saw a glint of expectation in his eyes, as though he were a fox on the scent of a hound.

"Lucy," he said "I do believe we're getting somewhere at last!"

# Chapter 39
# A Brief Interlude

"My sources tell me that the police know about the wig. They found glue in the waste basket in the room at the Regency."

"Yes, well, they can't trace me from a bit of glue can they? It's not as if I left anything containing my DNA in the room did I? "

"You slept in the bed didn't you? You could have left skin cells on the sheets."

"They didn't even know about me until days afterwards. All those sheets would have been through the hotel laundry system by then, and you know it."

"Well, I just hope for your sake that they don't find anything to connect you with that room, or with me."

"They won't. Now calm down will you?"

"Yes, right. I'm just getting a little nervous. They're floundering around as I expected them to but Connor is getting close without even realising it. I'll have to keep my eye very closely on the detective inspector."

"You do that. That's your department after all. I'm just the delivery girl."

"Just be careful that's all."

The man hung up on her, and the woman in turn replaced the phone on the hook. The Chocolate Woman, as the police now knew her thought it odd that the man would be nervous. He'd never once struck her as the nervous type in any of their dealings so far. In fact he was probably the coolest and most controlled person she'd ever met. She'd considered him to have nerves of steel and a heart of ice, he was so cold and detached in his speech and in the way he'd delivered her instructions. She had no doubt that 'nervous' wasn't something he really felt, just a phrase to incite her to be extra careful and vigilant.

She was confident that she'd left no traces at any of the crime scenes or at the hotel room. At lease, nothing that could ever be traced back to her. By following his instructions to the letter she'd ensured that no DNA, no personal items, not even a piece of paper that might contain a partial fingerprint had been left anywhere for the police to find. The man was good; she had to give him that. His knowledge of police procedures and of forensics was phenomenal. He could almost have been a policeman she thought, or perhaps a pathologist, but his knowledge came from all those years he'd told her he'd spent investigating various crimes for the newspaper.

She looked once again at the envelope that lay on the kitchen table. Picking it up she allowed her fingers to peel back the flap and play with the edges of the pile of crisp twenty pound notes that filled it to it's capacity. She enjoyed these paydays, and another ten thousand pounds would go a long way towards buying her way out of the country and enabling her to start the new life she'd planned when the job was over and done with. She'd collected it from the post office box as instructed that very morning, and now the cash would be added to her fees for the earlier jobs. She was becoming quite wealthy, and she liked the idea.

A few miles away, the man allowed himself to rest back against the soft leather backrest of his chair. He knew he'd chosen wisely. Tracy was the perfect woman to have become his angel of death, or Chocolate Woman as Connor and his people called her. How clever of him to have picked a woman with no connection to the case to do his dirty work. Tracy had been out of prison for less than a month when he'd approached her, and he'd been impressed by her attitude and her grim determination once he'd explained his aims. There weren't too many cold-blooded female killers around who'd do almost anything for money, but Tracy would. She'd just finished a ten year stretch for manslaughter, though he knew she'd been guilty of premeditation and had got lucky with her legal team and a soft jury at her trial. They'd only met once, when, heavily disguised, he'd explained his needs to her and given her the down payment of five thousand pounds that had bought her undying loyalty. She was intelligent without being too nosy, and she was just what he wanted. He'd planned everything meticulously, and then a chance meeting gave him the opportunity to further misdirect the forces of law and order and lead them up the proverbial gum tree when it came to the investigation of the killings he was about to enact.

Getting rid of Sam Gabriel had been a master stroke in more ways than one. Gabriel had defended her in court ten years previously at the outset of his career and had done his best for her but he'd been young and inexperienced at the time, and he'd lost and Tracy had gone to jail. She bore him no ill will however, but when he'd seen her coming out of the apartment that the man had rented for her, which he'd have known was obviously way beyond Tracy's limited finances, and Tracy had told the man about it, he'd known exactly what to do. First, he couldn't take the chance of Gabriel at some future date relating the news about Tracy and her new upmarket apartment to the police. She'd be a good suspect for the murders, being just out of prison and with a history of violence behind her and probably wouldn't withstand too much in the way of questioning. Secondly, killing Gabriel before his real plan had actually got under way was a stroke of genius because the police were now looking for a link between Gabriel and the Prentice case, and of course, there was no such thing. Fools! They could chase their tails forever and still come up empty handed. Sam Gabriel had been surprised when he'd 'bumped into' Tracy on the street, but had seemed pleased when she'd explained about her new job. He'd happily accepted the free sample of the new product she'd offered him. It had been the last time Sam Gabriel would see his former client.

From that day forward the man had only communicated with her by phone, and she'd been a loyal and faithful participant in his scheme. He'd just have to be careful now that things were coming to a head. She mustn't be allowed to give anything away. Though he was confident of the fact that she didn't know his real identity or have any information that could lead Connor and his team to him, he would be wary from now on. Tracy might yet turn out to be a liability, and of course, liabilities were one thing that he simply couldn't afford.

The man closed his eyes and allowed himself to daydream a little, to see in his mind's eye the face that reminded him of just why he was doing all of this and who he was doing it for. As the memory of that face pushed itself to the forefront of his brain, a smile played across his face. He still had his memories, and they were alive in his head.

For now, Tracy could wait, liability or not!

# Chapter 40
# Confession is Good for the Soul

The Mount Pleasant Hotel stands in its own grounds, a majestic building that was once the home of a titled lord, at another time a military hospital caring for war-wounded troops and then after a period of post-war decline bought and renovated by a burgeoning hotel chain, gradually being transformed into the four star pleasure palace that had been chosen by Roger Cahill the elder for his meeting with Connor and Clay. At first Cahill had resisted Connor's insistence that he be accompanied by his sergeant, Cahill's fear and distrust of all strangers only giving way when Connor insisted fiercely that he must have his sergeant with him to take down any notes required. He would be too busy talking to Cahill, he'd said, to bother about taking accurate notes, which would be essential to the interview. Cahill, being a former journalist recognised the validity of Connor's words and eventually though reluctantly agreed to Lucy's presence.

Connor and Clay arrived first, the tyres of the Mondeo making a satisfying crunching sound as they covered the expansive gravel of the approach drive to the hotel. That sound in itself served to give a feeling of opulence to anyone's arrival at the Mount Pleasant. *Nice touch*, thought Connor. A uniformed doorman held the main doors open for them as they entered the lobby of the hotel, and they soon found themselves in the 'Westminster Bar' which had been decorated to resemble a typical nineteenth century gentlemen's club, with leather sofas and armchairs, low and highly polished tables, a large open fireplace, and copious amounts of newspapers and up to date magazines covering a multitude of subjects placed neatly on small side tables for the reading pleasure of the guests.

Connor selected a table near the back of the room which would afford them a degree of privacy. There were no overlooking windows and Connor would have a clear view of anyone entering the room. He hoped that Cahill would be pleased with his choice. He ordered a tray of assorted sandwiches and large pots of tea and coffee in an attempt to make Cahill fell a little more relaxed when he eventually arrived. Connor hoped he wouldn't be late and that the tea and coffee wouldn't be cold by the time he arrived.

He needn't have worried. Barely ten minutes after the detectives had arrived, Cahill, accompanied by his son walked tentatively into the 'Westminster Bar'. Cahill the elder looked every one of his seventy eight years. He walked with a pronounced stoop and, as he and his son arrived at the table, having caught Connor's wave of greeting, Connor could see that the old man had bags under his eyes and those eyes showed a redness and had a hollow sunken look that told of Cahill's fear and lack of sleep. Connor had no trouble in recognising the look of a worried man. Cahill, he quickly decided, was no killer. This was without doubt a man in fear for his life.

"Hello Inspector, Sergeant." The younger Roger Cahill spoke to introduce his father. "This is my father, Roger Cahill. Dad, this is Detective Inspector Connor and Sergeant Clay."

Connor held out his hand, and as Cahill senior reached to take it in a handshake the detective could see the old man's hand shaking with trepidation. Whatever this man knew, it was enough to make him afraid of his own shadow by the looks of things. Despite his age and the trembling in his hands Cahill's handshake was firm and resolute. He and his son sat down opposite the detectives and Connor asked Lucy Clay to pour whatever beverages the two men required. Cahill the elder took tea, his son decided on coffee. No-one took the proffered sandwiches.

Connor hoped that no-one would query his expense requisite form. He noticed too the appearance of the old man. Cahill might be getting on in years, and he might be terrified out of his wits, but the man had style. He wore a crisp white shirt, a red and black spotted bow-tie, and a quality dark blue jacket that would have been expensive when new. His trousers were a slightly paler shade of blue from the jacket and showed neat, well-pressed creases down the centre of the legs, though they had a crumpled look that came from a relatively long journey in a seated position. Connor thought that he and his son must have driven for at least an hour to get that crumpled look. In many ways Cahill looked the typical news hack, ready to leap up from his desk and hit the streets in search of a scoop, though Cahill wouldn't be doing any more leaping at his age, Connor was sure of that.

"Mr Cahill, thank you for coming to talk to me. I appreciate how hard this must be for you," Connor began.

"Do you Inspector? Do you really think so? I doubt that you have any real idea of just how hard it really was for me to come here today. Do you realise that just by being here I could be exposing myself to the person you're looking for?"

"Listen Mr Cahill. I asked you to allow me to have a larger police presence here but you insisted on just me and the sergeant. You didn't even want her here at first, remember? We could have made sure of your safety if you'd let me have a few officers stationed around the lobby and the bar."

"What, and publicise my presence to all and sundry? He's probably watching everything you do you know, I hope you realise that Inspector. He probably also knows just about everything about this case as you do."

"And just how would he be able to do that Mr Cahill?"

"Because he's very clever and very resourceful, and always was. He'll no doubt have a source or two within the police force. He always used to. There are always one or two officers or civilian employees in every force who are willing to leak information in return for a small consideration Inspector. I hope you're not so naïve as to think there aren't?"

Unfortunately Cahill was correct as Connor well knew. It wasn't the same as being bent or downright dishonest, but he hated those within the police force who would sell their souls, *and vital information*, to the press. It was against all the regulations of course, but it happened, always had done, and probably always would.

"OK. Let's assume for a minute that you're right. What your man doesn't know, and can't possibly do so is the location of this meeting because only Sergeant Clay and I are privy to this location and even the sergeant didn't know about it until we were in the car. I kept it from her at your request, so I'd say we're pretty safe here wouldn't you?"

"He could have followed you."

"Yes, he could have, but hen I'm sure you'd have recognised him by now if he were here, wouldn't you?"

"He might be waiting to follow me when I leave and he could follow me back to here I'm staying and do me some harm there."

"Right. That brings me to my exact point Mr. Cahill. You'll be far safer if you tell me what you know and then allow me to arrange police protection for you, if I think it's necessary."

The younger of the Cahills broke into the conversation.

"Inspector Connor. Dad really does want to help you, but can't you see he's frightened? Even I didn't realise just how scared he is until I met him today. Like I said, he hasn't even told me where he's hiding out."

"I can see he's afraid Mr Cahill, but believe me, he needs to tell me what he knows."

"He's right Roger," said the old man. "If I don't tell him and then something happens to me, the killer could get away with everything and Mr Connor here might never find out who he is. He's bloody clever, like I've told you already."

Lucy Clay, realising that Cahill was about to divulge his secrets readied her notebook, pen poised.

"Please Mr Cahill," said Connor. "In your own time."

Cahill took a drink from his tea cup, then set the cup down in its saucer, looked around the room as though checking once more that they weren't being watched, and then he began his story.

"It all seems such a long time ago. When the Prentice case first began, I was the lead crime reporter for the Echo. We were only a small local paper of course but we tried to put out a professional and informative paper that could hold its own against the big dailies. I reported on the murder of course, and the local police were very helpful, as they always were to the Echo. Nothing confidential was disclosed of course, but enough to give me the bones of a good story and enabled me to keep the readers as well-informed as any of the dailies could. After Stride was cleared, and then Miller's conviction the whole case seemed to go away for a while, but then his murder in prison resurrected it for a while, and then of course the posthumous appeal came along. He was acquitted as you know and the case became front page news again for a time. My boss at the paper was very much into 'human interest' stories, especially those to do with the victims of crime so he sent me along to try and get interviews with those closest to the Stride and Miller Families, and the widow of the murder victim, Prentice. Terence Stride had killed himself of course, which added a certain pathos to the whole thing, but his wife hadn't yet committed suicide when I did my first set of interviews. It was clear to me from the beginning that the widow of the murdered man was by far the most unstable and suggestible woman I'd ever met. I'd ask her for example if she'd thought that either of the two men had been guilty of her husband's murder, and she jumped at the thought and immediately twisted it until she'd become convinced in her own mind that both Stride and Miller had been in it together and that the two of them had killed her husband for some reason. Of course, she couldn't explain what that reason could have been, and I saw that she was a seriously tragic and disturbed lady. I didn't give her wild stories and theories much page space to be honest, rather concentrating on the effects of the case on the families of the two dead men, who I thought were more deserving of a little sympathy by that time. After all, they'd both been innocent men and their families would have to live without them for the rest of their lives. They were just as much the victims of trauma as Elizabeth Prentice, who didn't go out of her way to elicit much in the way of sympathy, believe me.

Anyway, soon after I'd done my series of interviews one of the big dailies ran a weekly series of articles written by one of their whiz-kid investigative journalists. He'd fallen hook, line and sinker for Elizabeth Prentice's tales of conspiracies and cover-ups, and his editor allowed him to run with the totally implausible theories she'd fed him with. His own journalistic instincts and skills should have told him how stupid the whole thing was and his contacts should have been able to put him straight, but there was one thing that clouded his whole handling of the story Inspector."

"Which was?"

"He fell in love with Elizabeth Prentice! They were around the same age, and he became totally besotted with the woman. It became so bad that his stories became ever more lurid and sensational until his own newspaper refused to print them and he left his job under something of a cloud. It transpired that his love affair with the grieving widow was doomed from the moment he lost his job with the paper, because, once he was no longer in a position to give her rantings a national audience through his column, she dumped him. He was angry and crestfallen all at the same time and never held such a well-paid or prestigious position with any of the big dailies again. His career went right off the rails. Elizabeth Prentice ended up having a relationship with a police constable of all people would you believe? That only served to make our friend even more bitter and twisted. When he telephoned me a few weeks ago with the preposterous idea that he was going to write a book on the case and wanted to use my records and files of my interviews with the families, I just thought that he was off his rocker. I mean, who'd want to read all of that again after all these years? He did say though, that he was going to throw new light on the case and maybe even reveal the name of the real killer. I told him that my files were personal and private and not for public consumption and that he'd have to get his information elsewhere. Then he came up with the ridiculous story about someone being out to get us because of our connection with the case. I told him to bugger off. Well, as you know from my son, two days later I was mugged, all my credit cards and personal identity documents stolen and then there was the break-in at the house. When the killings began, I just knew he was behind it."

"Why didn't you call the police there and then Mr Cahill?" asked Lucy Clay.

"Because he threatened my son, Sergeant. When I refused to give him what he wanted, he said that he'd get what he wanted from somewhere else, and that he wanted me to keep our 'little conversation' private and confidential. He said that if I revealed that he was interested in the case to anyone he'd make sure something horrible would happen to young Roger here."

"You never mentioned this to me before Dad."

"I just thought he was being belligerent and melodramatic as he always used to be. It was only when I heard about the first murders that I realised he was probably seriously deranged and really meant what he'd said. I think, Inspector that his paranoia has built up over the years until he became convinced that he was still in love with Elizabeth Prentice, and she in love with him, and that he alone is responsible for bringing her husband's killers to justice."

"I see. Please tell me Mr Cahill what the name of this avenging nemesis is."

"Of course, I'm sorry. I should have told you that at the beginning shouldn't I? His name Inspector is Alexander, though he was always known in the trade as Sandy McLean, former chief investigative journalist of the 'Sketch on Sunday'. He's your killer, of that I've no doubt."

Lucy Clay immediately rose from the table.

"I'll get the name off to the station right away sir. We'll put a call out for this McLean."

"Wait Lucy. Do you have an address or location of any sort for this man Mr Cahill?"

"I'm sorry Inspector. In the days I knew him he lived in London somewhere, don't ask me the address. He could be anywhere now of course."

"And you're sure it was him on the phone?"

"Well, it was a lot of years ago Inspector, and people's voices do change with age, as I'm sure my own has, so I couldn't, hand on heart say with a hundred percent certainty that it was him, but he knew every detail of the case. He repeated certain things to me from articles we'd both written and he related things that only someone with his intimate knowledge of the case, and of Elizabeth Prentice would know. Also, why would anyone pretend to be him in order to get to my files and records and scare the life out of me like that?"

"Why indeed, Mr Cahill?" asked Connor thoughtfully. "Why indeed?"

Connor was about bring the interview to an end. He felt that Cahill had given him all he could for the time being. Further interviews might be highly productive, but for the moment Connor had a name and a likely suspect, though there were still many questions that needed to be answered. He needed to ask a couple of them before he left the Mount Pleasant.

"Do you know of any woman who might be helping McLean, assuming that he is the killer?" He passed a copy of the e-photo of the woman seen at the Regency Hotel to Cahill. "She looks like this, though the hair is probably a wig."

"I'm sorry Inspector. I don't know of anyone who resembles this lady."

"OK. Also, do the names David Arnold, Virginia Remick, Sam Gabriel, Andrew Forbes or Arminder Patel suggest any connection to the case to you? I already know about the connection with the Strides and Judge Tolliver, but these other victims appear random and unconnected as far as I can see."

"Virginia Remick, Inspector, was the grand-daughter of George Turner. He was the editor of the Sketch on Sunday at the time McLean was asked to leave. Turner thought that McLean had gone too far in his reporting of Elizabeth Prentice's claims and that he was making the newspaper look foolish. I seem to remember someone by the name of Arnold being involved as a witness of some sort, though only in a minor way. As you already know, I'm sure; Andrew Forbes was Prentice's partner. Were you just testing me with that one? I've no idea about Sam Gabriel or Arminder Patel. The names mean nothing to me."

Connor looked across at Lucy Clay. She had seen the significance of Cahill's words. They didn't have it all, but they had a connection. Connor was satisfied that at last he had a viable source of information, and a real and likely prime suspect.

"Shall I make that call now Sir?" asked the sergeant.

"What? Oh yes, please, make the call Lucy, then we'll arrange somewhere safe for Mr Cahill to stay in case we need to speak to him again. I don't want you disappearing again Mr Cahill. Is that understood? We'll protect you until we get McLean in custody, I promise you."

Roger Cahill nodded, took another sip from the tea cup, and relaxed for the first time in days. He believed Connor's promise of protection was a good one, and he felt as though by revealing what he knew, a great burden had been lifted from his shoulders. He was getting too old for all this, and now he'd got it off his chest he thought that the old adage was indeed true and that confession truly was good for the soul!

# Chapter 41
# Curry and Questions

Two days of relative inactivity followed Connor's meeting with Roger Cahill. After he and Clay had set the wheels in motion that he hoped would eventually lead to the apprehension of Sandy McLean the weekend had interceded in the investigation and things had slowed down almost to a crawl. Connor had also taken it upon himself to organise a 'safe house' for Cahill and his son. He didn't want to take a chance on anything happening to his only real source of information concerning McLean, so he'd detailed Detective Constable Simon Fox to 'baby sit' the two Cahills. D.C.I. Lewis had been furious when Connor had refused to reveal the location of his star witness, but Connor had decided that only he, Clay and Fox were to share the knowledge of the men's whereabouts. He'd explained to his boss that he considered the safe house's location a 'need to know' subject, and until Connor had learned all that there was to know from the elderly journalist then no-one, including his boss, would have access to the location for security reasons. Lewis wasn't happy, but accepted that Sean was acting in the best interests of both the Cahills and the investigation.

As for McLean, the man appeared to have simply vanished off the face of the earth. His last known address had been an apartment in Pimlico in London, but a visit to the address by the Metropolitan Police, made at Connor's request, had found the place deserted. The neighbours had informed the officers who attended the apartment that McLean hadn't been seen for over a month, which Connor thought significant if he was indeed the killer. He imagined the man being holed up somewhere, preparing his aconite parcels and communicating with his as yet unidentified accomplice by telephone or email. In that assumption at least, Connor was on the right track.

A knock on his door announced the arrival of Catherine Nickels. The pathologist stood on his doorstep armed with two bags containing an Indian take-away. Connor stood staring at her for a moment, her face a pleasant and welcome diversion after the rigours of the last few days.

"Now then Sean Connor, are you going to invite me in or stand staring at me until this food goes stone cold?" she said with mock seriousness.

"Sorry Catherine, yes, of course. Come in. I was just thinking how good you look."

"Flattery will get you everywhere Detective Inspector. Now, shall we eat?"

Catherine hadn't skimped on the unexpected treat. Together they devoured two sumptuous Madras curries, boiled rice, a selection of onion bahjees and vegetable samosas, a plateful of fresh crisp poppadums, and two bottles of chilled cobra beer each. Both studiously avoided making reference to the case in hand until the meal was finished. Catherine related to Connor the case she was working on, a young woman who'd died unexpectedly at the age of twenty one from a rare and relatively unheard of heart condition. Undetectable, she'd said. The poor woman had been a walking time-bomb, her heart waiting to explode at any given moment without anyone having an inkling that she carried the awful condition around with her. After dinner the two of them retired to the sofa in Connor's lounge where Catherine soon brought the conversation around to the aconite killer.

"The word on the grapevine is that you're making progress Sean."

"Well, a bit, though we still don't have a clue as to where our prime suspect might be hiding away. Like the rest of this case Catherine, it's all a bit of an enigma. Nothing seems to fit together the way it should although certain pieces are beginning to fall into place."

"Sean, you should be pleased. You're making progress and there haven't been any more killings have there?"

"No, not yet. It doesn't mean there won't be though, unless we get our hands on our man soon. Plus, Lewis is mad at me for not telling him where I've stashed the Cahills away. He thinks I don't trust him."

"Well, he is your boss Sean. Shouldn't you at least keep him informed about what you've done with them?"

"Look Catherine, Cahill told me that McLean boasted of having contacts in the police force all those years ago, he could still have one or more, I just don't know. It's not that I don't trust the boss, but he talks to people who talk to other people. He only has to let something slip and the wrong person could get wind of where they are, and my case could be blown away. As it stands, only three people know where the Cahills are, so if anything leaks then I know where to look for the source. Fox won't let anything out, he's incarcerated with the two of them and won't be leaving them for a minute and that only leaves me and Lucy Clay. I won't blab, so if anyone does find out where they are it'll be down to a loose tongue on Lucy's part, which I don't think will happen."

"You've got a point I suppose."

"Yes, and that's not all. I got a call from Charles Carrick in Birmingham today. He's been taken off the David Arnold Case. It seems that his boss and D.C.I. Lewis have been conferring and because the Arnold case is so obviously linked to our series of murders, it's been deemed wise to put them all together under one inquiry. Charles is sending me all of his files and the report on his interviews with Maggie Prentice. They don't amount to much apparently. She's gone all tight-lipped now that she thinks she's given us as much as we asked for in the beginning. She won't reveal another thing. Personally I think she'll plead insanity as her defence and will probably get away with it."

"My, my, you do sound down and depressed over it all Sean. I thought you'd be pleased to be making as much progress as you are."

"I am pleased Catherine. It's just that things don't quite add up in my mind. I normally have a feel for a case, but this one just confounds every ounce of logic I try to apply to it. Whoever is behind it all is an obvious master of deception. He assumes identities to throw us off the scent, not fake identities mind you but real people, and they all seem to be connected to the case. I know where and how some of the victims are connected now thanks to Cahill, but the others are still a mystery. There's something else that's bugging me as well."

"Go on Sean, what is it?"

"That's just it Catherine. For the bloody life of me I can't think what it is. Somewhere, recently, someone said something that didn't mean a lot when I first heard it, but then later I realised that I'd missed something vital. It's there at the back of my mind but I just can't place what it was, or who said it. As soon as I do, I know I'll be on the right track, I'm sure of it. I just need to review every piece of paper and every witness statement again when I get back to the office tomorrow. If it's there, and I'm sure it is, then I'll find it. I just wish to God I could remember it now. It's been driving me mad."

"Well, I'm sure it'll come to you. You've been under so much pressure to solve the case I'm not surprised that certain things are a bit confused in your mind. It's only natural to fail to remember something that might have appeared insignificant at the time but which now has some significance for you. It's a matter of the brain having to sort out the minutiae of the case and then pressing the correct recall button so to speak."

"I hope you're right Catherine, I really do."

Catherine rose from the sofa. It was getting late.

"Right then Mr Connor," she grinned. "I think that's quite enough of business for tonight don't you? Whatever you need to remember will be waiting for you when you get to the office in the morning, but for now I want to know whether I have to drive home alone at this late hour or whether a very nice gentleman might desire a little company to see him through the night?"

Sean stared hard at the beautiful pathologist. His reply, when it came, was exactly the one she wanted to hear.

"Upstairs! Right now if you please Doctor Nickels!"

# Chapter 42
# Pay Off

Tracy was becoming nervous. She hadn't heard from the man for nearly three days. After receiving her last payment she'd left the house only for a brief time to visit the local supermarket where she'd bought sufficient provisions to last her until the middle of the following week. He'd always been explicit in telling her to expose herself to as little public scrutiny as possible. He'd been good about getting rid of Sam Gabriel for her. That was essential to ensure that no-one knew she was in town of course, but he'd been absolutely furious when she'd asked to use part of his precious supply of aconite to dispose of Patel. She'd actually thought that he might kill her himself for having added another victim to the list. She'd explained however that Patel had assaulted her years earlier when they were both teenagers, and had laughed about it afterwards, bragging to his friends about what he'd done. She had never forgotten his hands as they'd groped her, pulling at her clothes, removing them before forcing himself on her in such an appalling way. Afterwards, he'd walked away, leaving her bleeding and battered on the ground.

"No-one will believe you," he'd mocked. "You're nothing but a little slut, and everyone knows that. You'd drop your knickers and spread your legs for any of the boys in town on a Saturday night, so why should they think you didn't do the same for me?"

She'd known he was right. She had a reputation for being 'easy', and Arminder Patel was from a good home, with a well respected father who ran the local newsagents shop. Arminder had never been in any trouble with the law, whereas most of the local police force knew the young Tracy Willis by name. She'd fallen in with the 'wrong crowd' at an early age and she was popular with the boys. It wasn't long before Tracy had realised that if she gave the boys what she wanted, her own standing in the 'gang' rose until she'd reached a point where she'd learned to trade her body for the things she wanted while being able to detach herself from the physical sensations of the act of intercourse, and anyway, they were her friends. With Arminder Patel it had been different. He'd forced her to do what he wanted totally against her will, and Tracy had vowed revenge. Why she hadn't told the other boys she really never knew. They would have broken Patel's legs at the very least, but no, something within her kept the secret of her violation until she could find a way to pay him back, and that opportunity came once she'd learned how to use the aconite, how much to give and how to insert it into the chocolates. Funnily enough, the man eventually said that the killing of Patel might actually suit his plans. Like Sam Gabriel, another seemingly random killing might help to further confuse the 'plods' as he called the policemen who would surely be trying to track him down. As for Patel, the stupid fool hadn't even recognised her after all those years! She'd even wished him a good day as she'd left. Perfect! Tracy had revelled in her moment of glory.

Now though, the man had left her in limbo, without instructions and with no contact. She'd expected him to call with further instructions, but so far there'd been nothing. What if he'd deserted her, left her to her own devices and skipped the country or something like that? Another even more frightening thought found its way slowly into Tracy's mind. What if the man were to do a runner, and then plant enough evidence to implicate her in all of the murders, so that she'd take the blame for everything? Clever bastard! She'd done it all of course, except Tolliver. He'd done the old judge himself, but they'd never believe that would they, and why should they? If he'd set her up for the murders there wasn't a lot she could do to convince the cops that she hadn't done them all, and would it even matter to them? Then there were the others.

She'd no idea who they were, but the man had told her he'd killed before, that it was easy, and that no-one would ever know about his 'beginnings' as he described them. What if he'd made sure that Tracy was the one who was eventually blamed for those as well?

She became suddenly afraid that that was exactly what he'd done. Why else would he leave her without contact for three days? He was supposed to tell her what to do and he'd abandoned her, just like every other low-life man she'd ever known. Tracy Willis was getting angry. Maybe, she thought, she ought to go to the police herself, and tell them that he'd made her do it, blackmailed her or something. They'd maybe go for that.

She almost jumped out of her skin when the phone began to ring. It was him!

The smooth voice at the end of the telephone line instantly allayed Tracy's fears. Five minutes later she was on her way out of the apartment, heading for the nearest station. An hour later she arrived at the place he'd designated in the phone call. This was the place where she would find the final payment for her services, the big one, the one that would give her the chance to get out of the country once and for all and start her new life somewhere warm and sunny, Spain perhaps.

As she waited on the deserted embankment by the river watching a family of ducks gently meandering along by the bank she caught sight of a small boat approaching from downriver. As it drew closer she saw the name on the prow of the tiny vessel. 'The Cormorant' came closer to shore and Tracy saw a man in the wheelhouse, waving to her. Thinking him to be a simple boatman who would often wave to pretty girls on the riverbank she waved back. She saw the man step from the wheelhouse, thinking he wanted a better look at her legs, *she'd always been proud of her legs*, and as he did so, he waved again. Tracy waved back and then the man appeared to be holding something in his hands, something long and black, and then he was pointing it at her and there was a muffled noise that seemed to emanate from the black thing, and then everything went blank in Tracy's mind. Her face literally exploded from the force of the bullet's impact, and Tracy Willis was dead before her brain had the chance to register the fact that she'd been shot. Her body pitched over the low parapet and fell into the dark waters below. The tide would soon carry it down towards the sea, where the man hoped it would disappear for ever. If not, it might be washed up on the riverbank in a few days and be just another unidentified murder victim with nothing to tie her to him of course.

The man placed the high powered rifle on the deck of the boat and lashed the wheel to hold the boat on its course. He'd stolen it from small boatyard a short time ago, and it had served its purpose. He quickly unscrewed the silencer from the weapon, placed everything back in the carry case he'd kept in the small wheelhouse and as the boat neared the river bank he simply stepped over the side and into the shallow waters of the Thames, his large fisherman's waders ensuring that his trousers remained clean and dry.

Once on dry land he removed the waders and packed them into the back pack he was wearing just for this very occasion, and then, satisfied with his day's work he watched as the little boat collided with the bank of the river a few yards downstream. The incendiary device he'd left on board would see it burn to a cinder when it ignited in a few minutes. Without waiting for the inevitable appearance of the flames that would soon engulf the little craft he simply turned on his heels and walked calmly in the opposite direction until he'd made his way to the main road. A quick hail and he had a taxi at his disposal. Half an hour later he was back in his own office, job done. He was soon on his way again, this time to Tracy's apartment where he used the spare key he'd kept since renting the place and there he callously smothered her crippled old father as he lay helpless in bed. Tracy had moved the old man into the apartment against his wishes, but now he was of no consequence and no-one would discover his body for a long time, as the man had paid a six month advance on the rent, and until the smell from the old man's decomposing corpse filtered out into the street the place would be left undisturbed. Tracy would be a concern no longer, and without any aconite involvement in her death to connect her to the others there was no way the police would think she was anything to do with the previous murders, especially as he'd carefully aimed at her face, destroying any chance of them matching her to the e-photo that had been circulating on all the TV news programmes.

The man was pleased with his achievement in disposing of his accomplice. He'd waited long enough, got her worried by not making contact, and then enticed her out into the open with the promise of a big pay check. *Stupid little whore!* She just couldn't have understood that she was a liability and as he'd said to himself so many times, he couldn't afford liabilities!

# Chapter 43
# Office Work

Connor put the phone down, ending his latest conversation with Charles Carrick. The West Midlands detective had been more than a little unhappy to say the least when he'd been removed from the David Arnold inquiry. He knew of course that the decision had been made further up the ladder of police hierarchy and that there was nothing that either he or Sean Connor could do about it, but at least the two could commiserate with each other. Connor had agreed to keep Carrick informed of his progress and had in fact just finished giving him a complete update on the case when Lucy Clay knocked and entered his office.

"Must go Charles, I'll be in touch soon," he said as he replaced the phone on its cradle.

"Inspector Carrick I presume Sir?" asked Clay.

"The very same Lucy. I've been bringing him up to speed on the case now that he's not directly involved any longer."

"I think its bad form, the way he's just been kicked off the David Arnold end of the case."

"In some ways I agree with you Lucy but the top brass made the decision and in truth it's probably the sane and logical one. Why tie up two D.I.s from two separate forces to investigate what is after all, one murder inquiry, separated by different locations?"

"I understand Sir, but it's hard for him to just walk away isn't it?"

"Never mind Lucy, I've agreed to keep him posted on developments, strictly off the record of course and he'll keep his ear to the ground just in case anything leaps up at him from his end of things. You never know. Now, was there something you wanted or were you just testing to see if my door hinges still work?"

"What? Oh yes. Harry Drew and I have been working on trying to find McLean. We've got the whole resources of the Met, Thames Valley and all the Home Counties Forces trying to locate him and I've put an alert out to all the provincial forces just in case he's holed up miles away from London. We'll find him soon, I'm sure we will. Do you really think he's our man?

"He's the best we've got at the moment Lucy. I'm seeing Cahill again in an hour or two. We'll see if he can tell us anything else that might confirm McLean as our man and hopefully something that might lead us to where he's hiding out."

"Need some company when you talk to him Sir?"

"But of course Sergeant. Be back here in an hour and we'll go in my car."

Lucy Clay left the office, leaving Connor alone with his thoughts. He was still trying to remember what it was that he'd heard that had piqued his investigative instinct only to disappear just as quickly, like a wraith in the night. Spread out on his desk were every statement and every police and medical report pertaining to the current investigation. He'd left Catherine in bed and arrived early at the office that day and had been hard at work trying to find the elusive words that would bring it all back to him, whatever 'it' was.

It was at five minutes to eleven, just before Sergeant Clay walked back through his door that he finally found what he was looking for.

"Bloody hell!" he exclaimed at the precise moment that Clay knocked on the door and entered as was usual without being summoned.

Clay could see that her boss was holding a piece of paper in his hand and it was evident to the sergeant that Connor had found something of great significance on that sheet of paper.

"Sir?"

"I've got it Lucy. I've been picking my own brains, and trying to remember what it was that I'd missed that was important, and I've found it!"

"What is it Sir?"

"Listen Lucy. I may be on the completely wrong track here, so please bear with me. I want you to go out there and ask young Drew to come in here. What is then discussed is strictly between the three of us, d'you understand? No-one outside the four walls of this office is to know what we've talked about unless I authorise it. Got it?"

Clay knew when her boss was on to something big, and she didn't hesitate for one second in walking out of the office and returning in less then thirty seconds with Detective Constable Harry Drew. As soon as the two of them were in Connor's office she closed the door behind them. At that moment in the investigation there were only three people in the whole world, the world was Connor's office, and Sean Connor was about to take a chance on the young D.C. in whom he was about to place a large slice of his trust.

"You wanted to see me Sir?" asked Drew.

"Yes Harry," Connor replied, using the young officer's first name for perhaps the first time in his life. Sergeant Clay and I have to go out for a while. While we're out, I have a very important job for you. Do you think you're up to it?"

"You can rely on me Mr Connor," Drew replied.

"That's exactly what I'm about to do young man, and big time," said Connor.

When he and Clay left ten minutes later Harry Drew remained behind in the office. When they'd gone, he locked the door, booted up Connor's computer and began the task entrusted to him by his boss.

# Chapter 44
# A Minor Detail

"So there's nothing else you can tell us that you think might help Mr Cahill?"

"I'm sure I've told you everything I can remember Inspector."

Connor and Clay had spent another hour in the company of the two Roger Cahills at the safe house arranged by Connor. There was a knock at the door followed by the appearance of Henry DeVere carrying a tray laden with tea cups, a steaming pot of Earl Grey and a supply of assorted biscuits. It had been Connor's inspired idea to ask the personal assistant of the late Judge Tolliver to allow the Cahills to stay in the judge's house with D.C. Fox until the killer was apprehended. Connor thought it almost impossible that the killer would return to the scene of Tolliver's murder, and the ex-guardsman DeVere was only too happy to do anything that might help catch the killer of his late employer and friend.

"I thought refreshments might be in order Inspector," said DeVere as he placed the tray down on the coffee table in front of the sofa.

"An excellent idea Mr DeVere, thank you."

DeVere departed as quietly as he'd arrived, leaving them in peace to continue their conversation.

"You're absolutely certain there's no more?" asked Connor, returning to the previous thread of their dialogue.

"Absolutely Inspector. I've had plenty of time to think while I've been squirreled away here, and I assure you that if there had been any further information I could give to you then I would have done."

"I know, and I'm grateful for everything you've told me. I just want to make sure that we haven't missed anything, that's all."

"I understand Inspector. It's just a pity that your people haven't been able to run McLean to ground yet."

"We'll find him eventually; have no doubt on that score."

"I hope you do Inspector for all our sakes."

"Are you sure you've got everything down Sergeant?" Connor directed his question at Lucy Clay who was sitting opposite him, beside the younger Cahill.

"Word for word," she replied.

Connor took a moment to sip from the tea that DeVere had brought. A thought entered his head. It might be that Cahill knew something, but didn't know that he held the knowledge, or considered it irrelevant.

"Mr Cahill, you were once an investigative journalist. Let me ask to hypothesise on something."

Cahill's interest was instantly aroused and he leaned forward to better hear Cahill's words.

"Why, if the killer is murdering everyone who he feels slighted or offended Elizabeth Prentice in her view of her husband's death, is Mary Stride still alive? Surely, once the killer had murdered her brother and sister logic would dictate that she would be next, or at least somewhere further down his hit list. So far Mary has remained splendidly isolated from the whole affair since Mikey and Angela died."

"A good question Inspector. Does she have police protection?"

"Sort of. We have extra patrols going past her house hourly during the day and a passive watch is being kept by the beat constable through the night, in addition to the motorised patrols."

"So, you have something of a puzzle Inspector. Perhaps she was never on the list, which I admit would be odd, as her siblings were both obviously on it. Then again, perhaps she is in league with the killer, which I would think absurd. More likely, and I must stress that this is just the opinion of an old man, is that either Mary Stride is for some reason exempt from the killer's attention or, and this is the more likely of the two scenarios, the killer is saving her until last, his piecé de résistance so to speak. I can't think of any other scenario that fits, can you?"

"A very good summarisation Mr Cahill and no, I can't think of anything that fits better than any of the things you've mentioned. Thank you."

Cahill seemed to pause for thought and came back with an addition to his previous words.

"Of course, there is some weight to the theory that she is exempt from the killer's attentions Inspector."

"There is?"

"Yes, I've only just remembered. Many years ago McLean's editor ran a series of pieces based on some of McLean's previously unpublished 'human interest' articles on the Prentice case. I seem to remember one in which Mary Stride berated her own parents; her father for having killed himself, and her mother for not believing in him and for then taking her own life in what the teenage Mary described as 'a coward's way out' when she realised what she'd done and thus leaving the eldest daughter, Mary with the task of looking after her two younger siblings. Of course, if it had happened today the children would all have been taken into care and looked after by the State but thirty years ago things were different. Mary Stride had a hard life Inspector, and she must have found it difficult to cope with a disabled and blind brother after her mother's death. My point is that the killer may have decided that Mary's condemnation of her parents was enough to absolve her from his need to take his revenge directly out on her. I know it's a wild theory, but it could just be true."

"I didn't know she'd publicly condemned her parent's suicides Mr Cahill. Thank you for that, and yes, you could be right in your theory. I think though that we might have to increase the watch on Doctor Stride, Lucy. If the killer is saving her until last we need to be vigilant. After all we don't actually know how many names he has on his list."

"Consider it done Sir," Clay replied.

"Couldn't you put her in a safe house like us Inspector Connor?" asked the younger Roger Cahill, who had been relatively silent throughout his father's discussion with the detective.

"In an ideal world, yes Mr Cahill," Connor replied. "But my boss is already hopping mad because I won't tell him where you two are being kept, and he'd go over the edge if I asked him to fund another witness protection scheme when we don't know for sure that Mary Stride is in fact an intended victim of the killer. We can't speculate on his intentions to that extent I'm afraid."

There was little more to discuss that morning, and Connor thanked the Cahills for their time and DeVere for his help as he and Clay prepared to take their leave of the house. As Lucy Clay walked through the front door and headed down the path towards the car, Connor stopped and turned to the elder Cahill.

"Mr Cahill, before I go there's one more thing I want to ask you."

Cahill instinctively realised that Connor was about to ask him something important and he summarily dismissed his son and cocked his head to one side so that he wouldn't miss a word.

"The last time we spoke you said something that didn't really sink in the first time you mentioned it," said Connor in a hushed tone.

For the next two minutes the two men conducted a whispered discussion on the doorstep and Connor eventually shook the old man's hand before walking to join Lucy Clay in the car.

"Was there something you forgot to ask him earlier Sir? You seemed to be getting very intense back there."

"Oh, it was nothing really Lucy; a minor detail, just a minor detail."

# Chapter 45
# A Window to the Past

Tracy was gone. That was his one remaining major irritation out of the way. He doubted that the girl would ever have been in a position to bring the police down on his neck, but this way he'd made sure of her eternal silence.

There was only one thing left to do and his plan would be complete. He only needed to be careful for a little while longer and his long wait for vengeance would be absolute. Elizabeth would have been proud of him, he was sure of that. Obtaining the aconite had been the hardest part. No reputable company in the country would supply him with the poison in the quantity he required, even with the fake I.D. and diplomas in medicine and homeopathy he'd purchased via a slightly unscrupulous internet website. Luckily, his work had, over the years brought him into contact with similarly employed people who had access to the information he required to obtain his supplies from elsewhere. Thus it was that the Ho Sin Import and Export Company of Hong Kong, themselves a less than reputable organisation with links to the illegal drugs industry on the island and mainland China had been only too happy to meet his needs, for the right price of course.

His first killing, the one they didn't even know about had been the easy one, the one that proved to him that he could get away with murder. Two shots and a quick kill, and everything was in place for what would follow.

Tracy had been his next acquisition and a good one at that. The gullible and easily-led girl had just the background he'd been looking for. He'd waited patiently for her release from prison and had then found it quite easy to convince her to work for him. The promise of riches beyond her limited dreams had been the convincing factor, and the murders of Sam Gabriel and Arminder Patel, had, in the end played into his hands as they would help to further deflect the police from the real nature of his plan. Watching them running around like fools, trying to make a connection between 'Tracy's victims' and his own had been a source of great amusement for him, but now the time was drawing near when he would have to bring his master plan to a close.

He'd perfected the means of adding the aconite to the chocolates long ago, after studying chemistry, the use of poisons and pharmaceutical procedures in his spare time. It had to be aconite of course. The Stride woman had used it to good effect all those years earlier, and it had been a dreadful way to die, he'd remembered. What a fitting way then for his own victims to die, to suffer the horrors and pain of a poison they wouldn't even know they'd ingested. As for the police, he'd learned of their theory about dissolving capsules being made to insert into the chocolates and so on. They were close, but not exact in their thinking. He'd simply injected the poison, coated in tiny bubbles of the same materials used to make pharmaceutical hard-shell capsules into the chocolates using the thinnest and least detectable syringe on the market and had then had the chocolates re-coated by the Prentice woman. She'd been an excellent foil for his task as well, and her creative skills had helped considerably in creating the perfect murder weapons, the poisoned chocolates! She'd dealt with David Arnold so well the man thought she'd have made an excellent career killer, but the police had her now. She was of no consequence, and no threat to him, having never seen him in person. He'd dealt with Tolliver himself of course, but Tracy had been his 'angel of death' when it had come to despatching Virginia Remick and the Strides. When she'd told him how she'd visited the Stride house and fooled Angela into thinking she was a new district nurse, he'd been impressed, especially when Tracy described to him how she'd offered to 'help' making tea and ensuring that she was able to drop a lethal dose of aconite into the brother and sister's cups. She'd even taken the time to watch them die after they'd taken her upstairs to show the 'nurse' Mikey's room and his facilities for self-care, then coolly gone back down the stairs to clear away the tea cups and any evidence of her being there.

She'd been a cool customer had Tracy, and she'd wanted to 'do' Tolliver as well, but the man had insisted on doing that one himself. The old judge knew him of course, and welcomed him into his house without realising that he was about to die. The man had waited until DeVere had gone to the shops before presenting himself at the house and had then easily convinced the old judge to share a drink with him, and had offered Tolliver a drink of his own 'special reserve' scotch whisky that he carried in a hip flask in case he needed a shot of the stuff. As he poured it into two whisky tumblers it had been easy to slip four of his specially prepared aconite capsules into the judge's drink. They dissolved quickly, though the aconite would take some time to enter the judge's bloodstream and begin its deadly work. It had been the last drink the judge ever took. The man was long gone by the time the poison took effect soon after DeVere had returned.

His reminiscences over for the time being, he returned to the present. Not only had he almost completed what he'd set out to do, but sooner or later the police would manage to work it all out, or at least enough to bring them closer to him than he would find comfortable. He couldn't allow that to happen of course. He'd come too far to be caught, had waited and planned too long to exact revenge on those whose stupidity and lies, deceit and duplicity had led to the eventual mental break down and the death of his beloved Elizabeth.

He allowed his mind to stray again for a few minutes, remembering the times he'd spent in the arms of the only woman he'd ever truly loved. His mind left the present and became a window to the past as the recollections of another time flooded his thoughts. He'd entered her life when she being ridiculed by the press, her neighbours and work colleagues, all of whom thought she'd gone too far in trying to ensure that her husband's murderer was brought to justice. Nobody had understood her properly, at least not until he arrived on the scene. Even the local press reporter who should have been more sympathetic to her story had eventually walked away, the arrogant sod! Now the police had him squirreled away somewhere for his own safety while he presumable filled their heads with his own twisted version of the story concerning Elizabeth. Ah, Elizabeth. He thought of the long days and nights together, the passion of her love-making and the warm afterglow as he'd lain in her bed, her head gently resting on his shoulder as she drifted off into a peaceful sleep. Then of course the ridicule had begun, and Elizabeth had begun to change. She'd become twisted and bitter at the world, but never with him. She knew he believed in her and in the righteousness of her campaign against those who'd wronged her, and her husband. He'd promised her that if anything happened to her he would never rest until those she felt responsible for her husband's death, and for her subsequent torment were punished.

It was a promise that had taken him a long time to fulfil, as he'd progressed in his career and made a good a life for himself, while waiting and planning, always planning. Eventually the time had come when he felt confident in putting his plan into operation. Some of those involved in the original case were dead of course, but that didn't matter, they had families, and he'd destroy them the way their fathers or grandfathers had destroyed his beautiful Elizabeth.

Now, all that was left was to dispose of Cahill, the last of the mockers, the doubters, but first of course he had to find out where the police, or Detective Inspector Connor to be precise, had hidden the old man.

The fact that his own mind had gone down exactly the same road to madness as his once-beloved Elizabeth's had never once entered his head, and was highly unlikely to do so as he studiously began working on the problem of locating the unfortunate final target for his wrath.

# Chapter 46
# The River Gives up its Dead

Connor and Clay breezed back into the station and made their way straight to Connor's office without speaking to a soul. They barely acknowledged the "hellos" or the "good mornings" that emanated from various officers as they passed through the room. During the drive back from the late Judge Tolliver's house Connor had filled Lucy Clay in on his conversation with Roger Cahill. The two of them now eagerly awaited the report that they hoped to receive from Harry Drew who was still where they'd left him, working behind closed doors in Connor's office. It was a novel experience for Sean Connor to have to knock on the door of his own office and to have it opened from within by a junior officer.

"Well Harry? Any luck" he asked the young detective.

"I did as you asked, Sir, and accessed the computer files for the original Prentice investigation. Unfortunately they were incomplete in as much as the age of the case meant that only the barest of details were recorded on the file. Witness statements, interview records and the names of every officer who was involved in that investigation are still in existence but I had to go to the central archives to obtain them. This is the full case file."

He pointed to an extremely large brown cardboard box on the floor beside the desk that bulged at its seams. Connor looked aghast at the mounds of papers that Drew had so far extricated from the box and which were now positioned in obvious piles of varying meaning on his desktop.

"Go on Harry, tell me if you've come up with anything yet."

"I'm afraid not. All the witness statements are present and correct but they make no reference to what you're looking for. The individual officers who took the statements are there of course but there's no complete dossier on the others. All of the senior officers who were involved at the time have now either retired or died. Judging from what you told me earlier you wouldn't be looking for them anyway, would you, Sir?"

"No Harry, I wouldn't. Look, you're doing a great job, keep at it, don't give up, there's a good chap."

"I won't give up. There's a lot of paper here but some of it is easily discarded as being irrelevant to what you need. It'll still take some time though, maybe a day or two to sift through everything."

"Right then. The sergeant and I are going to grab a quick lunch, then we'll be back to check on your progress. Have you eaten yet?"

"I had a sandwich a while ago. I'm fine thanks."

As Connor and Clay ate a frugal lunch and sipped hot coffee in the police canteen they were joined by D.C.I. Lewis. Their boss seemed to have softened his attitude since his earlier rebuke to Connor about keeping him in the dark over the matter of the safe house.

"Well Sean, how's it going? Any progress?"

"Not much Sir. Cahill was able to give us plenty of background information on McLean, but nothing that would help us in trying to track him down. Most of his intelligence relates to the McLean of thirty years ago, and is well out of date."

"Yes, of course, it would be wouldn't it? Well, never mind Sean, I'm sure something will turn up soon, you mark my words."

"Thank you Sir, I'm sure it will too," Connor replied as Lewis rose from his chair and made his way from the canteen, presumably heading back to his office.

"He's mellowed a bit, Boss," said Clay.

"No-one can be angry for ever Lucy. Lewis is under pressure to get results so he's allowed to vent his spleen from time to time."

"He's been on the force a long time hasn't he Sir?"

"Yes he has. He'll be retiring in a year or so, or at least that's what I've been led to believe, so he won't want to go out with an unsolved murder case on his record will he? He must have been on the force for over thirty five years by now and he's seen a lot of comings and goings over the years."

Their lunch concluded, the two walked back to Connor's office where Drew was still employed in going through the reams of paperwork that lay strewn across Connor's desk. Leaving him to it, Connor and Clay moved into the main office section of the incident room where ten officers were still hard at work collating and checking every piece of information on the case in the hope of finding something of help in tracking down the elusive McLean. The only news so far that day had been of a neutral variety. It would take at least three or four days to recreate the deleted files from Forbes's computer.

As they moved from one to another of the officers Connor was suddenly hailed from one corner of the room. Sergeant Gareth Jones was waving a piece of paper in his hand as Connor approached.

"What is it Sergeant?" asked Connor as he approached the Sergeant's desk.

"This has just come in Sir. It's an e-mail response to the call we put out to all forces to be on the lookout for McLean."

"You've found him?" asked Lucy Clay, unable to disguise the excitement in her voice.

"Well, yes we have," said Jones, "but I don't think you're going to like it."

"Go on Sergeant," said Connor, a sinking feeling appearing in his stomach.

"It's from the City of London Police. Apparently a body was fished out of the Thames three months ago. It was in a pretty bad state of decomposition, having been in the water for an estimated month or so but there was evidence of the man having been shot twice, with a high powered rifle. There was no identification on the body, which was fully clothed, but here's the thing Sir. When you gave us the description of McLean to circulate, it included reference to a tattoo on his right forearm?"

"That's right. A sword with a pen running through it."

"The pen is mightier than the sword, a good one for a reporter" said Clay.

"Well Sir," Jones continued, "when the City boys saw our request a Sergeant Musgrave put two and two together and called me right away. This e-mail is from him and shows the tattoo from the arm of the man in the river."

Connor grabbed the piece of paper in the sergeant's hand and peered intently at it for a minute. When he spoke again, the anger and frustration in his voice was heard through the length and breadth of the incident room.

"I knew it; I just bloody well knew it! That bastard has fooled us again!"

"Sir?" was all Lucy Clay could say as she saw the rage building in her boss's expression.

"We thought Andrew Forbes was the first victim didn't we? Well, I think we were bloody wrong, just as the killer intended us to be. I'm guessing that he killed McLean a long time ago, knowing that he could then use his identity to fool everybody and leave us a false trail leading to a dead man, and d'you know what Sergeant? We damned well fell for it, hook line and bloody sinker!"

"But he was shot, Sir. There was no aconite present in the body, was there, Gareth"? asked Clay.

"None reported in the autopsy," said Jones.

"Of course there wasn't," Connor snapped. "If there had been and the body had been found sooner there'd have been a chance we'd have been on to him earlier. This way, the body stayed unidentified for months and we've just got lucky in identifying the remains. He probably hoped the body would drift downriver and end up in the sea, and then we'd never have found it, and would have gone on searching for McLean for ever and a day."

"Excuse me Mr Connor, but there's more." This was Sergeant Jones once again.

"Go on Sergeant, you might as well ruin what's left of my day completely."

"It's the ballistics analysis. The other day a woman's body was washed up on the banks of the Thames, just inside the City police's jurisdiction. The River police picked her out of the water and she'd been shot too, also with a high powered rifle. Now here's the funny part. When the bullet taken from her was analysed it cross referred straight away to the ones taken from the male body that we now assume to be McLean. The woman has been identified, though they had to do it from fingerprints and dental records as the bullet used was a high velocity soft tipped one that exploded on contact and took her face apart. Her name was Tracy Willis and she'd only been out of prison for a couple of months after doing a ten year stretch for manslaughter."

Jones fell silent and waited for the D.I. to respond. When he did Connor had a knowing look on his face, though that look was mixed with one of frustration.

"Sergeant, I think we've just found out what happened to The Chocolate Woman. That's why we haven't been able to trace her and why she hasn't been active since the last killing. He used her to do his dirty work and then disposed of her like a piece of junk. He shot her in the face so that we wouldn't be able to link her to the description we received from the hotel."

"D'you really think it's her?" Clay asked her boss.

"I'm sure it is Lucy. I told you this bastard was clever. He must have recruited her when she left prison, unless he knew her already, and promised her something in return for helping him. That's why she was so hard for us to trace. She had no connection at all with any of the victims as far as we know so we'd never link her to the killings unless we got very lucky."

Connor was as yet in the dark about Tracy's connection with Sam Gabriel and Arminder Patel, and so was still working on the theory that the victims were all connected to the Prentice case. So, just when he'd thought that his case was coming together at last the trapdoor had been pulled from beneath his feet and the investigation was back to square one, or, was it? Somehow, though his face was etched with disappointment, Connor knew that the solution to the case lay not in the murky waters of the River Thames, in the cold-room of the City mortuary or in the mind of the elderly Roger Cahill, but much closer to home; in his own office in fact, somewhere in the mountain of papers that Constable Harry Drew was wading through even at that moment.

# Chapter 47
# The Key

The mound of paperwork on the left hand side of Connor's desk had grown considerably since they'd last visited Harry Drew. The height of that mound corresponded roughly with the decrease in the size of the one on the right side of the desk. Obviously Harry Drew was working to a system and a methodical one at that.

"Anything for me yet, Harry?"

"I'm afraid not Sir, but I'll get there eventually, I know I will."

"Listen Harry, I want you to change direction a bit. The files will tell us a lot, but they only concern the direct investigation of the case. They'll give us the forensics, the dates and times of the interviews of witnesses and suspects and who carried them out, and the commanding officer's report at the end. What they won't tell us is the one thing I really need to know, and I need to know it fast."

"Just tell me what you want me to do."

"I'm not sure how you'll go about this Harry but I think you may have to go back to the computer for the information we require. I want to know the names, the ranks and the present locations if known, of every officer who was stationed at this police station at the time of the Prentice murder."

"Am I allowed to know why I'm looking for that information?"

"Find it for me first young Harry, and then I'll tell you everything I know."

"Right Sir, leave it with me," said Drew as he once again fired up the computer on Connor's desk. As Connor led Lucy Clay back out of the office, allowing Drew to work in peace he turned and spoke to the man at the desk.

"And Harry?"

"Yes?"

"Remember what I said. Only myself or Sergeant Clay are allowed in that office and I don't care who you have to upset in order to enforce that order; understand?"

"Perfectly Sir."

"You know something I don't, don't you?" Clay asked him two minutes later as they sat opposite each other at one of the spare desks in the incident room.

"Maybe Sergeant, and then again maybe not. When I'm sure one way or the other I'll let you know but for the moment I want to play my cards very close to my chest. I'm nursing a suspicion based on what Cahill told me the other day as we were leaving him, remember?"

"Right," said Clay in comprehension of her boss's thinking. "I'll say no more until you're ready."

The sergeant had an idea where Connor was going with his theory, but she also knew that to voice it at this stage would be too much for her to expect from him. When and if he had the confirmation he required he'd make his move, and Lucy Clay would be with him by his side as always. She looked up at the clock on the wall and watched the second hand as it ticked its way around the face of the timepiece. Each second seemed to last an eternity and the minute hand appeared to be on a go-slow, and in such a fashion she sat and passed the next ten minutes, wondering when Connor would rouse himself from the almost trance-like fugue he'd fallen into. Lucy was too good and too experienced a sergeant to interrupt her boss when she knew him to be deep in thought so for now she just sat there, watching the interminable seconds ticking by, and she waited.

Eventually, Connor roused himself, and he stared at his sergeant intently before speaking.

"If I'm right Lucy, then the solution to this damned case is within our grasp. If on the other hand I'm wrong and we move too soon, then my career, yours and possibly every officer who's worked closely with us on this case could be in serious danger of evaporating before our very eyes."

"Do you want to share your theory with me now then?"

"I'll tell you as much as I dare for the moment, and then the rest if it's confirmed, as I suspect it will be by Harry Drew. He's the one who holds the key to cracking this case now Lucy, believe me, but I can't tell him exactly what to look for. He has to find it by himself because if I'm wrong then at least the reasons for me being wrong will have some independent back-up and credibility."

"It's not like you to be this mysterious."

"I know Lucy, but listen. Do you remember when we first spoke to Roger Cahill, the elder one I mean?"

Lucy nodded and stayed silent, waiting for Connor to continue.

"We were so wrapped up in his story concerning McLean and his involvement with the Prentice widow that we both overlooked one small sentence in his statement. That was the thing that came back to haunt me, the thing that kept nagging at me for days until I could recall where I was when I'd heard it and what it was I'd heard. He told us that after Elizabeth Prentice had ended her relationship with McLean she began dating a *police officer!* If I'm right Lucy, that police officer was probably a young constable at the time, possibly one who'd been involved in making house to house inquiries during the investigation rather than someone directly involved in it. I think that in the course of his daily beat patrols he met Mrs Prentice and that they eventually became lovers. *He's* the one who became bitter and twisted and ended up with the vendetta against all of those who'd slighted Elizabeth Prentice, and that probably included her ex-lover Sandy McLean. It's always bugged me throughout this case that the killer always managed to be one step ahead of us, as if he knew exactly what we were doing and when we were doing it. Now I have a good idea how and why."

Connor paused, long enough for Lucy Clay to ask,

"You think you know who it is don't you?"

"Let's just wait and see Lucy, let's wait and see. Like I said, Harry Drew is the man who can confirm what I suspect to be true and, having said that, I have to admit that I sincerely hope with all my heart that I'm wrong!"

Despite the hubbub of activity all around them in the incident room, as Connor fell silent and Lucy Clay sat staring at her boss with a perplexed expression on her face, at that moment, in the small area surrounding the desk where they sat, one could have heard a pin drop.

# Chapter 48
# The Meaning of True Love

Connor and Clay re-entered Connor's office just as Harry Drew was printing off a document from the computer printer on the small desk in the corner of the room.

Lucy Clay closed the door to the office very quietly and the two detectives waited in a hushed silence as Drew looked at the paper in his hand. A quizzical look appeared on Drew's face as he read down the list of names that had appeared as if by magic from the police computer's archives.

"You've found something haven't you Harry?" came the question from Connor.

"Well, I think so, though I'm not sure if it's what you expected to find."

"Let me see please," said Connor quietly, reaching out his hand to take the document from the young detective constable who still had that look of quizzical puzzlement on his face, as though he wasn't sure what it was he was supposed to find in the first place and, now that he'd found it, he didn't quite know what it meant, though Connor obviously did.

The list of names on the sheet of paper was quite long, though in almost every case the annotation beside the names stated, 'retired', deceased' or just 'present status unknown'. Only one name leaped out from the page at Connor as he scanned it and he nodded his head as though it had been exactly what he was expecting to find. Slowly, with an air of resignation about his movements his shoulders seemed to sag a little as he passed the paper to his sergeant who had patiently waited for him to speak or do something without interruption.

Lucy Clay looked at the paper as her boss had done and realised why he'd been hoping against hope that his most recent theory was wrong. It wasn't! As she perused the document that she held in her hand she saw that it contained a list of all the officers who had been employed at the station during the course of the original Prentice murder inquiry. It listed those involved in witness interviews, house-to-house inquiries, and the more senior officers whose task it had been to drive and carry out the detailed investigation of the evidence. Of all the names on that list one screamed out at her from the page, as it had done to Connor. It was the name of the only officer still employed at the station, though he was no longer a uniformed police constable as he had been in those long ago days, when he'd carried out house-to-house inquiries on the street where Elizabeth Prentice had lived.

"It's D.C.I. Lewis!" she gasped incredulously.

"Yes Lucy, I'm afraid it is," said Connor with a note of resignation in his voice.

"But Sir, he's... I mean, he's the boss, he's the man who's led the inquiry all along."

"I know he is Lucy. That's why he was always one step ahead of us. That's why we could never get close to the killer because Lewis knew exactly what we were doing and changed his identity to keep leading us along the numerous false trails he'd laid for us. When we look a bit deeper I think we'll find that he had a long and lasting relationship with Elizabeth Prentice, and that he became totally wrapped up in her campaign against those she thought responsible for her husband's death, or at the very least for their sins of omission in allowing whoever she perceived to be his killer to escape justice. I don't know why, but he's waited all these years before carrying out his act of retribution against those people or their families."

"He must be sick sir."

"Very sick Sergeant, without a doubt. Now, I think it's time we had a word with Detective Chief Inspector Harry Lewis. Come on Drew, I want you with us."

Harry Drew joined Connor and Clay as they made their way to the office of their senior officer. The door was closed when they got there and Connor, leading the way, knocked hard before pushing the door open, only to reveal an empty office within.

"He's gone Sir," said Clay.

"I can see that Sergeant. The question is where has he gone to?"

At that moment Sergeant Tom Daly, the station administrative officer came bustling into the D.C.I.s office, unaware of their presence.

"Oh hello Mr Connor," he said to the D.I. "Is the D.C.I. not back yet?"

"Back from where Sergeant?"

"Well Sir, he came to see me a while ago. He said you wanted a transcript of the last phone call that D.C Fox had made from the safe house. I told him that you'd ordered that no-one but yourself should have access to that information but he reminded me that he was your boss, and mine, and anyway, he said you'd asked him to get the information because you were busy on another part of the investigation."

"Did that transcript have a record of the telephone number of the incoming call sergeant? Think man, it's important."

"Well yes, it would have done. All official incoming calls are screened and identified by the caller's number being recorded on the top of the transcript form."

"Bloody hell!" Connor cursed. "So there was nothing to stop him calling the Telecoms people and finding out the address that corresponded to the number the call came from?"

"Of course not Sir. Look, is there a problem?"

"You'd better hope not Sergeant. When I said no-one was to have access to that information, I meant no-one, and that included Lewis, or the chief super or even the damned chief constable!"

"I'm sorry," muttered the administration officer, but Connor and Clay, closely followed by D.C Drew were already running towards the stairway on their way out of the building. Connor pushed a piece of paper into Drew's hand, gave him hurried instructions to make a short detour and then to get hold of D.C Kelly and for the two of them to follow on in a squad car to the Tolliver house.

As Clay pulled the Mondeo to a halt in the deserted confines of the close where the Tolliver house stood hidden behind its well-matured grove of trees Connor sensed that all was not well with the place. Everything just *looked* too quiet.

"Let's take it nice and slow Lucy," he ordered as they quietly got out of the car and moved towards the house. "We don't want any nasty surprises now, do we?"

"Right, Sir."

We're going to take a look through the windows first and try to ascertain what's going on in there before we do anything. I'll take the study, you take the dining room. They're both on the ground floor at the front of the house. If we don't see anything we'll move around to the side and check the other rooms."

The two officers moved almost silently towards the ground floor windows that Connor had indicated. As he arrived at the window of the late judge's study Connor saw a sight that almost made his blood freeze in his veins. Lewis was there alright, and D.C Simon Fox, Henry DeVere and the two Roger Cahills were on their knees, with their hands positioned behind their heads at the far side of the room. Lewis had them all covered with a menacing looking rifle and none of the men confined in that room could have moved without the renegade officer seeing what they were doing and thus making themselves an instant target for his firearm. Connor gestured across to Clay who answered his frantic waving with a nod and the sergeant moved to join her boss as he peered over the sill of the window. After taking a few seconds to assess the situation she asked,

"What now Boss? Any ideas?" she whispered.

"I think we have to approach this one head-on Sergeant, as I don't think that time is exactly on our side. Lewis is highly unstable and he could pull that trigger at anytime."

"Lead on then, I'm with you all the way," said Clay as Connor began to edge his way towards the front door of the house.

Together the two officers entered the house, making as little sound as possible, though the heavy front door betrayed their presence by making annoying creaking sound as the hinges protested at the sluggishness of movement as Clay tried to close the door without announcing their presence.

"Sorry," she whispered.

Connor simply placed one finger over his lips and beckoned her onwards in his wake. They padded across the hall and stopped outside the study door, listening intently for any sound emanating from within.

"If that's you out there Sean," Lewis's voice boomed from within, "I suggest you come in and join the party. I was wondering how long it would take you to realise where I was."

Sheepishly, Connor pressed the door handle down and slowly opened the door to the study, motioning for Clay to stay where she was.

"Oh Sean, really! Do bring the good Sergeant in with you as well. We don't want to leave her standing alone out there now do we?"

Connor and Clay joined the unhappy band in that room and were soon on their knees, as helpless as the other captives.

"Surely you must realise that it's over. You can't get away from here," said Connor, attempting to reason with his boss.

"Do you really think that concerns me now Sean, after all these years? You've no idea what it's been like, planning and waiting for the right time to put these fools out of their misery. They all made my poor Elizabeth's life one of despair and melancholic misery, and they all deserved to pay."

"Sir, Harry, listen. You don't have to do this. You've let your judgement be clouded by things that happened a log time ago and by the words of a woman who was stricken with grief and was prepared to lash out at anyone and anything she thought had let her down in her search for justice for her husband. She became unhinged, and you've done the same. It's not too late though. You can get help."

"What? And end up in a psychiatric ward or in a special hospital with all the other crazies who I've helped to put away. Cone on now Sean, we both know that's not going to happen."

"Then tell me at least why you killed Arminder Patel and Sam Gabriel. What did they have to do with your revenge? They had no connection at all with Elizabeth Prentice."

"Oh Sean, you can be so naive. Don't you realise that they had nothing to do with the Prentice case? They were Tracy's victims, not mine. Gabriel had to die because he recognised her and could put her in town at the time of the murders, and you might have traced her through him eventually and Patel, well, that was personal to Tracy."

"Look Sir, we can work this out. Why kill all these people when you only want Roger Cahill, and he's an old man, so why not leave him be, and let the whole thing end right now?"

"He could have helped her more. He could have supported her story. Instead he ridiculed her and left her to fight for justice on her own. By the way Sean, I had to get his files because one day I foolishly gave an unauthorised interview to a reporter outside Elizabeth's house. I said that I believed she was a wronged woman and that I had every sympathy for her. Not much I agree, but it would have been enough for you to latch on to me if you'd found the file first. Cahill here was that reporter of course, though he never printed that interview in his paper. He was too busy putting her down and making fun of her with his lying articles about her."

"I wrote her story," said Cahill from his position on the floor. "I gave her space in the paper to tell her side of things, but when she began to get unrealistic and sounded as if she was 'losing it' my editor pulled the plug. She lost the plot Mr Lewis, and so have you."

"Shut up!" Lewis screamed at Cahill, "or I'll kill you right now."

As Cahill fell silent Lewis swung the rifle in his direction and appeared to be taking aim at the old man's heart. In doing so he missed the faintest of movements that came from the crack that had appeared in the internal door to the study, the one that led from the dining room. As Lewis took a step towards the cowering figure of the elderly journalist the door suddenly swung open and a voice commanded;

"I'd suggest you drop the gun Mr Lewis. Right now!"

Harry Lewis turned to see Detective Constables Drew and Kelly standing in the doorway, both armed with standard police issue revolvers which were pointing directly at him.

"Ah, very clever Sean. You arranged a little surprise for me, I see."

"I said drop it Sir," Drew demanded in an even sterner tone.

Slowly, Detective Chief Inspector Harry Lewis lowered the rifle to the floor. The two young detectives moved into the room and Kelly kicked the rifle into the far corner of the study, where it was quickly retrieved by Lucy Clay who'd sprung to her feet the instant Lewis had lowered the rifle.

Five minutes later, with the hostages safely removed to the drawing room where DeVere poured them all a stiff drink according to their individual preferences, Connor and Clay, together with the constables were left in the presence of Lewis who now sat quietly behind the desk that had belonged to Judge Tolliver. In deference to his rank, he hadn't as yet been cautioned or placed in handcuffs though he'd been told to keep his hands in full view on the desk top.

"Well Sean, "he said as though addressing Connor across his own desk back at the police station. "It looks like you've won eh?"

"I wouldn't call it winning," Connor replied. "I've worked for you for, what, nine years? I've always respected you as a bloody good police officer. Yet, here you are, a self-confessed serial killer. You're no better than some of the scum we've nailed between us over the years. Why? How could you throw away a damned good career because of some twisted and distorted memories from the past?"

"You see Sean, you'll never understand. You don't know what it's like to be so much in love that everything in your world revolves around that one single person. When Elizabeth died I had nothing left to live for except to carry out her wishes and seek justice for her and her husband. That cause kept me close to her all through the years."

"That 'cause' as you call it has cost you your career and probably your freedom for the rest of your life."

"So you say Sean, so you say."

With that, Lewis slowly yet imperceptibly began moving his right hand back towards himself.

"Please keep your hands where they are Sir," said Drew, ever vigilant.

"Ah yes, sorry Constable. I just thought that you, Sean would like to know exactly how I managed to dispose of old Tolliver right here in his study."

Connor nodded to Drew, who released the grip on his police revolver. Lewis reached slowly into the inside pocket of his jacket and extracted a small pewter hip flask.

"A little drink first Sean, just to whet the whistle. It's a long story."

Lewis took a long swig from the flask. Connor estimated that he'd drained it completely.

"Finest single malt Scotch," said Lewis. "Simple, wasn't it? Don't worry Sean, it won't take long. There was enough to kill a whole field of racehorses in ten minutes in there. Tolliver's dose was smaller and took a little longer to hit him after I'd left to meet you for lunch as it happened, but it must have been quite a sight to watch him writhe around in his death throes, don't you think?"

Lewis began to tremble as the tingling sensation hit him almost instantly.

"Bloody hell Sir," Drew exclaimed. "He's poisoned himself."

"What can we do for him?" asked Lucy Clay as she looked on in horror.

"Nothing Sergeant, nothing at all," Connor replied, calmly.

None of the officers in that room would ever forget the sights of the next few minutes as they watched the man they'd always followed and respected die from the effects of the massive overdose of aconite contained in the hip flask. Only when the convulsions had finished and Harry Lewis lay contorted in death on the floor before them did Lucy Clay break the shocked and terrible silence that had gripped them all in those minutes.

"You knew he was going to do that didn't you?"

"I had an idea he would Lucy. Perhaps it's better this way. He'd never have lasted long in a special unit after all. There would have been too many lunatics wanting to make a name for themselves by doing him in. This way he escaped a knife in the back in the shower one day or some other ignominious death and I think that despite what he did, we at least owed him that."

"But what about Mary Stride? We'll never know why he didn't kill her too."

"Oh, I think we do know Lucy. She hated her parents for what they'd done to her by leaving her to care for her family. In Lewis's twisted mind she was thus absolved of her part of the blame because her whole life had become one of suffering like his own. It's over Lucy, finished, and I can't wait to get out of this bloody place."

Lucy Clay nodded. Drew and Kelly left the room and joined the others in the drawing room as Connor picked up the telephone to call for an ambulance and scene of crimes team.

Much later, after the hullabaloo of the day had died down Sean Connor returned to his office to inform Charles Carrick of the events of the day and to write out his report on the aconite killings. As he finally put his pen down and allowed himself to relax his thoughts turned to the rest of the evening and realised that Lewis had been wrong on all counts. Sean Connor *did* at last know what real love was, and, armed with that knowledge he picked up the phone to call Catherine Nickels...

Dear reader,

We hope you enjoyed reading *Purple Death*. Please take a moment to leave a review, even if it's a short one. Your opinion is important to us.

Discover more books by Brian L. Porter at
https://www.nextchapter.pub/authors/brian-porter-mystery-author-liverpool-united-kingdom

Want to know when one of our books is free or discounted? Join the newsletter at http://eepurl.com/bqqB3H

Best regards,
Brian L. Porter and the Next Chapter Team

# About the Author

Winner, Best Author, The Preditors & Editors Readers Awards 2009, and also Winner of Best Children's Book, and Best Artwork for *'Tilly's Tale'* (under his Harry Porter pseudonym), and with a Top Ten Finisher Award for his thriller *'Legacy of the Ripper'*, Brian L Porter is the author of a number of successful novels. His works include the winner of The Preditors & Editors Best Thriller Novel 2008 Award, *A Study in Red – The Secret Journal of Jack the Ripper* and its sequels, *Legacy of the Ripper* and the final part of his Ripper trilogy, *Requiem for the Ripper*, all signed for movie adaptation by Thunderball Films (L.A.), with *A Study in Red* already in the development stages of production. Both *A Study in Red* and *Legacy of the Ripper* were awarded 'Recommended Read' status by the reviewers at CK2S Kwips & Kritiques.

Aside from his works on Jack the Ripper his other works include *Pestilence, Behind Closed Doors, Glastonbury, Kiss of Life* and *The Nemesis Cell*, and the short story collection, *The Voice of Anton Bouchard and Other Stories*.

Brian has also become thoroughly integrated into the movie business since his first involvement with Thunderball Films LLC and is now also an Associate Producer and Co-Producer on a number of developing movies, as well as being a screenwriter for many of the movies soon to be released by Thunderball.

Two sequels to *Behind Closed Doors* are planned, both featuring Inspector Norris and Sergeant Hillman. Watch out for *A Tainted Inheritance* and *An Unfortunate Recuperation*.

He is a dedicated dog lover and rescuer and he and his wife share their home with a number of rescued dogs.

For more about *Purple Death* please go to www.inspectornorris.webs.com.

Purple Death
ISBN: 978-4-86750-241-9

Published by
Next Chapter
1-60-20 Minami-Otsuka
170-0005 Toshima-Ku, Tokyo
+818035793528
8th June 2021

Lightning Source UK Ltd.
Milton Keynes UK
UKHW012103221222
414357UK00004B/111